The Enclave

Fred Allen

Juanres
thank you
for reading my
novel

Fred Allen

Copyright © 2001 by Fred Allen

ISBN 0-7414-0752-3

Published by:

INFINITY
PUBLISHING.COM

Infinity Publishing.com
519 West Lancaster Avenue
Haverford, PA 19041-1413
Info@buybooksontheweb.com
www.buybooksontheweb.com
Toll-free (877) BUY BOOK
Local Phone (610) 520-2500
Fax (610) 519-0261

Printed in the United States of America

Printed on Recycled Paper

Published October, 2001

FOREWORD

The Enclave von Freiderhoff now emerges from a period of gestation that extends for more than forty years. A period sufficient – according to my oldest son, Brian, - to bring forth a herd of elephants.

This novel is a work of fiction but it is inevitable that it will reflect impressions gained in a variety careers, life in nearly all parts of Canada and several other countries that extend even beyond the gestation period mentioned above to include those wonderful years of growing up in beautiful Fredericton, New Brunswick.

These include the days at York Street and Charlotte Street public schools where a variety of teachers made valiant efforts to convince as to the value of education. Most memorable were the extremely fair minded principal at Charlotte Street PS, Rolph Nevers, and the indomitable Grade V teacher Emma Betts, also at Charlotte Street PS, who was so strict but so fair and whose teaching of arithmetic succeeded in introducing me to discipline and order that have served me well.

Unfortunately my successful experience in Grade V - I was repeating the year after a disastrous experience in York Street PS – did not extend beyond Grade VI and the first half of Grade VII when I encountered teachers who practiced a form of favoritism that is reflected in most schools that draw students from "both sides of the tracks."

When I look back over nearly seventy-nine years there are so many people to whom I must express my gratitude. First to Desmond Pacey, Alfred Bailey, Conrad Wright and Bill Smith all professors at the University of New Brunswick who saw some of the promise that Emma Betts had seen so many year earlier when the University as an adult - although not necessarily mature - student.

Readers will find a few more details describing my early years in the Post Script at the end of this book and for more details they must await my fourth book which will be devoted to lifetime impressions including ideas, observations, regrets on missed opportunities and, most of all, the sanity preserving component of laughter.

But there are a few other people who deserve special mention. My daughter Judy Taylor who took time from her busy life as an RN and being the world's best grandmother to our five great-grandchildren to read my books and make valued observations. To my oldest son, Brian, who offered wise counsel although even in his present career as a 747 Captain he has some difficulty in forgetting his Air Force career where jet jockeys always tend to look down on "grunts" or "brown jobs" such as me. My sincere thanks to my second son Terry also for wise counsel and to his son, our grandson, Jamie, who joined with my youngest son, Michael, in the Herculean effort required to drag me out of the age of the quill pen and into the age of the word processor.

Others who have taken time from their busy lives to read my books and make valuable contributions include nieces Betty Jantz and Pat Mills and their husbands Arnold and

Steven respectively, my nephew Danny Boyne and my sister Doris Fanjoy of Fredericton (Nashwaaksis).

Special mention must go to my old friend Sally Pengalley who was an indefatigable colleague in our struggle to protect teachers' pensions against the self serving designs of the Provincial Government and the apathy of teacher leadership. Sally demonstrated outstanding talents as an eagle eyed proof reader and offered both encouragement and many valuable recommendations on both the form and content of my first three literary efforts.

Also honorable mention must go to my old friend Lt - Col Ed Schrader and his wife Linda who kindly agreed to read my three books and have offered many valuable suggestions. Ed retired in 1999 after nearly fifty years with service in just about all the units in the Royal Regiment of Canadian Artillery where he always served with quiet distinction.

But above all I must thank my wife of fifty-four years, Nell, whose patience in the face of my endless procrastination made this book possible.

Fred Allen

Thornhill, Ontario   June, 2001

THE ENCLAVE

INDEX

CHAPTER I

THE ENCLAVE von FREIDERHOFF

It was early in the afternoon of Saturday May 25th, 1968, as the tour bus made its way along the Freiderberg road parallel to the main front wall of the remaining wing of the old Mansion. As the bus passed the now gateless arch representing the main entrance to the Mansion the tour director drew the attention of the tourists to the large plaque on one of the gate posts on which could be read the inscription "Enclave von Freiderhoff" and the date "1768" directly below the large block letters in gold denoting the name.

As the bus moved slowly past the gate the tour guide announced that this was another of the historic sites they would be visiting on the first day of their guided tour. He tells them that this estate was presented to the first Baron von Freiderhoff in 1768 for services rendered to the royal family and the Mansion was built between 1760 and 1790 and remained intact as one of the great family houses of what is now Germany until a portion was destroyed by bombing and fire late in World War II. He tells them that they will have the opportunity to take photographs but advised them that the mansion was still a family residence and privacy should be respected. He also told them that the ninth Baron von Freiderhoff continues to live in the mansion. He then drew their attention to the buildings in the background in the other side of the small stream, which he identified as the barracks of an American armoured regiment surrounded by high barbed wire topped fences.

When the bus came to a stop a little farther down the road where the elevation of the road gave a better view of the old mansion for taking photographs the tour guide gave the tourists a brief history of the Enclave von Freiderhoff. The designation of "Enclave" was a special distinction conferred upon the estates of aristocratic families, who had provided

1

service of particular distinction to the Royal Family. Conferring the special status of "Enclave" was equivalent to creating a tiny kingdom in itself over which the head of the family would exercise near full hegemony. With the fragmentation of the state the significance of the "Enclave" designation had lost much of its meaning but this particular property remained exempt from federal taxes although subject to the ever-increasing local taxes.

A few of the tourists lefr the bus to take photographs and the tour director again reminded them that the Mansion remained a family residence. He added that the current resident, the ninth Baron von Freiderhoff, had been one of Germany's most decorated heroes of World War I and had risen to the rank of Field Marshall before retiring in the late 1930s.

Inside the old mansion Sandra von Freiderhoff heard the tour bus pass along the road and could hear the muffled voice of the tour director. Tour buses were a daily event from late spring until early fall and, judging from the language, this must be a group of either English or American tourists. These bus tours only represented a minor nuisance to the residents of the Mansion as the tourists were reasonably circumspect in observing the privacy requests of the tour directors.

It was a very warm late spring day and Sandra, or Sandy as she was known to most of the other residents and her class mates at the exclusive girl's boarding school she attended, decided that she would go for a swim in the small stream behind the house. The stream which originated in a spring fed lake a few kilometers away had been dammed behind the house producing a reasonably sized pool which the family used for swimming and cooling off during the very warm summer months. The water was both cool and clear and had, thus far, escaped the contamination of agricultural and industrial wastes that was killing so many similar streams. The

2

area leading from the house to the stream had been land-scaped with a closely manicured lawn leading down to the water's edge. This section of the stream ran through a layer of firm red clay and this provided a highly suitable bottom for the pool and permitted comfortable wading in the shallows. Some years earlier a small diving board had been mounted on the dam to complete a fairly well equipped private family swimming pool.

There were tall trees on both sides of the stream and a thick hedge about five feet high followed it behind the trees on the other side and this hedge marked the property boundary between the Enclave and the land, formerly part of the estate, but now the property of the German federal government and leased to NATO and the American Armed Forces. The barracks built on this property was currently occupied by an American armoured regiment.

As Sandy, dressed in a long flowing gown - in the form of a large beach towel - over her bathing suit, left her room and came down the front stairs she noted that the old General was in his study and continuing his painstaking reading of a Braille book as she passed the half open door. She also noted that Gerda was busy in the kitchen. Mannheim was nowhere to be seen but he was probably in his room pouring over the pile of American magazines that Woody Washington had brought home the previous evening. Before she reached the rear entrance to the mansion she had picked up an enthusiastic companion. Plato, the family black Labrador dog had noted her apparel and recognized that the robe and bathing suit meant swimming and Plato was all in favor of that.

Sandy was home on the final school break before graduation at the end of June and this break would be about ten days to allow for preparation for final exams. Because the school was not that distant Sandy was home most weekends except for the four months each year devoted to language training at girls' schools in England and France. Helga, her official guardian, would be home the following day and had promised to spend a few days helping Sandy prepare for her exams.

Helga was a very special person in Sandy's life, a mixture between mother and big sister. Helga had been only twelve when she had found the note that had been slipped under the front door of the mansion. The note was from a desperate mother who pleaded with its reader to take good care of her baby and saying where the baby could be found in the rose bushes at the corner of the Mansion. Helga had rushed out to the location indicated, gathered up the baby and returned to the mansion where Gerda had helped her to bathe and feed the baby which was very thin and obviously under-nourished. It had also been Helga who had insisted on applying to adopt the baby when efforts to locate the baby's mother were unsuccessful. They had great difficulty in persuading the old General that the baby should be adopted because he insisted that this child was just another product of the irresponsible coupling of the same inferior people who had contributed to Germany's decline. However, his hostility declined as Sandy grew into a very pretty and lively child and Sandy recalled the many times she had seen the trace of a smile flit across his face as a result of something she said or did.

Sandy was not sure if she actually loved the old General the way she loved Helga and Gerda and, for that matter, Mannheim who had always been very kind to her. The old General was really not that lovable. He was always very stern and sad. Then there were times when he was out with Mannheim and Sandy would sit in his study and look at all the pictures. It was so sad that they had all died and that they had died so young. It was at times like these that Sandy felt love for the old man.

Sandy arrived at the stream but not before Plato had made his enthusiastic running plunge into the refreshingly cool water. Sandy removed her robe and joined him but while the water was very refreshing it was quite cold and it was several minutes before her body became adjusted to the sudden change in temperature.

CHAPTER II

JASON CREIGHTON(BUCHALTER)

On the other side of the stream, inside the barracks of the 8th US Armoured Regiment, Jason Creighton was spending a lazy Saturday but with a lot on his mind. He had arrived at the base late on Thursday following a sudden move from a communications training center in California where he and four other members on his course had been unceremoniously yanked off the course after merely two weeks of a scheduled twelve week course. They were told that this was to meet an emergency shortage of communications specialists in an armoured formation in constant contact with Russian units in the NATO Occupation Zone. Jason had his suspicions. Why would the US Army, in its infinite wisdom, take five soldiers only two weeks into their specialist training - and already earmarked for the Viet Nam buildup - and suddenly whisk them away to Germany? Certainly there was a shortage of communications specialists with the US Forces in Germany but that was true everywhere. And why take partially trained specialists?

Jason Creighton suspected that somehow or other his father had something to do with this sudden move. Jason's true identity was not Jason Creighton but Jason Buchalter and his father was Senator Buck Buchalter a two term Senator about to be re-elected, practically unopposed, to his third six-year term and was the ranking minority member of the Senate Armed Forces Committee. He certainly had the power to make things happen but Jason just couldn't imagine how he could have found him.

Jason reviewed his activities for the past year in an effort to find just where he might have slipped up. He had moved to New York a year ago with full family blessings. He was an accomplished musician and his success in this endeavor had been his mother's prime interest in life for as

6

long as he could remember. His mother had also been a fine concert pianist who had gone as far as Carnegie Hall but never quite into the first rank of concert pianists. His mother had spared absolutely no expense in hiring the best available music teachers to tutor her talented son and as the only surviving child of one of the richest industrialists in North America there was absolutely no shortage of financial resources. His parents, supported by his music loving grandfather, decided that the target should be the School for Concert Pianists operating under the auspices of the famous Julliard School of Music with a maximum annual intake of six exceptional students. To ensure admission to that very select school Jason was sent to New York to study for a year with one of the finest music teachers in the US.

The year in New York had gone very well up to a point but then Jason had added the pleasure of sexual activity to the pleasure of his music when he met a young aspiring actress a few years his senior who was attracted to him by his music and, quite possibly, the beautiful condominium his mother had arranged to be available to him for his year in New York The music was wonderful and the sex for the young stud was out of this world until the young actress decided to return to her first love, a handsome young actor, her own age, who had just landed a leading role in a major Hollywood production.

Jason was heartbroken and temporarily lost all interest in music. He followed his love to California but was further frustrated in his efforts to reestablish contact when the Hollywood movie moved to location in South America. At eighteen years of age Jason soon realized that it was the sex he missed more than the starlet and there was no shortage of prime sex in Southern California for a young man of ample independent means. He had kept in touch with his mother to ensure that he retained access to the money supply. He pleaded to her that he just needed a little time by himself in "his own space" before returning to his studies of music. He

7

did not tell his mother where he was and this was possible because he maintained all his banking arrangements through the bank in New York with which he had dealt while in that city. Jason dealt only with his mother knowing that his mother's ambitions for him provided him with a measure of leverage that would not be available in dealings with his father.

Jason Buchalter's false identity as Jason Creighton was the product of security cover, which had been arranged by Jason's father for his year in New York. The son of a wealthy friend had been kidnapped in New York and Jason's mother was absolutely terrified at the possibility that Jason might suffer the same fate. She pointed out to her husband that Jason would be a prime target of kidnappers as the son of a US Senator and a mother who was the sole heir to the Conrad fortune. To ease her fears Buck Buchalter arranged with a major security company to provide a protective cover story for Jason and this consisted of three completely separate identities supported by full documentation and two of these would be unknown to everyone but Jason, Spencer Graham - the Senator's Chief of Staff - and the head of the security company. The Senator convinced his wife that the "need to know" principle of intelligence should be observed and the second and third false identities be unknown even to them. In actual fact, the Senator considered his youngest son, while admittedly talented, to be a bit of a pain in the ass and he had little interest in knowing the other false identities. The "need to know" principle worked on Jason's mother and for the first six months they used the identity of Jason Parker. Jason's father remained quite happy with this arrangement until Jason's mother started leaning on him after Jason's actual location had been unknown to her for nearly three months.

In California Jason, now known as Jason Creighton, met a very pretty little girl from the Midwest who was totally committed to the anti-war effort and reserved her favors only for those boys who agreed to support her chosen cause. Jason

Creighton became a convert to the cause although, initially at least, he had greater enthusiasm for the sex than for marching around waving placards bearing anti-war slogans. In the group to which Jason had allied himself there were about a dozen boys who were prime targets for the draft and they had formulated a plan. They would not wait to be drafted but they would volunteer and as volunteers they would be given a choice of trades training to follow their basic training. They would all select a trade for which specialists were in very short supply and they decided on the trade of communications' specialist based upon advice of someone who was on the inside. Then, when they had completed their trades training, they would all take off for Canada. This action would have a much more serious impact on the war effort than skipping the draft before receiving any trades training.

Then on Tuesday, just seventy-two hours earlier, Jason and four other students had been suddenly yanked off the course and shipped to Germany. Included in the draft to Germany were two other members of the antiwar plan but the three of them had been separated when assigned to different units at the reception center in Frankfurt. Jason had arrived in his current location late on Thursday and Friday had been devoted to medicals, shots, drawing equipment and briefings. The three partially trained communication specialists arriving at Jason's new unit were assigned to qualified specialists for "in job training". The communications briefing had been conducted by a tall, redheaded, Staff Sergeant who introduced himself as S/Sgt Mombirkett and used the introduction to warn them that he expected a high standard in both the performance of their duties and their general military deportment or they would be dealing with him personally. The word went around that Mombirkett was one "hard ass" non com who meant everything he said.

During the briefing there was a knock on the door and a voice asked the S/Sgt if he could come in. Mombirkett replied with an emphatic "Yes, Sir!" and called the room to

9

attention. Through the corner of his eye Jason saw a young, tall, very black officer enter the room and approach the lectern at the front of the room. "Men," said the staff sergeant, "this is your Commanding Officer, Lt-Col Pelladeau. Do you wish to speak to the men, sir?" The young Lt Col offered just a few words of welcome telling the new arrivals that they had been selected to participate in accelerated training in the "in job training program" and that they would learn quickly with the aid of the qualified communications' specialists with whom they would be working and who were also present at the briefing. He reminded them that they were in a very dangerous location and that as representatives of their country abroad he would accept nothing less than the highest standard of conduct. He then left the room but not without Mombirkett once again bring the class to its feet with an ear shattering command "Class, Attention!"

Jason got the impression that Mombirkett would be his section chief and he would probably be, as advertised, a real "hard ass". But the communications' specialist, Henry (Hank) Wilson, to whom he was assigned, seemed to be a real nice young guy just a few years older than Jason. He remained with Jason for most of the day and helped him through his "reporting in" procedure. From a high point at the rear of the barracks, and just outside the barbed wire topped high security fence, Hank pointed out a few features of interest. They could make out the buildings of a small town about a mile away and Hank informed him that there were a few pretty good restaurants on the main street and two bars or gasthauses that were very popular with the troops. He also pointed out the large building on the other side of a small stream and identified it as the Enclave von "something or other" - a long German name - and the mansion house for an estate that had, at one time, included just about everything in sight. An old German General - actually a former Field Marshall - lived in the Mansion with a small support staff and, it seemed, two granddaughters. The old General was also referred to as the Baron by local inhabitants and could be seen

10

occasionally being driven around the town in a very old but elegant Mercedes-Benz staff car usually with the top down. The story about the old General was that he had been on Hitler's staff until 1938 when he was forced to resign because of ill health. The old General was now in his eighties and blind.

Hank advised that the old Mansion and its grounds were out of bounds to all ranks except on invitation by a member of the household. One of the HQ squadron cooks was a regular visitor to the mansion after establishing a relationship with the housekeeper.

That evening Hank took Jason down to one of the bars for a few beers and he found that the music, while not quite his cup of tea, was loud, enthusiastic and, apparently, very popular. He noticed that the group providing the music were all American and he recognized the tall lead guitarist as the non com who had briefed them earlier in the day. During the evening two requests brought up a couple from the audience, a large black man and a tall attractive blonde German woman. Both duets were very well received and Hank identified the big black man as a cook from their unit and the woman as the housekeeper at the old Mansion. It was Friday and the special Friday evening program always attracted many girls from town and cities in the area to whom Hank referred to as American groupies or just German girls looking for American husbands. Jason was pleasantly surprised at how many very attractive young girls made the weekly trek to the market place. As the evening wore on Hank and Jason sitting alone attracted a number of appreciative glances from many of the girls.

Late in the evening the small orchestra took a break and the Master of Ceremonies announced an impromptu amateur contest and called for volunteers. Jason had made the mistake of telling Hank about his musical background and, over Jason's protests, Hank volunteered Jason as a participant in the contest. Jason tried to disengage but the crowd insisted and he reluctantly made his way to the small bandstand. There was no piano just a keyboard but one with which Jason was familiar. Even without music, he was able to perform three numbers. The first was a melody from a classic, the second was a popular hit from the sound tract of a current movie and he concluded with a rousing rendition of the Beatles hit "Hey Jude" and this brought the house down. Jason was not really that much of a vocalist but, for this number, he was able to get the audience quickly involved and his personal exposure was limited. HHank was even more impressed as their tabletop suddenly filled up with glasses of beer and they were surrounded by a crowd of very attractive girls who were obviously both willing and able. Hank had a steady girlfriend who was not there that evening and declined some obvious invitations. Jason decided to stay with his mentor and they returned to their quarters at about midnight just a little tipsy but having resisted the many very promising advances. Jason decided that the bar was well worth another visit, which would take the form of a reconnaissance with more specific objectives.

Hank had been very impressed with Jason's performance on the keyboard admitting that he had thought Jason had been just blowing smoke when he had told him about his music studies. "Man," Hank told him, "You play one mean keyboard! You really knocked them dead. Someone else who was really impressed was Red Mombirkett who plays guitar with that group. He came over to our table while you were playing and said he thought he had seen you somewhere before and I reminded him that you had been in on his briefing that day. He was some impressed!"

After lunch on Saturday Jason decided to take his small portable keyboard and find a quiet place and work on a melody that had been running through his mind for days. He made his way out the back gate and down the hill towards the small stream. At a point, nearly directly behind the old

12

Mansion, he found a comfortable shady spot under one of the tall trees. His attention was attracted for a few minutes by the tour bus passing in front of the mansion and he listened to the voice of the tour director as he told the tourists about the history of the mansion and the family living there. As the tour bus finally passed out of earshot, Jason turned his attention to his keyboard. He turned the volume down low and played a few chords. There was no sound. Jason turned up the volume, still, no sound. He checked the battery compartment and cursed softly as he found he had forgotten to install the batteries. But his ear did pick up sounds from another source and it was the unmistakable sound of a girl's laughter accompanied by subdued sounds of splashing.

The stream in front of him and directly behind the mansion had been dammed forming a pond about twenty-five meters across by about forty meters long. The objective was to form a swimming pool and this became obvious when he noted the small diving board that had been mounted on the low dam. There in the middle of the pond was the source of the nearly musical girlish laughter. Jason could see a blond head and the black head of a large dog and the blond head, obviously that of a girl, was the source of the laughter as she attempted to get the dog to tow her to shore by hanging onto his collar. The dog - she called him Plato - was having no part of her plan and swam to the edge of the pool as she followed him. As they stood up at the edge of the pond the dog did just what came natural to him and shook himself vigorously as the girl sought protection from the spray of cold water. She softly scolded the dog as she draped her body with the big combination beach towel and robe. Plato, completely unaffected by her scolding and having enjoyed his swim, now turned his interest to the mansion from which he detected odors and sounds that suggested he might just be able to scrounge an early afternoon snack.

The girl now leaned against a tall tree that appeared to come directly out of the lawn beside the pool and proceeded to rub herself vigorously with the heavy towel. Now Jason could see the girl fully for the first time and his immediate reaction was that this was probably the most beautiful girl he had ever seen. She appeared to be in her late teens, very blonde, quite tall with long slim legs, slender hips and firm well developed breasts. Her face was oval shaped with full red lips and eyes that he was just sure would be blue. He just couldn't take his eyes off her as he watched in amazement as she slowly peeled down her skin tight one piece bathing suit and let it curl around her feet. The beach towel was now pinned between her shoulders and the tree and he felt quick involuntary arousal as he gazed upon her total frontal nudity. Now he could see all of her from the top of her blonde head all the way down to the golden mound that provided ample proof that she was indeed a natural blonde; she was so indescribably beautiful. Then, as he watched, she moved her hands up her body in a caressing motion that ended as she cupped her full breasts one in each hand. It was only then that Jason realized she was looking directly towards where he was sitting. He was now also aware that such an enticing view might just have drawn him forward, ever so slightly but, nevertheless, leaving him without his full original cover. He continued to watch as she now draped herself in her long robe, picked up her bathing suit and started across the lawn towards the old mansion. Jason sat still afraid to move but he was almost certain that just before she disappeared from his view she turned and looked back and once again her gaze was directly at where he was sitting.

Sunday was a lazy day in the barracks. During the morning Hank had dropped in to check with Jason and made sure that he was prepared to commence his training the following morning then took off to meet his girl friend in town. His girl friend had borrowed a car and they were going to an area lake for a picnic. He said that he would have invited Jason except that it had been a couple of weeks since he had seen the girl and he was reasonably sure that the picnic

14

would include some special dessert, the latter stated with a broad suggestive wink.

Jason wished his newfound friend the best of luck and hoped that he would enjoy the dessert. After lunch Jason ensured that batteries were installed in his portable keyboard and headed down to the spot beside the stream where he had spent such a pleasant few minutes the previous day even without his music. Under normal circumstances Jason would have defended himself vigorously against any charges of voyeurism. But this was different. He just had not been able to get the vision of the girl out of his head since the previous day. He had even gone to sleep in a heightened state of arousal and it was only his complete fatigue at that point that prevented the natural consequence of completely involuntary release while he slept. Regardless, he clung to his personal claim that he was not a voyeur, but that same melody was still running through his mind and he wanted to try and set it to frames of music and he just couldn't think of a nicer spot than down by the stream in the shade of that big tree. If the girl reappeared, well, that would be just a fringe bonus.

Before settling down in nearly the identical spot he had occupied the previous day, Jason checked his lines of sight very carefully. He ensured that he had a clear vision of the pool and that his own location was concealed as much as possible from the other side of the stream. He put on his earphones and commenced his efforts to recapture the melody. He continued with appreciable success for nearly an hour and utilized the memory capacity of the keyboard to store the melody planning to set it to paper when he returned to his quarters. He had not seen any sign of the beautiful young girl but he noted that the big black dog that she had identified as Plato had appeared and was stretched out on the lawn beside the water. He was suddenly aware that he was no longer alone, that someone was watching him. He turned his head and there she was behind him not more than ten feet away.

Dressed in that long, white beach towel robe. She spoke in German in a very stern tone of voice.

Jason removed his head set and, using a phrase from his Guide to Germany handbook, told her what he hoped amounted to his confession that he did not speak German. She immediately switched to halting but thoroughly understandable English. "What are you doing here? Why are you watching me?"

Jason decided that honesty was the best policy. "To answer your second question first I was watching you because you are so beautiful. The answer to the first question is that I am composing a melody on my keyboard"

The honesty worked and he noticed that she was blushing as she translated his words. "But that does not give you the right to look at me....she groped for another word, to glare at me, no, to leer - that is the word - at me. Do you always look like that at things you think are beautiful?" Again she was blushing.

"Yes, I do look at things, sorry, objects, people I think are beautiful. I go to art galleries to look, not leer, I never leer, at paintings that I think are beautiful. There is absolutely no law against that."

"But this is private property," she protested.

"No, that is private property, "said Jason pointing to the other side of the stream. "Oh, yes, this is private property but it is the property of the American Armed Forces. So you are trespassing. Perhaps, I will arrest you for trespassing. Another question; why shouldn't I look when you obviously knew I was here and you made those suggestive movements with your hands. Was that not an invitation to me to look?"

And now she was really blushing. "No, that is not what I meant. I just wanted to show you that I could do what I liked on my side of the stream. Sure, I knew you were there but I don't like to be stared at by strange men especially American boys." The latter was intended to put him into the category of just an inquisitive boy who really just didn't know what he was looking for. "And just what is that thing you call a keyboard." She came just a little closer and bent over to examine the keyboard, which was now across Jason's lap.

Jason lifted the keyboard suddenly and, startled, she stepped back. "It's only a keyboard, don't be afraid, it won't bite you."

"Do not be so silly," she replied a little angrily. "I know it will not bite but what is it?" She continued.

"It is like a small piano," Jason replied. "Listen, this is the melody I was composing and" now Jason was fibbing just a bit, "I composed it just for you." He recalled the melody from the keyboard's memory and played it as he turned up the volume. She listened apparently entranced. "Oh, yes, it is like a little piano and, yes, that is very pretty music. I play the piano, do you?"

"Yes," answered Jason, "I have played piano for many years."

"We have a big piano, it is what you call a grand piano. Would you play this pretty melody for me on our piano?"

"Yes, but you must promise me that his is not a trap and you will not arrest me for trespassing when I cross the stream. I have been instructed that the mansion is out of bounds to us."

"Don't be silly," she replied. "Anyone can come into the mansion if we invite them. You will meet Gerda's friend

Woody. He is American and he comes to our house many times".

They made their way carefully across the top of the low dam and, now joined by Plato, walked up to the steps leading to the rear entrance of the mansion. Just inside the door they were met by a tall, blonde German woman whom Jason recognized as the same woman who had joined a big black American for several duets at the bar Friday evening.

The girl introduced the woman as her very special friend, Gerda, who was their housekeeper. Then turning to Jason she blushed on realizing that she still didn't know his name, "This is........Jason Creighton interjected Jason, he is going to play our piano for me."

"Ah, Sandy liebling (and now Jason realized that the girl's name was Sandy)" said Gerda, in halting English. "I have met, no seen, your friend already. He played for us at the gasthause on Friday evening. Woody and I heard him and he is very good! But be as quiet as possible, the General is in his study."

As they walked down the centre hall of the mansion Jason was very impressed by the heavy oak walls. The high ceilinged rooms he could see through open doors on each side of the hall all appeared to be furnished with heavy ornate furniture and one, obviously the dining room, had a table that must have been at least thirty feet long. As they reached the music room, which was not far from the main entrance and off the main drawing room the girl, now identified as Sandy, pointed silently at another door leading off the drawing room and Jason assumed that it was the old General's study. The music room was nearly circular in shape and it reminded Jason of a concert stage and it appeared that it might have been designed to acoustically enhance the instrument located at very close to the geometric center of the room. The glass doors to the room seemed be of particularly

18

heavy construction and Sandy left them open. She announced with a shy little smile that Helga had told her not to be alone in a room with a boy or her reputation would suffer. "I don't really understand what that means but I love Helga and believe her when she tells me something".

Jason was impressed. This was not only a grand piano in the great tradition of concert pianos but was probably the most magnificent grand piano he had ever seen. He recognized the maker's name proudly emblazoned upon the front of the piano just above the keyboard as the famous maker of the world's greatest concert pianos. He ran quietly through a few scales and he was pleased to note that the instrument was in fine tune and was now even more convinced that the room had been designed with the acoustics of the piano in mind. He then played lightly through the melody that he had professed to have written especially for her and she was delighted. She indicated for him to move over and then proceeded to replay the melody herself and did so quite accurately showing both a fairly high standard of musicianship and an excellent ear.

"That was very good." said Jason. "You play very well and play by ear which is quite unusual. Let's try something else." He proceeded to play one of his great favorites, an Etude for Piano by Chopin. This was one of the more complex pieces that he could play from memory without music because he had played it so often. It was also a great favorite of both his mother and Grandfather Conrad.

"That was so beautiful," said Sandy. "I think that I could do it but I'd need the music." They hadn't noticed but through the open glass doors to the music room they now saw that the study door had opened and the tall figure of the old General had appeared.

"Sandra," The voice came from the doorway, "That was Chopin. I didn't know you played Chopin and you played it

19

so well. That piece was a favorite of my wife and she played it for me many times."

"Oh no Grandfather, that was not me playing it was my new friend Jason." It was now that Jason remembered that Hank had told him that the old General was blind. He swung his long white cane as he came towards the open music room doors.

"Jason, who is this Jason?" he asked.

"Jason is an American. He is my new friend and he will teach me to play Chopin." She was speaking in German and when she told Jason later just what she had said he realized that the slight exaggeration was purely to aid in the introduction but knew he would be more than willing to accept the assignment.

A sound something like "harumph" came from the old General as he stopped at the doorway leading to the music room. "An American?" He was now speaking in near perfect English. "I do not care much for Americans but he does play very well."

They had been in the music room for more than an hour when they saw a young man dressed in a chauffeur's uniform - Sandy identified him as Mannheim Hillstrom, Gerda's nephew - knock on the door of the General's study and watched the two of them go out the front door. They now noticed that the General's highly polished old staff car had been brought around to the front and was parked in front of the main entrance. As they watched, the impressive old car drove off with Mannheim at the wheel and the old General seated very upright in the back seat.

"They are going to the Post Office," announced Sandy. "The General has a post office box there and he and Mannheim go there once a week to pick up his mail. All of the

20

mail and magazines are about chess games the General is playing. Manheim reads the mail to him and positions the chess pieces for all his games. Sometimes he plays games by phone but Mannheim deals with all the correspondence and telephone calls. Come with me I want to show you something."

Sandy led Jason to the now open study door and Jason realized that this was more a library than a study but much of the space of the room was taken up by three tables and on each table was mounted a chess set. Jason's grandfather Conrad had been an avid devotee of the game of chess and had attempted to teach Jason at least the basics of the game before his stroke but Jason was only really interested in music. However, he knew enough about the game to be very impressed by at least one of the chess sets, which occupied the table in the center of the room. It was the most beautiful chess set he had ever seen. The figures were obviously carved from ivory and inlaid with what appeared to be gold and silver. Sandy noted his interest and told him that it had been a present to the General's great grandfather from the King of Prussia and that there were only two like it in the world.

Sandy sat down in front of the General's desk and pointed to the books on the desk. Several of them were open and obviously all in Braille. Now she pointed to all the pictures mounted on the wall behind the desk. She identified them as the General's three sons, his two daughters, his wife and his three grandsons.

"This, "said Sandy, indicating one of the pictures" was his second son, Victor. He was Helga's father. She is my guardian and friend. His body lies at the bottom of the Atlantic; he was a U Boat Commander and only 35 years old. This was his oldest son, Wilheim, he died at Stalingrad when he was a Major General and only 36. His youngest son, Jurgen, was a Major in a Panzer regiment who was killed at

Falaise in France. He was only 27 years old. " She drew his attention to two of the young women and told Jason that these were his daughters both of whom died in the war. One was killed in the huge air raid on Hamburg and the other was killed by the Russians when they over ran her husband's estate in Silesia. Helga's mother was also killed in that raid on Hamburg when she was visiting her sister-in-law. "

She then pointed to the pictures of three teenage boys, all in the uniform of what she described as that of the Hitler Youth. "You see they look so much alike because they were triplets. They all died on the Eastern Front when they were only seventeen and all of them lie where they fell on the battlefield in unmarked graves. In fact only the body of the General's youngest son was returned for burial in the family burial ground." One other picture was of a very beautiful young woman who Sandy identified as the old General's wife who had died in the influenza epidemic of 1919 when she was only in her thirties. "They all died so young and it makes me very sad to sit here and think of them." Jason noticed that tears had welled up in her eyes.

There was a moment of silence and she continued. "Yes, it makes me so sad, they were so young. Why did they have to die?" Tears were now streaming down her cheeks. "The old General is very stern and gruff and difficult to love but I do love him when I sit here and think of all these dead young people."

Jason was very touched as he followed her back to the music room. They spent a couple of hours at the piano as Jason tried to show her what he called the Chopin touch. He showed her that all the great composers and pianists had distinctive characteristics and Chopin's was his very light and deft touch on the keys. Jason was delighted with the way she appeared to quickly learn this first lesson.

Later they went back down the long hall to the big kitchen. Gerda had been joined by the big black American who had done the duets with her at the gasthause on Friday night and Gerda introduced him as Sergeant Woody Washington. They were also joined by Plato who had come in from outside with expectations of a snack.

Gerda and Woody commented on Jason's performance on Friday evening and he explained to Sandy that his friend Hank had volunteered his services to the impromptu amateur program. He told her that it had been a new experience for him and he had not been sure as to what he should actually do. Gerda, in heavily accented English interjected that Jason was much too modest, that he had been the hit of the evening and Woody added similar comments to the critique. They mentioned the Beatles number that he had played in which he had encouraged, and received, the participation of the crowd. Sandy was very impressed.

"The Beatles?" She asked. "You play the music of the Beatles? You must teach me." Jason promised he would now realizing that he would agree to anything just to ensure the continued company of this amazingly beautiful girl.

Woody had just completed setting the large kitchen table and Gerda reminded Jason. "He is a cook you know but here, in my kitchen I am the only cook. I let him set the table, peel the potatoes, wash the dishes, but he does not cook, not in my kitchen!" She concluded with emphasis. "And now, sit down and we'll have a little early supper."

Sandy excused herself to change and as Jason took a seat at the table he was joined by Plato who quite obviously believed that the newcomer might be the best prospect to provide table scraps. Before serving Gerda suddenly became very serious. She was holding a long wooden spoon and she placed the end of this spoon squarely in the middle of Jason's chest.

23

"You know Jason I think you are a very nice young man. Anyone who creates such heavenly music must be a good person. I just want you to understand that Sandra is a very special person. She has been the joy of this house for many years and we love her very much. She is not like those silly girls at the gasthause. I give you fair warning, do not hurt her or I will have my big friend here," indicating Woody," search you out and he is very strong."

Jason protested that they were just friends and that his intentions were strictly honorable but feeling that the latter assertion might not be completely true.

Sandy reappeared still bubbling from her experiences of the afternoon. She was now wearing a beautiful short pink dress that fitted her like a second skin. Both Gerda and Woody told them that they had been listening to the sounds from the music room and it had sounded so beautiful. Jason pointed out that much of it had been Sandy playing with Sandy interjecting "But not the Chopin. Even Grandfather heard that and said he enjoyed it and Jason will teach me how to play the beautiful music from Chopin and then I will play it for grandfather."

Gerda served a delicious thick broth containing large pieces of heavily spiced meat accompanied by warm home-made bread and pure country butter. It was absolutely delicious and Plato agreed as he moved around the table scrounging a little from each of them.

Mannheim returned from driving the old General and immediately prepared a tray and took it to the old General. When he returned he and Jason were formally introduced and Mannheim immediately broke into a lengthy soliloquy of praise for America. He spoke slowly in perfect, albeit ac-cented, English and took great pains to ensure the correct pronunciation of each word.

"Oh, yes, " he pronounced. "I will go to America some day and I will become a very fine American citizen. Already I am studying American history and I can tell you all the names of the American presidents. I can recite both the Oath of Allegiance and Lincoln's Gettysberg Address. I know that I must make myself stronger and improve my health but Woody brings me Ameican magazines and I send for medicine and equipment that will make me healthy and strong. You must come to my room and I will show you."

After they had eaten Sandy and Jason accompanied Mannheim to his room. Jason was taken aback by the contents of the room. First there were stacks of magazines around the walls of the big room. Jason readily recognized many of the magazines as those publications that could be found beside the check out counters of most super markets and on the lower shelves of magazine racks in book stores. Above the stacks of magazines were shelves loaded with all kinds of containers with labels advising of miracle cures, hair removal, complexion enhancement and health food supplements. There were also a number of pieces of equipment of the type designed to develop specific areas of the body.

"You see, "said Mannheim. "I have all of these things to help me to prepare for my medical. This is why America is so great. It is truly the land of the free where everyone has the same opportunity to become a citizen and they even make available all of these wonderful things to help us to meet their standards. Jason, if you see anything advertised in an American magazine that might help me please cut it out and bring it to me."

Jason just nodded his head in what he hoped Mannheim would interpret as an affirmative. But Jason was really speechless He had never seen so much phony patent medicine, and equally phony physical equipment in one place in his life.

On their way back to the kitchen Sandy explained that Mannheim had his heart set on going to America but the years of upheaval from the time he and Gerda had left Russia and made their way through the Displaced Persons Camps had taken their toll on Mannheim. Despite Gerda's valiant efforts her nephew's health had been damaged irreparably. But hope springs eternal and Mannheim clung to his dream. Sandy described Mannheim as a very good person, He was very kind and loyal to all members of the family including the old General who could be a very difficult taskmaster and for whom Mannheim had assumed the role as chauffeur and personal servant. He was also the "jack of all trades" for all matters relating to maintenance in the household. Sandy commented that it was really sad but Mannheim circle of friends consisted of few others than members of the household. He did not seem to like girls and it was her opinion he was what the girls at her school called gay. The word describing Mannheim's sexual orientation came from Sandy's lips very naturally and Jason was at a loss when he recalled his reaction later. It was just that he was surprised that the word came so easily from the lips of this seemingly innocent and beautiful young girl.

As they walked across the lawn towards the pond they were accompanied by Plato who, apparently, had decided that Jason had met with his stamp of approval after revealing himself as a soft touch when he had made his rounds scrounging at the kitchen table.

As they reached the narrow walk across the top of the dam, Sandy told him that she would be back from school late on Thursday and reminded him that she would hold him to his promise to teach her how to play the beautiful music of Chopin. He promised that he would be there Thursday evening. This was easy; nothing short of World War III would keep him away from this incredible person. She thanked him and kissed him very lightly on his cheek.

"I like you Jason Creighton." She whispered softly. I think you are a very nice person and you make beautiful music. But please don't try to ......me." Jason was shocked as he recognized the German equivalent to the English f...word). "Helga and Gerda tell me that I must not do that because bad things can happen if I let a boy do that to me."

Jason was absolutely speechless. The word was the very last he would expect to hear from those beautiful, innocent lips. He was red-faced and tongue-tied and she looked at him in wonderment. When he finally recovered he told her "That word, Sandy, you should not use that word! Nice girls do not use that word!"

"But what is wrong, it is only a word and my friends at the school use it all the time and they are nice girls. You know what I mean and isn't that what words are for?"

At this point, at least, Jason was in no mental condition to challenge her logic but the word was still ringing in his ears as he made his way across the dam.

When he arrived back at his quarters he found that sleeping accommodation had been rearranged and his new roommate was Hank who told him that this was S/Sgt Mombirkett's idea so they could study together for the remainder of the "in job training" program. Jason had found Hank very agreeable so he had no complaint with this arrangement.

Hank was already in bed and Jason watched him stretching languorously. "I'm really beat" Hank announced. "That dessert was so delicious, I had three helpings!" This remark concluded with a knowing snicker. "Boy oh boy, does that little girl ever want to go to America. And how was your day?"

"Just wonderful!" Jason replied. "That was, without a doubt, the most wonderful day of my life." He told Hank about his day at the Mansion starting with his experience at the stream the previous day. He told Hank all the details, the music, the old General, the food right down to when he and Sandy had said goodbye. He described the gentle kiss on his cheek and then the shocker when the equivalent to the English "f…" word came from those innocent lips. He also told Hank that he would be spending most of the following weekend at the mansion teaching Sandy how to play Chopin.

Now it was Hank's turn to be speechless. When he finally broke the silence it was with an emphatic "Jason, you son of a bitch, you are either the biggest bullshitter in this man's army or the luckiest. You spent the day with that gorgeous young blonde at the mansion after seeing all of her goodies yesterday and she kissed you on the cheek when you left, made a date with you for next weekend, and, then, softly told you that she would not let you fuck her. My God I have never heard anything like this in all my born days. Do you realize that while I have been gazing at that mansion for two years, I have only seen her three or four times and, until this actual moment, I didn't even know her name was Sandy. Every goddam man in this unit who isn't radically queer has been drooling at the very thought of that beauty and Jason Creighton walks in on practically his first day in Germany, has her willfully expose her goodies to him, invites him into the mansion to teach her music, introduces him to all the members of the family including the old General, feeds him, kisses him on the cheek, talks dirty to him and makes a date for next weekend. My God Jason it is so incredible that I believe you. But do you realize what you have done? In two days you have achieved the wettest of wet dreams of every man on this base who has caught the slightest glimpse of that beauty to whom you now refer very casually as Sandy. This is the girl that stouthearted studs talk of with the deepest reverence. They refer to her as prime table stock and one of our aspiring poets made the ultimate statement when he said that he would use her shit for toothpaste!"

28

CHAPTER III

Lt Col JULES PORTEOUS PELLADEAU

Lt Col Jules Pelladeau, Commanding Officer of the 8th Armoured Regiment, arrived in his office at shortly before 7 a.m. on Monday, May 27th. His Second in Command informed him that Squadron Commanders had been advised to be in the Conference Room at 7.30 a.m. for the regular weekly briefing as per Regimental Standing Orders. Jules had been absent the previous Monday on Temporary Duty to NATO HQ in Brussels and was now looking forward to receiving reports from his Squadron Commanders as well as reports from his HQ Staff on the progress being made on a number of programs that he had set in motion since taking command less than a year earlier.

Jules Pelladeau was quite young for his current rank and command especially when his African American background was taken into consideration. African American "streamers" were few and far between but then few African Americans had either the academic or family background of Jules Pelladeau. He had graduated third in the 1954 class at the Point. He had been All-America at tight end on a very successful football team and had had a couple of great games against Navy. He had been awarded a very well deserved Rhodes Scholarship and, while at Oxford, completed his Masters Degree in European history in less than eighteen months and earned a "blue" as a member of the Oxford boat in the famous Oxford-Cambridge boat race.

In the twelve years after Oxford Jules Pelladeau had completed two three year tours of duty with armoured regiments and armoured formation HQs in Korea and Germany and one three year tour of duty in a faculty appointment at West Point where he had lectured cadets on European History. While back at the Point Jules had applied for and had been accepted in the Cornell Doctoral Program indicating that his field of study would be Modern European History and that he would select the theme for his doctoral thesis after a faculty advisor had been chosen to work with him. After the mandatory year in residence at Cornell, Jules was notified that he would be eligible to participate in the university's extension program and this would permit him to continue his military career, report on a regular schedule to his faculty advisor and return to Cornell when he was prepared to present his Doctoral Thesis to the Doctoral Committee of the Board of Supervisors.

To assist him in completing his Ph D program Jules requested that his next posting be to Germany. Not only was his request granted but he was promoted to command the front line armoured regiment to which he would be posted. When the Extension Department of the University was advised of his posting they informed. him that they had requested Lt Gen Carl Reichold to act as his faculty advisor. General Reichold had earned his Ph D in the same program that Jules was now entering and was also stationed in Germany. In fact, General Reichold was the Corps Commander of the armoured formation to which Jules' regiment was assigned.

Jules' father, Major Romeo Pelladeau was well known in military circles. In 1942 he had been the catering manager of a small luxury hotel in the French Quarter of New Orleans. When Dwight Eisenhower was assembling his HQ Staff one of his staff officers approached Romeo Pelladeau and found he would be very interested in the appointment as Director of Food Services for Eisenhower's Headquarters. He joined Eisenhower's HQ in England late in 1942 as a Warrant Officer and was commissioned less than a year later. He quickly earned a reputation as an outstanding food services director with a special talent for those major catering events attended by international dignitaries and which were far beyond the talents of most directors of food services.

At the end of the war Romeo was a Major and he accompanied Eisenhower to NATO and, when Eisenhower was elected president, Major Pelladeau requested a posting as Director of Food Services at West Point where his only son had accepted a special appointment to the corps. This posting was arranged with the firm understanding that Major Pelladeau would continue to be available to return to the White House to assist in the catering for all major international events.

Jules' mother was from the island of Martinique in the West Indies where her family dated back to one of the original governors when an ancestor of Mrs. Pelladeau had been the product of an affair between the governor and one of his slaves. The Porteous family had survived and thrived in the islands and continued to enjoy a prominent social position in both Martinique and the adjoining islands. Elizabeth Porteous had been educated at an excellent girls' boarding school in England and went on to take both her undergraduate degree and MA from Tulane specializing in Early Childhood Education. In New Orleans she had met the very handsome young Romeo Pelladeau who was the very popular catering manager at a local luxury hotel. They were married in 1930 and their only son, Jules Porteous Pelladeau, was born in New Orleans in 1932. Elizabeth Pelladeau was the assistant headmistress of a girls' private school in the New Orleans area when her husband was recruited into Eisenhower's staff. She returned with her young son to her family home in Martinique for the duration of the war. She rejoined her husband on his return to the US after the war and she accompanied him on his postings to NATO in Europe, back to Washington and then to West Point. For many of these years Elizabeth was employed as either a teacher or headmistress of fashionable girls' schools but her top priority was always the early education of her only son.

While attending the girls' school in England Elizabeth Porteous, already fluent in English and French, had shown a definite flair for languages, and had become fluent also in both German and Spanish. Her background in the French language led to some very interesting exchanges with her husband who was also fluent in French and also in the Cajun dialect. He was very light skinned and the descendant of the original Acadians who had been expelled from Nova Scotia and New Brunswick two hundred years earlier and during that period there had been numerous permutations and combinations with African Americans and a variety of other nationalities. On the other hand Elizabeth Porteous Pelladeau was very proud of the purity of her African American ancestry and, while very fine featured, Elizabeth was very black.

Jules had been an excellent student and a very fine athlete. He was All State in the State of New York in football despite attending a relatively small upstate school. He also received a number of honorable mentions in both track and field and basketball. He was heavily recruited by major universities but he never had any doubt as to where he would be going to college. In 1950 he received a presidential appointment to West Point. While the appointment came from President Harry Truman it was made at the request of General Dwight Eisenhower. His mother had some reservations about a military career for her son but she fully appreciated her husband's love for his chosen profession and his ambition to have one of the first black officers of general rank come from his family.

In 1950 West Point could be a rough place for minorities. The corps had its share of "rednecks" who were not averse to making life miserable for the relatively small number of African Americans and Hispanics who received appointments. But while Jules was certainly not the first African American to attend West Point he was probably the first to rate special consideration. Everyone on campus knew exactly who Jules was. This was not only because of his success in academics or athletics but everyone knew very well that he was under the watchful eye of Major Romeo Pel-

32

ladeau who carried an awful lot more rank that that denoted by the oak leaves on his shoulders. This was *THE* Romeo Pelladeau, the personal friend of generals and presidents. It was never that Jules asked for or expected special treatment because he just went with the flow and strived to meet the highest standards demanded by the corps. However, his connections protected him from some of the difficulties encountered by other members of the corps from minorities.

He was 22 years of age at graduation, third in his class and had been twice an All American tight end in football and had also received a number of honorable mentions in basketball.

On this Monday morning Jules would be meeting with his squadron commanders and members of his headquarters staff. When he had been promoted and given command of this very select regiment he had been pleasantly surprised but had been prepared for the possibility of resentment from officers he had jumped or superceded. His regimental second in command and two of his squadron commanders fell into this category but he found them totally loyal and supportive. Certainly, he thought, the influence of Romeo Pelladeau did not extend this far. Jules had developed his own ideas on command from his tours of regimental duty and by studying the commanders he had admired and his personal accomplishments had given him a level of self confidence that allowed him to introduce these ideas. They were implemented immediately and smoothly.

Following the staff meeting Jules received progress reports from all of his staff and junior commanders. There would be a major NATO military exercise in late August and all the squadron commanders were advised to keep the Second in Command informed on the state of readiness of all weapons and equipment. Strength of units was to be maintained at the war establishment plus 10% as prescribed for front line units. The head of the Special Weapons Section

33

was instructed to brief him later in the day on all current nuclear weapon codes.

After the meeting the Second in Command (2IC) who had been in command during Jules' absence brought Jules up to date on amendments to formation standing orders which had been received during the past week. The only one requiring early action was one that had quite obviously started with the Department of Immigration and was on the subject of mixed race marriages which would result in Americans returning to the United States accompanied by a spouse of a different racial origin. Jules' 2IC advised that there was one application in the unit that fell into this category and it was the application of Sgt Woodrow Wilson Washington to marry a German national of Caucasian ethnicity, Gerda Hillstrom, who was housekeeper at the von Freiderhoff Mansion. The new standing order directed that Commanding Officers should make every effort to personally interview all such applicants and determine their suitability for American citizenship.

"I would think that the irony of the situation will not escape the notice of anyone." Said Jules with a smile and his 2IC nodded in agreement. "I wonder if the creator of this standing order thought for a moment that there are at least a few of us African American commanders over here and if they really want our opinion on mixed marriages." His 2IC chuckled appreciatively and volunteered to undertake this assignment.

"No," replied Jules. "I think I'll take this one myself. I have always been just a bit curious about the Enclave von Freiderhoff and this might be my only opportunity to visit the place. Just ask my clerk to advise the Mansion that I would like to call upon them on Thursday morning and have the prospective groom come to see me at 3 p.m. today."

Later in the morning Jules received a telephone call from Lt Gen Carl Reichold the corps commander. General Reichold advised Jules that he had received a request that he act as Jules' faculty advisor in his doctoral program and that he had accepted with pleasure. He told Jules that his own Ph D from Cornell was in the same academic field that Jules had chosen and he now looked forward to meeting Jules and deciding the most effective manner in which the General could aid the younger officer in his program of studies. He also told Jules that he had noted that Jules' predecessor at the 8th Armoured Regiment had been an important member of the General's standing NATO committee on the deployment doctrine for armoured units and hoped that Jules would continue in this role. The duties were not particularly onerous but they would have a major presentation when all the representatives of the NATO countries attended the annual NATO conference in August.

Jules agreed immediately and they arranged their first meeting for the afternoon of Tuesday, June 4th, at 3 p.m. and agreed that these meetings could be used to discuss academic matters and preliminary planning for the proposed NATO program. An extended schedule of meetings would be arranged at the first meeting.

Jules had heard of Lt Gen Carl Reichold; in fact all officers serving in armoured units knew about the General. He had graduated from the Point near the top of his class in 1942 and had served with distinction in both the invasion of France and the advance through Northwest Europe and ended World War II as a very young regimental commander. He had grown up in Minnesota in a family of German origin, was fluent in German and had made All America as a center on the Point's ice hockey team. He had served again as a regimental commander in Korea and, having paid his dues, earned all the required decorations, he could be now classified as a "streamer" and in line for accelerated promotions.

He had also been back to West Point for two separate tours of duty on the academic staff.

At 3 p.m. Sgt Woodrow Wilson Washington was ushered into his office. Jules had had an opportunity to review Woody's personnel file and found everything on the file to be quite satisfactory. The Sergeant was 37 years of age and had been in the service for fifteen years with a short shift in Korea at the conclusion of that war or police action. Jules noted that the very large man now sitting in his office had attended university in Florida but there was no mention of credits earned. Jules immediately suspected that this was one of the many football casualties and when he asked Woody if he played football Woody's short succinct answer was "Not any more."

Woody's annual fitness reports indicated that he was a good average soldier. His superiors described him as a hard worker and always willing to do more than his share in any work project. The only negative remarks came on the subjects of imagination and ambition. Nothing really that bad there, the Sergeant was just a contented soldier putting his time in until pension.

"We have your application for permission to marry a German national named Gerda Hillstrom who, I believe, is employed as housekeeper at the Enclave von Freiderhoff. Tell me about her."

Woody was very nervous and Jules gave him a few minutes to put his thoughts together. "Gerda, is a very special woman," commenced Woody. "She has had a very hard life. Her family had been relocated in Russia in the 1930s as part of a religious experiment and then they were caught up by the war. Of all her large family only Gerda and her nephew Mannheim survived the war and the DP Camps. She came to work at the Mansion as a chambermaid nearly twenty years ago and has worked her way up to her present position of housekeeper. I have known her for nearly four years and know she would make a fine American citizen. I have been teaching her all about America and she already speaks fairly good English. I have been proposing to her for over two years but it was only recently that she accepted me."

"Yes, Sergeant, I'm sure that your Gerda would make a fine American citizen but have you explained to her about the racial prejudice that still exists in our country and how mixed marriages always attract vicious comments from the bigots. Do you think that she could deal with that? Many German girls, in similar circumstances, have been very unhappy in the States and many have returned to Germany leaving some very unhappy families."

"Yes, I have tried to explain that to her. Our plan would be to remain in Germany until I retire and then look for employment in upstate New York or New England with a family needing a strong back - perhaps a chauffeur - and a good cook - Gerda is a wonderful cook - and after we saved up a bit of money we might try to open our own restaurant. We have decided upon either New England or upstate New York because the anti-race sentiments would not be as rampant there as in the south. I assure you sir that our expectations would be very reasonable. We both would like children but when my retirement comes up in five years it might be a bit late for that. We would consider adopting one or two orphans from areas of poverty in third world countries. When you meet Gerda I'm sure you will find that everything I say is true. Her employer is the old General's granddaughter, Helga. She lives and works in Frankfort but she is home for a few days nearly every week and she handles the management of the property. She always tells me that Gerda does such a good job in looking after the General and the household when she is away.".

"Well, Sergeant, that's just about it, I will be meeting your Gerda and, hopefully, the General's granddaughter, later in the week. There shouldn't be any problem. You are both mature adults and know what you are doing. My only comment is that surely this is some indication of progress when we find an African American Colonel interviewing an African American Sergeant on the subject of mixed marriages."

Woody's broad smile indicated that the irony of the situation had not been lost on him.

On Thursday morning Jules drove up to the main entrance to the Mansion. He recalled driving past the building so many times and had always wondered just what it would be like inside. The remaining building was just one half of the original mansion. The other half had been destroyed by a combination of bombing and fire during the war. There were several small utility buildings now occupying the land upon which the ruined wing had previously stood. One of the utility buildings was quite obviously used as a garage because Jules could see, through the open door, the shape of the very large old staff car that carried the old General through the town about once a week. Parked beside the garage was a much smaller car but Jules recognized it as a top of the line luxurious Mercedes Benz two seater.

Jules rang the doorbell and could hear the melodious chimes announcing his presence from the other side of the heavy oak door. Through the glazed, frosted glass panel on the door he watched as a figure approached the door and swung it open. Standing in the doorway was a very tall and beautiful blonde woman. This was quite obviously not Gerda but Jules thought that he detected a hint of surprise in her eyes.

Jules introduced himself speaking in German. "I am Lt-Col Jules Pelladeau, Commanding Officer of the 8th Armoured Regiment and I am required to interview one of your servants, Gerda Hillstrom, whom one of my sergeants has applied for permission to marry."

The slight look of surprise remained in her eyes as she listened to his near perfect German introduction and she replied in near perfect English. "Ah, yes, Colonel, I have been expecting you. Your German is excellent but I was looking forward to practicing my English on you. Please come in."

As they went down the hall past the drawing room Jules noticed that a door off the drawing room had opened revealing a tall, elderly man. "What is it, Helga?" a voice asked.

"Oh, Grandfather, it's all right. This is Colonel Pelladeau from the US army. You will remember I told you that Gerda's friend has applied for permission to marry her and the Colonel must speak to her." They spoke in rapid German.

"Ah yes, of course. Gerda and the big black American she has been seeing. Americans, I am not that fussy about blacks; in fact, I really I don't like Americans that much."

Jules felt words expressing his impression of Germans right at the tip of his tongue but withheld any such remarks saying instead, in carefully measured German. "Yes, General I apologize for this intrusion into your home. I assure you that it will only take a few minutes."

"An American who speaks such good German," muttered the old General as he retreated into his study.

As Jules passed the still open study door he was halted in his tracks by what he saw in the middle of the very large combination library and study. There, mounted on a large table, was the most magnificent chess set he had ever seen and reacting involuntarily to the layout of the pieces he announced "that is the Sicillian Defence." This was a classic strategy but one used only by experienced players of chess.

And now this comment stopped the old General in his tracks as he was moving towards his desk using his long white cane to guide him. "Yes, Colonel, you are correct, that is the   Sicillian Defence. And if you had the white figures what your strategy be." Jules answered immediately and the old General swung his cane emphatically. "Yes, that is exactly right. That is precisely where most players make their mistake and lose the match. Indeed, you are a chess player and quite obviously a student of your famous compatriot Bobby Fischer of whom I have read so much."

"Yes, and it is not my intent to boast, but I was playing against chess masters when I was twelve years old. I spent my summers with my grandfather who was a chess master and both my mother and father were devoted to the game. You are absolutely correct, I have been an avid follower of Bobby Fischer in his career."

"That is so very interesting. Perhaps you would like to have a game with me some time. Yes, I am blind, but I have total recall of the board. My servant makes all the moves for me in my games by mail and telephone but it would be very challenging to have a real live opponent. Helga plays with me occasionally but her mind is usually on other things and as you know so well Colonel, chess is a game of complete concentration."

"Yes, I would be delighted to have a match with you General. How about Saturday afternoon at three o'clock?

"Yes, yes, yes" replied the General with some enthusiasm. "I will look forward to it and I apologize about my earlier remarks about Americans, it's probably the blacks that I don't understand."

Again a retort was on the tip of Jules' tongue when he noticed that Helga had put her finger to her lips pleading silence and he withheld the remark.

As they continued down the hall Helga thanked him for withholding his remark. "I ask you to excuse him, he is a very old man and still lives in a different age. But in his response to the promise of a real chess match against a real live player of obvious experience and skill he showed the first enthusiasm I have seen for years. For nearly thirty years his whole life has been chess. In his study you may not have noticed but he has three large tables with chess sets mounted on each and he plays all three games simultaneously by phone and by mail. His servant, Mannheim, handles all the phone calls and correspondence but he does not find it the same as competing with a live competitor face to face. Sometimes I agree to play but he is quite right I have too many other things on my mind and I'm not much of a player to start. He is very good, probably close to the level of chess master and he sometimes gets angry with me when I make silly moves. He is a perfectionist and probably has always been of that nature in other things besides chess. Obviously, he does not know you are black. It's not really that difficult to realize what he would have done had he known you were black. I doubt if he would play with you; I doubt if he would even speak to you. He has given instructions that Woody - Gerda's black man as he calls him - only enter through the rear entrance and remain in the kitchen. Of course he doesn't know that they are sleeping together. All I ask is that you remind yourself that he is just an old man. Despite some ideas that must seem very strange to our generation he has an amazing mind and even at close to 84 years of age he has near total recall of everything that has happened in Germany since the turn of the century. He really needs a challenge and I think you would be it!"

"All right! All right!" Jules answered. "I'm convinced. But I give you fair warning. Ayrians and master race proponents have never been among my favorite people, and that should be obvious to all but the totally blind. Whoops, sorry about that. I'll play chess with him. I'm even looking forward to it. To be able to play three games at one time with total recall of the boards from memory that's pretty amazing and suggests a formidable opponent."

Helga stopped before entering the kitchen. "You remember my comment that he has total recall but that is up to 1938 or the actual date that Adolph Hitler had his famous meeting with Benito Mussolini in the Alps at the Brenner Pass. That was the day he walked out of Hitler's HQ, got into his staff car and personally drove himself back here. That was the point at which my Grandfather gave up all hope for the Germany he had loved so much. You have heard the expression "Stop the world, I want to get off". Well, on that day, the world stopped and my Grandfather got off. When you sit in his study playing chess just let your eyes wander over all of the decorations, awards and the pictures. Grandfather raised his sons in the proud tradition of the Germany he knew and they raised his Grandsons the same way. When you sit in that study you will realize that he has nothing left but old photographs of dead young people and his guilt."

Helga continued "I know full well that you are proud that you are African American; so is Woody. But Woody accepts the old man. He realizes that his words come from a different time and Woody tells us that he has heard even more hurtful remarks back in the United States. Your secret is yours for so long as you want to keep it but you might even find it to be an interesting experience if you wish to talk about the old Germany with my Grandfather."

Gerda and Woody were both in the kitchen when they entered and the table was set. Helga announced that Gerda would allow just about anything in her kitchen except that she was the only one allowed to cook and, no matter what your activity was, eating must be included. The table was set and she served up heaping ladles of aromatic stew. It was absolutely delicious and Jules could see a great future for Gerda and Woody in the restaurant business in the United States.

Jules was impressed. Gerda was everything that Woody had said she was. These were not starry eyed, horny young lovers but mature people demonstrating mutual respect more than the less permanent and less reliable bond of animal attraction. He would have absolutely no problem in recommending the approval of their application for permission to marry.

Helga accompanied him down the long central hall to the main entrance. As they reached the entrance she stopped and turned to him. "Thank you for understanding, Colonel. I think you are a very nice person and a very good officer. You seem to really care about your men and I'm sure that they will care about you."

"Thank you for your very kind remarks, pretty lady. Please don't get me wrong, I'm not hitting on you - you know what I mean by the word hitting?" Her indication was that she understood. "But I would like very much to have lunch with you some time. I'm in Frankfort at least once a week. Would that be possible?"

"Yes," she replied, "I think that would be possible. I'm very busy between my work in Frankfort and here but here is my card. Just call me when you are coming to Frankfort and we will try to arrange something. But I warn you that hitting on me will not do much for your batting average and I assure you that the color of your skin will have absolutely nothing to do with you striking out."

CHAPTER IV

SANDY, JASON AND CHOPIN

It was about seven-thirty on Thursday evening that Jason rang the bell at the front door of the old mansion. Helga came to the door and looked at him quizzically as she opened the door. "Yes?" she asked, but before he could answer Sandy arrived calling out in great excitement "It's my friend Jason, Helga, he has come to teach me Chopin!" She had rolls of music under one arm. "See, Jason, I have brought home the music. My music teacher at school loaned it to us." Her enthusiastic exuberance had totally taken over the situation as she ushered them towards the music room. She sat at the piano and commanded "Now, Helga, just listen!" as she put sheets of music on the piano music holder and commenced to play. "You'll see, Jason, I have been practicing and I love your Chopin so much." She played Chopin's Etude for Piano through from start to finish with occasional glances at Jason and Helga as if looking for their approval. Jason thought she played the piece very well and was quite obviously trying very hard to apply the Chopin technique of the very light touch that Jason had shown her the previous Sunday.

They heard the door of the old General's study open and heard his voice from the doorway, "Sandra, is that your American again playing Chopin."

Sandy was absolutely bubbling with excitement as she told him. "No, no, Grandfather. That was me playing. I have been practicing so that I can play Chopin for you the way Jason is teaching me."

"Yes, that was very nice. I like Chopin." He said as he withdrew, muttering, into his study. His final words appeared to be "but I do not like Americans."

"Yes, Sandra, you played that very nicely but who is this Jason?" Jason was sitting beside Sandy on the long piano bench but they were speaking in rapid German and he didn't really understand.

"Jason is my new teacher and he is teaching me Chopin which Grandfather likes so much. He plays so beautifully. Just listen." Now she was speaking English and she moved over on the bench and Jason put another selection of the Chopin music on the stand and played it through partially from the music and partially from memory. The voice of the old General was heard again but this time from inside his study as he correctly named the piece of music, adding "That was very beautiful!"

Helga now spoke in perfectly unaccented English. "Yes, Jason, or whoever you are, that was very beautiful and you already seem to have made some conquests. But this has happened so quickly and I look forward to having someone explain to me what has happened. Does Gerda know about this?"

"Oh yes, yes" said Sandy, still bubbling with excitement. "Gerda knows. She heard Jason play on Sunday and she and Woody had heard Jason play on Friday night at the gasthouse."

"Very interesting, very interesting. So you are really a bar room performer?" Still speaking in English she now directed this remark to Jason.

"Oh, no!" Answered Jason. "I am just an American soldier who has been studying music for years. I must compliment you. I have played on many concert grand pianos but this is absolutely the finest instrument I have ever played."

"And it should be. You will recognize the name of the maker. They have not made grand pianos in years and it cost

45

me a small fortune to have it tuned a few weeks ago. But I am still uncertain as to just what has happened while I was away."

"Well, really nothing, " replied Jason. "It was only that I found your sister very talented and she really has a feel for music. I played a piece from Chopin for her and she really loved it and her Grandfather also liked it and told us that it was a piece that his wife had played for him. I told Sandy that I would teach her how to play Chopin and now she has brought many sheets of music."

"And what is this about the gasthause. "Helga was now speaking to Sandy." Surely Gerda and Woody have not been taking you to that bar."

Sandy giggled in amusement. "Oh, no, they know I'm too young but I would like to go there sometime even just to hear Jason play that Beatle tune "Hey Jude" that the girls at school are always talking about. It is a great favorite of theirs and they were so envious when I told them I had my own personal teacher who played Beatle music for me. Jason please play "Hey Jude" for Helga.

Jason ran through the Beatle tune quickly but explained that it was much more effective with vocal accompaniment. "As far as playing at the gasthause, one of my friends volunteered me for their amateur program. It was not my choice but the crowd there were very kind."

By this time Helga had mellowed a bit. Jason realized that his first impression had been correct. This was a very beautiful woman and, quite obviously, very protective of Sandy. "Yes, Jason, who ever you are. You are a very talented musician. But as for becoming Sandra's teacher, I must think about that. And where does this name Sandy come from. Her name is Sandra and she was named in the memory

46

of Gerda's little sister who died in a Displaced Persons Camp."

"But, Helga," said the object of Helga's remarks, "Everyone else calls me Sandy. All the girls at school call me Sandy. It's just short for Sandra. Even Gerda calls me Sandy sometimes."

"Well I'll leave you to your lessons for now. Remember I will be taking you to your friend Meta's on Saturday for the rest of the weekend so you can study with her for your exams next week."

"Yes, I'll be ready," said Sandy. "I will be studying by myself tomorrow and I may come to you for help with my accounting course."

"I'll see you in the morning," Helga aaid as she walked away down the hall towards the kitchen. "I don't want you staying up late tonight."

Sandy giggled a bit and winked at Jason in what appeared to be a conspiratorial gesture. "And now she has gone to speak to Gerda and Woody. But really she is very good to me and has always been very kind. And, after all it was Helga who found me and arranged my adoption when they could not find my parents."

"Found you?" Asked Jason, "What do you mean when you say she found you?"

"Well, someone, they think it was my mother, left a note under the door at the Mansion and told them to look for her baby in a certain place on the grounds and, when they looked, Helga found me. The note pleaded with them to look after me and they did for all these years. Helga was only about twelve years old and, suddenly, she had a baby the easy way."

47

"So your name is really not von Freiderhoff and the old General is not really your Grandfather, then?" Asked Jason.

"Yes it is. At least that is what is shown on my adoption certificate. I don't really have a birth certificate and I really don't know exactly how old I am or when my real birthday is. We celebrate September 12th because that is the day they found me."

"You are full of surprises, aren't you?" Said Jason. "Well, I have a surprise for you." He opened a large parcel he had brought with him. "This is a recording deck but instead of recording on large reels of tape, it records on narrow strips of tape inside these little cassettes. Then, all you have to do is plug the cassette into this slot, press a button, and you can play back whatever you record. I have tried it out and it works very well. The sound quality is not perfect but it's pretty good. Let's try it out. If you will play that second Chopin piece again I'll record it and we will play it back."

Sandy played the Chopin piece again. Once again she made a determined effort to use the very light touch that Jason had told her was a characteristic of Chopin's music. When she finished Jason inserted the cassette into the cassette player, rewound the tape, turned up the volume control and watched the smile of delight light up Sandy's face. "That's really me? "She asked. "It's so beautiful. Thank you Jason thank you, thank you!" In her excitement Sandy kissed Jason full on the lips. She quickly drew back blushing profusely. "Oh, I'm so sorry, it's just so exciting to listen to what I have played."

"No apology required," said Jason. 'You may kiss me anytime you like." To illustrate his offer Jason puckered up his lips in the ready position.

"No, Helga tells me that I am not to kiss boys on the lips because that is what boys do when they want to........you." Again that German equivalent to the English four letter word. The same word she had used when they had parted beside the dam on Sunday. Again, Jason nearly choked at the manner in which the forbidden word slipped naturally off her lips.

"Sandy, please, pleeeaaase, don't use that word. Nice girls don't use that word."

"But it's only a word and you know what I mean and that's what words are for. Wait, I just had an idea."

"Ok, I'll listen but I don't want to hear that word again. Promise?"

"Oh, all right," said Sandy. "My idea is that you could record some of those Beatle tunes and show me how to operate the cassette player and if you could just loan me the recorder for next week I could play the cassettes for my friends. I don't think they believed me when I told them I had a private teacher who could play Beatle tunes. This will prove it and they'll just go wild with envy and they'll all want to meet you. Please, loan the recorder to me."

"Well, I don't think I could ever say no to you Sandy. But what about these girls, just what do they speak like?"

Sandy blushed slightly and told him, "They only speak German and they say much worse things than I do"

They started recording some Beatle tunes which included "Hey Jude", "Hard Day's Night" and "I Saw You Standing There," as Jason played from memory and Sandy operated the recording machine. "And now, "Jason announced," just once more and this one will be for my mother." He played through Chopin's Etude for Piano and asked Sandy to play it back. He then set this cassette aside saying he would take this one with him. Mannheim came to the music room and they saw him signaling outside the closed heavy glass door. When he saw they had completed the music he opened the door and told them that Gerda had prepared a late snack for them and that they should come right away. Jason told Sandy to go along with Mannheim and that he would be along in a few minutes. He then took the cassette for his mother and used the small microphone to add a few comments. After meeting Sandy he was no longer certain as to his plans for the future but he wanted his mother to remain confident that he intended to be available for the intake of the next special course at Juliard. He then joined the group in the kitchen just as Mannheim was leaving with a tray for the old General.Gerda again provided a delicious snack. Woody was there and he and Gerda invited Jason to join them at the gasthause on Saturday night. Jason said he probably would be there with his roommate. When Jason took his leave after about half an hour Sandy walked with him to the edge of the stream accompanied by Plato. They sat on the wicker lawn bench beside the end of the dam.

"So you will be going to that bar with Gerda and Woody on Saturday night while I am studying with my friend?" Sandy asked as they sat on the very comfortable bench. "I will tell them to chase all the pretty young girls away because you are my friend and you have no need for these other girls. Try and come a little earlier tomorrow evening and we will play those Beatle cassettes we made tonight. I just can't wait to play those to my friends. They will be so envious. You are so good to me Jason Creighton. I have a surprise for you, just close your eyes and promise not to move your hands"

"I promise," replied a completely mystified Jason until her round full lips closed on his in a long lingering kiss that Jason felt to the very tips of his toes. Her mouth was slightly open and her tongue flicked very lightly against his with nearly the effect of an electric shock that summoned near instant arousal. Involuntarily, Jason reached for her but already she was gone and as he opened his eyes, she was standing a few feet away with an impish smile on her face. "No hands, you promised" now she was giggling. "The girls tell me that the boys' hands are dangerous and that is what they use when they try to.......you." There she used that forbidden word again and Jason just shook his head. "Where in this world did you ever learn to kiss like that?" he asked.

"From the girls," she replied. "Girls are much better kissers than boys," and Jason was not prepared to argue.

"Just remember that kiss when you go to the bar on Saturday night and remember that just maybe, I will kiss you again sometime."

As Jason made his way across the top of the dam the kiss was still on his lips and her promise was still resonating in his mind and he knew that he would never forget that kiss. Jason was hopelessly in love.is voice trailed away as he realized that Jason was just sitting on the edge of his bed with a glazed look in his eyes. "Hey, man, are you listening? Are you high, or something? I just told you that I - your ever-loving roommate - has fixed you up with Tina who is Grade A prime ass. She was there last Saturday but with a marine officer. She has asked specifically to meet you. Do you hear me? This is strictly Grade A Officers' Stuff. Just wait till you see her! What in the hell is the matter with you?"
"Hank, please, just leave me alone. I'm in love with the most beautiful and the most amazing girl in the world and I expect to spent the rest of my life with Sandy."

"Oh, cut the horseshit buddy. You've only been with the girl twice, probably haven't even got into her drawers and, already, you're planning to take her home to Mommy. For Christ's sake, Jason wise up. Sure she's beautiful but what in the hell makes you think that you can grab her, put her on your white stallion and ride off into the sunset. Wake up, man, and smell the roses. Often you'll find its pure horse-shit."

And now Hank gave up in disgust. Jason just continued to sit there with that stunned look on his face. Whereas on the previous Sunday night he had wanted to tell

CHAPTER V

JULES AND LT GEN CARL REICHOLD

It was about a quarter to three on Tuesday afternoon that Jules presented himself at the HQ of Corps Commander Lt Gen Carl Reichold just on the outskirts of Frankfort. The armed guard at the information desk checked the appointment schedule and advised Jules to go directly up to the General's office which was on the Penthouse floor. On his arrival outside the office he was greeted by a Lt Col who introduced himself as one of the General's aides and was advised that the General would be with him in a few minutes.

Jules had only been seated outside the office for a couple of minutes when the door opened and the General came out to greet him and escort him into his office. The General told his aide that he would be tied up for the remainder of the day and that he would only be receiving Code 1 calls. He carried on a brief conversation with his aide telling him that Colonel Pelladeau would be a fixture on his schedule every second Tuesday unless specific orders were received to the contrary. The aide was also advised that Colonel Pelladeau would be joining the NATO Standing Committee on Armoured Equipment and Tactics and he would participate in the presentation to NATO Defence ministers at the annual meeting in August. He also asked his aide to arrange with the mess staff to bring up some coffee at about four- thirty.

When they were inside the General's office Jules was impressed with his surroundings. This was, quite obviously, the General's administrative centre. His operational centre was probably underground either in this building or in the neighborhood. "Did you have trouble finding us?" asked the General with what Jules recognized as an "opener".

"None whatsoever," replied Jules. "A Lt Col must always know how to find his General by the shortest and most direct route. Besides, I was just next door for lunch pointing to the huge Bank of the Rhine Complex which started only about two hundred meters away.

"The Rhine Group is a very busy place. The largest banking consortium in Europe and pretty close to the Japanese banks which are now the largest on the world. Are they handling your port folio? I don't think we have many Lt Cols who have sufficient assets to be of interest to Jacob Wiseman and his group. There I go again, one of my problems, name dropping, but I did meet him at a seminar they presented recently to brief military commanders on specific economic problems that may have strategic implications."

"No, actually I was doing a bit of peripheral research that might bear on my selection of the subject for my thesis. While visiting the Enclave von Freiderhoff last Thursday the old General's granddaughter, Helga von Freiderhoff invited me to call upon her for lunch on one of my visits to Frankfurt and she is the VP of Public Relations at the Rhine Group."

Jules saw that the General was suddenly deep in thought and his eyes lit up in recognition. "Now that's a coincidence," the General said. "I've actually met the lady. Very impressive and she would be hard to forget. Breathtaking is probably the adjective I'd use to describe her. During our seminar with the Rhine Group we had a social evening at the CEO's suite in that central building over there. The CEO was accompanied by the very beautiful young lady of whom you now speak. She had no official part of the program but the word from those who spoke to her was that she was very intelligent and very well informed. Well, Colonel, if we must do what you refer to as peripheral research I'm sure there are worse places to start than with someone as attractive as this lady."

54

"And now, Colonel, it looks as though we will be here for a while." He removed his jacket and invited Jules to follow suit. "I'm not that good at taking notes so I trust you will have no objection to my using a tape deck."

"None whatsoever," Jules answered. "In fact I hope to do extensive taping on cassettes in my discussions with the old General. His granddaughter has indicated that that should not be a problem so long as the product is to be used for academic purposes."

"That's fine. We should have no problem in that regard. If you are ready Colonel why don't you kick it off?"

"Thank you General, first I would like to spend some time introducing you to the subject. My perspective has changed significantly since I spoke to you last week and arranged this meeting. This change in perspective has resulted from the nearly eight hours I have spent with Field Marshall, the Ninth Baron Erich von Freiderhoff in two separate meetings, one on Saturday afternoon and the second on Sunday afternoon. These meetings became possible when I was introduced to the old General. If you have no objections I will continue to refer to the Field Marshall as the old General in the same manner as he is referred to in his own household. I visited the old General's Mansion on a strictly administrative matter. His daughter, Helga von Freyderhoff greeted me at the door and the old General's attention was drawn to the discussion we were holding in the drawing room outside his study. His granddaughter introduced me to her grandfather when he came to the study door. I came to the immediate impression that the old General is completely blind and uses a long white cane when finding his way around the house. His granddaughter explained why I was there. His housekeeper's good friend Sgt Washington had applied for permission to marry Gerda Hillstrom an employee of the household for many years. She explained that I was there because the approval of a mixed race marriage required an interview by the applicant's Commanding Officer."

"Please note that thus far the entire conversation was being conducted in German and this had the old fellow just a bit confused. His first comment was something about Gerda and her black man whose movements, on the General's instructions, had been limited to the kitchen and the rear area of the house. He muttered something quite audibly about not liking black Americans or, for that matter, not caring about Americans in general. Just imagine my position. There was a retort on the tip of my tongue but, for some reason, I held my tongue and that just might prove to be the most fortuitous act of my entire life."

"Then," Jules continued, "just as the old General was walking back into his study I caught a glimpse of the most impressive chess set I had ever seen in my life. The set was mounted on a large table and it was obvious that a match was in its opening phase. I have been playing chess for nearly thirty years and I even have a number of wins over chess masters. I just happened to comment upon the black pieces on the board and noted that this quite obviously the Sicillian Defence. This immediately caught the old General's attention.

"You play chess Colonel?" the old General asked.

"Yes, I truly love the game and I have played many years."

"Then, tell me Colonel, "said the old General, "if you were playing white at this juncture what would be your next move?"

I answered immediately that my next move was not that important by my strategy would be and that would be to attack his King line. This is the strategy I have learned as an avid fan of Bobby Fischer. I had used this strategy many times and had played against it

The old General's immediate response was "Exactly, that is precisely the most effective strategy! Yes Colonel, you are a player of this game of chess. I detect the possible influence of your compatriot Bobby Fischer of whom I have read so much. Perhaps you will join me for a game sometime." His granddaughter was standing beside the old General and I detected a near imperceptible nod of encouragement which, she told me later, was generated by her grandfather's enthusiastic response to my comments on the game in progress. It was only then that I noted there were three, not one, chess matches in progress. There were two other tables in the study each reflecting a chess match in progress.

Helga von Freiderhoff anticipated my question and told me "Yes, my grandfather loves the game of chess and he plays games by both mail and telephone aided by his personal servant. Sometimes I play with him but I am no match for his skill."

The old General now broke in. "Yes Colonel it is always more challenging to play against a real live opponent especially one with your experience. How about Saturday afternoon?"

"Again I noted a nod of encouragement from his granddaughter. Yes, General, that would be a great honor. Shall we say three o'clock?"I asked.

"Yes, yes, that would be fine. " was his response. There was actually enthusiasm in his voice. "Helga, tell Gerda that we will have a guest on Saturday and tell Mannheim that I will require his services on Saturday." He then moved to his desk at the back of his study.

His granddaughter actually thanked me for accepting his invitation. She commented on the enthusiasm she had heard in his voice, something that had been missing for so many years.

"General, in a way I think I should apologize for including all of this that may appear to you to be irrelevant detail but I assure you I think it is very important that you have the same understanding of this situation as that which I have arrived at through my exposure to this detail. I hope that by the time I finish this introduction you will also recognize the truly amazing opportunity that is presenting itself through this opportunity for discussions with the old General."

"Absolutely no apologies required. You have my complete and undivided attention. In fact I find the possibilities suggested by this situation very fascinating and I think I know just where you are going."

"Thank you General. That's a real relief. Such a situation and the possibilities offered would only be recognized by someone with a very keen understanding of the period that will come under examination. This was the reason that I was so pleased when the University Doctoral Board asked you to act as my faculty advisor. I knew that your thesis focussed on German political and military structure between World War I and World War II. I have studied your thesis and it will serve me very well if the Board accepts my proposal for a thesis. We will go into greater detail but I can only assume that you already expect that my discussion with the old General will provide some very important material for my thesis."

"First I would like to try and provide you with the historical perspective. Field Marshall the Ninth Baron Erich von Freiderhoff is the last male survivor of the von Freiderhoffs. His brother, the Eighth Baron, was a World War I air ace who died in France in the final days of that war. The estate known as the Enclave von Freiderhoff was presented to the family about two hundred years ago by a grateful monarch in appreciation of services rendered. At that time the designation Enclave carried with it a number of privileges. The original estate consisted of nearly eight thousand hectares and included the town of Freiderberg and a number of villages. The Mansion representing the family home was built between 1760 and 1790 and was regarded, at one time, as one of the finest family homes in Europe. Financial considerations have reduced the estate to a little more than one hundred hectares and the Mansion was reduced to the one wing left standing after both bombing and fire during World War II. What is left of the Mansion is still pretty impressive as a family residence. In all there are about thirty rooms including twenty bedrooms on the second level.

"The furnishings are all either oak or mahogany and extremely valuable but the upkeep must be a heavy drain upon the resources of the granddaughter who appears to be the only member of the family with a steady income. I suspect that the property is heavily mortgaged after most of the original estate was sold off to meet expenses. In fact what was formerly the family's hunting lodge and the surrounding heath, which the family used as its exclusive hunting preserve, is currently leased by NATO and my regiment uses it as a training area for tanks and other armoured vehicles. It is about thirty-five miles to the north.

"My first impression of the old General was that he could have stepped right out of an old war movie in which he had been cast as a German general or, at least, a German senior officer. He is eighty-three years old and his presence is very impressive. He is very slim and over six feet tall. He even has several of the old dueling scars that many German officers regarded as badges of honor. His English is really quite good but he prefers to converse in German. He served as a military attaché in both London and Washington just

59

before the First World War. In WWI he was the most decorated German officer and at the end of the war he was the
youngest Major General in the German army. His wife died
in the influenza epidemic of 1919. He had three sons and two
daughters and all were killed in World War II. There were
three grandsons who were caught up in the Hitler Youth and
all died on the Eastern front

"And now just a few words about the old man's study
which may very well be our theatre as we proceed with our
discussions. This is a very large room and actually represents
a combined library and study. The three huge tables bearing
the chess games in progress dominate the room. The chess
set on the center table is the one that originally caught my
attention. All the figures are hand carved ivory with extensive gold inlays. The other two chess sets are very nice but
really nothing when compared with the one I originally
commented on. The one thing that was remarkable about the
library is that I have yet to discover any publication of a later
date that 1938. There may be some of a later date but nothing
I have found in my two visits to the room.

"On the wall behind his desk are all the family pictures
and beside the pictures, almost like a big exclamation mark,
stands the Heidleberg Sword of Honor. The amazing thing is
that the old General won this as the outstanding cadet for
three years in a row, in 1902, 1903 and 1904 and this is the
original Sword of Honor presented to him in perpetuity. Not
just a replica, not just possession for a year but the original
sword became his when he won it three years in a row. This
was an honor that he really cherishes. I could hear the pride
in his voice when he told me about it between games and this
pride reflects just how important this honor was to him and
his family.

"I will never forget his granddaughter's comment when
she thanked me for not responding angrily to his racist remarks when we originally met and for agreeing to play

chess with him. She had said "really all he has left are old photographs of young dead people and his guilt."

General Reichold now offered a comment. "My God, Colonel, you really seem to be into this project. Your sensitivity and intelligence promise to produce a very important academic work and perhaps even more. There might even be a very good book in all this. Perhaps this would be a good point for us to stop for coffee. I'm quite sure that it is on the way up. It's four-thirty and they are usually very punctual."

"Just one more point," said Jules. "Our discussions will probably go in some detail into the post WWI period but I would like to return for just a moment to the strange composition of the old General's library. You will recall that I have yet to find any publication dated after 1938. I do not think that it is just a coincidence that it was in 1938 that the old General walked out of Hitler's HQ, got into his staff car and drove himself back to the Enclave. The only conclusion we can reach is that in 1938 the old General reached a level of total frustration in his disillusionment with Hitler and just gave up and we should not regard this as only a retreat; actually it was a total withdrawal."

There was a knock on the door. It was exactly four-thirty and coffee had arrived.

As the steward poured the coffee and set out the small tray of sandwiches and pastries the General checked his tape deck. He listened very briefly to the quality of sound on a few words that had already been recorded and loaded a fresh tape cartridge. Actually he had not been completely candid with his visitor. In reality, the General was very good at taking notes but he preferred using the tape deck in one-on-one sessions because while he would listen intently it also gave him the opportunity to study the person making the presentation. He would remember what Jules had said, at least in outline, but then he would be able to review everything in detail when he played back the tape later that night. Through experience he had found that his assessment of the presenter was at least as important as the material.

The General was pleased that Jules had read his thesis because it certainly represented an excellent background and even a starting point for his own thesis. Reichold had encountered the name of the old General many times in his research for his own thesis but until his name came up in Jules' original telephone conversation Reichold hadn't realized that the Field Marshall was still alive. He found the prospect of extensive dialogues with the old General very exciting.

After about 15 minutes the steward silently reappeared and took away their dishes after ensuring their coffee cups were filled. General Reichold turned on his tape deck to indicate that Jules could proceed.

Jules continued. "General I think you will understand that this is an introductory session. My objective in this session is to paint the broad picture for you. It is my intention to conduct two sessions a week with the old General and all will be sandwiched between chess matches. With your concurrence I plan to meet with you four or five times in which my material will be divided into four or five areas of interest. First I will try to get the old General to discuss the philosophical origin of Germany's fascism and trace its development starting with the Teutontc belief in the superiority of the Ayrian race and how Hitler and his band of demagogues used this theory to appeal to a proud people so humiliated by their defeat in World War I and the Treaty of Versailles. My second area of interest will concentrate on the efforts of the old General and his fellow patriots to deliver their beloved country from the crippling economic burden imposed by the schedule of reparations demanded by vindictive former adversaries. Third, I will try to get the old General to review the efforts of his group to restore some vestiges of the once proud German military. I expect that some of these efforts will consist of developments veiled in the guise of economic activities such as the building of the autobahns and revitalizing other facets of the transportation infrastructure such as river traffic and major ports.

"My fourth area of interest will be to try to lead the old General through some of those sand table and map based exercises that were used in the development of the highly successful tactics designed for their armoured units and the all important techniques to be applied to effective battle procedure.

"Finally, I think I will have the opportunity to get a few comments from the old General on those days with Adolph Hitler. After all there was a time that he was one of Hitler's most trusted advisors. A remark he made the other day provides an inkling of the promise offered by this area. We had just completed a chess match which he had won and he was very pleased and feeling just a little expansive. Somehow or other I was able to turn the conversation to Hitler. He was deep in thought for several minutes before he responded. "Ah yes, Adolph Hitler, a very evil man. We underestimated him when we made the mistake of thinking we could use him but he used us!"

General Reichold was very impressed. "Colonel, that approach sounds just great to me and promises to produce a very important thesis. If I did have any other ideas you have just blown them away. If any ideas occur to me I will introduce them as we proceed. Of course much of your project depends upon the old General's cooperation but it seems that you have his confidence and, what may be even more important, you have the confidence of that very impressive young lady, his granddaughter."

"Yes, General, you are absolutely correct on that latter point. But so far, so good. We had a very pleasant and productive lunch today. She is a very strong young lady who appears to be completely in control of her life. And she really is a head turner. When we entered the large hotel dining room today I could see heads turning and heard utensils being dropped all over the room. She is very smart and so beautiful. Her relationship with her grandfather is a little strange but while she quite obviously loves him her comments about him range from real concern and affection to remarks such as "he's really such a silly old man". In a way I truly believe she still blames him for the loss of her father and mother but she is always ready to put things in their historical perspective. Today she made it very clear to me that I will have her cooperation just so long as I do nothing that will hold the old man up to ridicule. She emphasized that her grandfather must not know that I am black and all members of the household have been sworn to secrecy on that subject although she assured me that warnings were unnecessary because they were all so pleased with the renewed vigor shown by the old man since our chess matches began. They all appear to be devoted to the old man in their own ways.

"There is absolutely no danger that I will expose the old man to ridicule and it is not only because he is so important to my project. I have only spent about seven hours in his company and while I am not enamoured with many of his ideas, I have already developed a great respect for his intellect. The first evidence I offer as to the power of his intellectual capacity is to point out that here is a man who is totally blind who can play three chess matches simultaneously. Just think about it, he has total recall of the positions of all the pieces on all three boards at all times even when there is a time lag of days between moves on some of the games he plays by mail. The sole assistance he receives is from his personal servant who follows his direction in placing the pieces. I have played against chess masters who play against twenty or more competitors at the same time but they can see the boards as they go around the room. I have played against as many as twelve other players at the same time myself and did so successfully but I always had full view of all the boards.

"This high powered intellect comes through in other ways and ways which promise great things for my project. The few wide-ranging discussions we have already had between our chess matches indicate that this old man, at eighty-three years of age, has a memory capacity with total recall. Once again that is total recall up to 1938. Certainly he knows that Germany lost the war. He realizes that Germany is now divided but he lost all interest in world events since 1938. He recalls the Olympics of 1936 but only to mention Hitler's disappointment with the success of that black American and his explanation that Jesse Owens' feats had been explained as merely an aberration. But he has no knowledge of the Marshall Plan and that is unfortunate because I was looking forward to engaging him in a comparison of the conditions of the Treaty of Versailles with the impact of the Marshall Plan. But on all other events up to 1938 he remembers everything; events, places, people, dates, everything. His memory is encyclopedic.

"Another thing I have learned about the old General is that he is fiercely competitive. In every chess match he fights fiercely until he has no choice but to concede at which point he stands, bows to me, extends his hand and offers his very grudging congratulations. Defeat does not rest easily on the shoulders of this very proud old man. After a defeat he will sit very quietly for several minutes, sightless eyes closed as he seems to be reviewing all his moves in the previous game. When his analysis is complete, he sits up very erect and this is the signal for us to continue. When he wins a match he is delighted. I, also, stand up and bow to him, congratulate him and he shakes my hand vigorously. Then he becomes very expansive and he is receptive and cooperative to just about any direction I choose to lead the discussion. I know just what you are thinking General. Perhaps it would be much better for our project if I let the old man win more often. I wouldn't dare. He is much too smart. He would spot that ruse immediately and all would be lost. He now has a very accurate understanding of my skill level and would recognize an intentional mistake immediately. I have already mentioned how proud he is and that intense pride would never accept a victory that had not been earned honestly. No, that strategy would be highly counter productive but rest assured I have my hands full every game and the old man will certainly win his share of the games without any assistance from me.

"Something else that must be understood about this old man is that he is totally obsessed with the game of chess. All of his energies and efforts are devoted to the game. The only books he reads are books in Braille on chess. The two magazines he subscribes to are about chess. One is in Braille which he reads and the other is read to him by his servant. Any psychiatrist would offer the very obvious diagnosis. The game of chess for the old man is his escape. It is my diagnosis, as I said earlier, that this is much more than an escape, it represents a total withdrawal.

"Well, General, that concludes what I wanted to do for this session. As I told you earlier, it is my intention to tape all future sessions with the old General. I told his granddaughter of my intention at lunch today and she had no objections beyond the one stipulation I identified earlier that nothing should hold him up to ridicule. I believe I have already expressed my intentions in that regard. Also the tapes will all be in German originally. I have been conducting all of my discussions with him in German and I was gratified that he was impressed with my command of the language and I understand that you have been fluent in German since the days of your youth.

"Yes, German was always a second language with my family and I have always been very happy that that was the case. It was very helpful throughout undergraduate and

66

graduate studies and it has been very useful in my tours of duty here in Germany. The young lady we have discussed here, Helga von Freiderhoff seemed to be suitably impressed with my German when we exchanged a few words at the seminar I referred to earlier. On the other hand I was very impressed with her command of English as I overheard her speaking with some of the other officers. It seems, Colonel, that you have taken full advantage of your service here in Germany to become fluent in the language. I find it very discouraging that so many of our career officers do not take advantage of their tours of duty here in Germany to learn the language. I had the advantage of three generations of people speaking German in my home."

"My service here in Germany has been very important to my language training but, believe it or not, my mother really got me started and she was a French national from Martinique who became an accomplished linguist attending an exclusive girls' school in England where they spent a number of terms here in Europe for language training. She also insisted that I learn French and I also got the French from my father who was not only fluent in French but also in some of the Cajun dialects. He could trace his ancestors all the way back to the Acadians who settled in Louisiana when they were expelled from Nova Scotia and New Brunswick about two hundred years ago. The Cajun has been of limited use but my father and I had great fun with it when we visited Quebec and New Brunswick on holidays some years ago. The modern Acadians we encountered up there were really impressed when we started speaking Cajun to each other."

"Well," the General interjected, "I'm sure they were and I'm impressed too. I will have no problem in submitting a preliminary report to the university telling them that you are embarking on a doctoral program that will be both highly imaginative and that will be of significant academic merit. I am also impressed with your enthusiasm for the study area and the impression you seem to have made on both the old

General and his granddaughter as well as your faculty advisor who will look forward with great interest to our next session. I would like to schedule our sessions for the same time every second Tuesday and I will arrange my timetable so that they will be open ended so we will be able to continue for as long as the session requires. Changes to this schedule may be arranged by mutual consent."

"Thank you General, you are very generous with such a time allocation from your busy schedule. What I propose is that we commence each session by playing over the tapes I have recorded and then I would like to review the major points through discussions in which I will be able to incorporate your comments by also taping them on cassettes"

'Fine " said the General. "Then it's agreed that we will meet every second Tuesday at 3 p.m. That means our next meeting will be on Jun 18th. I will look forward to that date."

After Jules departed the General remained in his office for a few minutes. He unloaded his tape deck and he filled in the details that identified the tape and put it in his brief case. He would review it later that night. He always made it a point after any one-on-one session to review the session while it was still fresh in his mind to firmly identify and confirm his original impressions. He reviewed his original impression of Lt Col Jules Pelladeau and decided that the file of outstanding fitness reports on Pelladeau he had reviewed earlier in the day were right on target. This was a very impressive young man who would be arriving on the level for promotion to general rank at precisely the right time given his ethnicity and the increasing demand for "political correctness" in structuring promotion slates.

As Jules left the office building he was also suitably impressed and very pleased with his day that had commenced with the very pleasant - and productive - lunch with Helga. He was already looking forward to his next chess match with the old General scheduled for Saturday afternoon with another session on Sunday afternoon. He had really enjoyed the keen competition of the matches they had already engaged in and thought he just might encourage the old man to schedule the occasional evening session as well.

CHAPTER VI

THE SENATOR AND MRS BUCHALTER

It was nearly nine a.m. on Friday, June 7th, in Washington, that Spencer Graham's phone rang. One of the interns had advised him that the Senator's wife was on the line trying to reach the Senator. Spencer had learned from experience the value of that minute or so that you could easily delay picking up a phone and speaking, and to use it to think about the announced caller and trying to anticipate just what the call would be about. He knew that Pat Buchalter had flown home to Columbus the previous day on one of the Compass Inc corporate jets and that she and the Senator would be participating in several rallies and fundraisers on the weekend in Illinois and Wisconsin. What would she be calling about? He just had a hunch that it would be about her missing son Jason. This was not as much a guess as a reasonable extension of the laws of probability. Since Jason had disappeared from her sight four months earlier, 75 per cent of her calls related to Jason. Now having prepared himself Spencer picked up the phone. "Hello, Pat, the Senator is at a committee meeting but should be in the office by ten."

Spencer had been on target. "Spence, I've heard from Jason again but this time he has sent me a cassette as an indication that he is still really serious about his music. The cassette includes a Chopin piece that has always been a great favourite of mine and he plays it beautifully even if the sound is a bit limited on a cassette but the piano he plays has marvelous tones and he tells me that it is the most beautiful concert piano that he has ever played on. The only voice on the tape other than Jason's is just a few words from some girl praising Jason's playing and I think that I detect a little bit of an accent in the girl's voice. Jason assures me that he is continuing to work on his music and has every intention of entering the course at Julliard not later than the semester that commences in January. I'm still worried because his original target was the semester commencing in September. Spence, what am I going to do? Where can he be?"

Spencer had to be very careful because he knew very well just where Jason was and for a very good reason. He had made all the arrangements for Jason's sudden move to Germany because if he had not acted, Jason, on this very day, would be on a fast boat to Viet Nam and Germany was a hell of a lot healthier than Viet Nam even in 1968. Spencer reassured Pat that she shouldn't worry as long as Jason was providing proof that he was continuing to work with his music. He had no more knowledge of Jason's whereabouts since her call one week earlier which was truetrue, but an answer classified by committee counsels as disingenuous. "Pat, Buck will be in the office by ten and I'll have him call you."

"Spencer, I'm going to try another approach. There is something distinctive about the concert grand on which Jason recorded this piece of music. I have a friend who has played concerts all over the world and he has told me that he can recognize the signature of the really great concert grands. I'm flying down to Dallas the first of the week to see Daddy and I'll meet the maestro later in the week. I want to play this cassette for Daddy because it is one of his favorites and if it is one of his good days he will really enjoy it. And by the end of the week I just might know where Jason is and just who this mystery woman is. Tell Buck I'll call him later."

Spencer quickly reviewed all of the information he had taken in from the call. He quickly identified just what he would tell Buck and what he would not tell Buck. The speedy classification of all information into a variety of categories was an absolute must for Chiefs of Staff for all Senators, the President, the Vice President and members of the cabinet. First Buck would be informed that Pat had called and that she had advised that she had received the cassette from Jason. He would be informed that Pat would be visiting Daddy in Dallas early in the week. "Daddy" was Howard

Conrad, Sr., Chairman of the Board (Emeritus) of Compass Inc but confined to his bed since suffering a severe stroke ten years earlier. The information on the maestro would be withheld because Spencer knew that this would be Umberto Fillini the noted concert pianist who had been tuning Pat Buchalter's piano for many years and whom Spencer was very nearly convinced was really Jason's father. Spencer had not quite closed his case on Umberto and Pat but he was already close enough to be able to make a preventative strike should Pat threaten to break the story of the Senator and the nubile young intern. Yes, he thought, the timing of using this information would be critical and it must be used for prevention instead of preemption.

While waiting for the Senator to come in Spencer Graham reviewed his current position. Within a few years of age 60 he was the Chief of Staff for one of the most powerful men in the Senate. A man who was often mentioned as the next GOP presidential candidate after Nixon completed his presidency consisting of either one or two terms depending on what could be a very fickle electorate. Spencer found the prospect of becoming the Chief of Staff in the White House very attractive.

Spencer Graham was another of the West Point grads that spotted the landscape of upper echelon Washington. He had graduated in the top twenty-five percent of his class in 1936 after spending his youth in the Far East with a father who made a career of the diplomatic service. When Spence entered West Point he was fluent in both Japanese and Mandarin Chinese and this certainly set him apart from all of the other members of the corps and, for that matter, 99.9% of serving officers with all three Armed Forces. While setting him apart, the linguistic skills did not really do that much for Spencer Graham's career. After Pearl Harbor Spencer quickly found himself assigned to Intelligence and he remained there for the rest of the war.

At the end of the war Lt-Col Spencer Graham found himself caught on the career seniority lists with hundreds, if not thousands, of other Lt Cols with similar seniority. But many of these other Lt Cols had something that Spencer never acquired in his appointments as intelligence officer at many levels. He did not have any command experience or the combat decorations that accelerated career movements. When the Korean conflict came along Spencer was still a Lt Col and, with the action once again focussed on the Far East, Spencer found himself right back in intelligence. In 1952, even before the Korean war was over, Spencer bit the bullet and resigned his commission and made the plunge into politics. He was successful in his first try and became the freshman congressman for a solid GOP district in northern Indiana close to the Ohio border. He was re-elected in 1954 but in 1956 there was an opening in the Senate brought about by an unexpected retirement. The Governor of Indiana asked Spencer if he was interested and Spencer jumped at the chance. But what the Governor did not tell Spencer was that the Governor intended to run for that same seat at the end of Spencer's two year appointment and the only reason he had appointed Spence was that he knew he could beat him in a general election and the Governor was right.

In 1959 Spencer had heard on the West Point old boy's net that Senator Buchalter, Ohio's now senior representative in the upper house, was looking for a Chief of Staff when his original Chief of Staff decided to return to Compass Inc. from whence he came, to accept a very senior position. Spencer knew the Senator very well having worked with him for two years in the senate and his four years in Congress. He also knew that Buck had disapproved of the Governor of Indiana's personal ambitions that had left Spence out in the cold. This disapproval may have arisen directly from that element of loyalty possessed and highly valued by former members of the Corps but, regardless of the motivation, the Senator preferred to play his cards straight up at least where other members of the GOP were concerned.

Spence had immediately applied for the position as Chief of Staff and heard later that he was on the short list from the very beginning. At the time of his only interview it was obviously a lock and the Senator's search was over. It proved to be a perfect fit from the start. Just two old soldiers working together with an understanding of each other that could only be the product of shared experiences.

In nearly ten years Spencer had become recognized as one of the very best Chiefs of Staff in Washington. He had a thorough knowledge of the system and what made it tick. He knew where all the bodies were buried and whose closets contained some useful skeletons. His loyalty to the Senator and his family was without question and he worked 12 to 16 hour days to ensure that he always possessed all that he needed of that vital currency of power, knowledge.

Spencer Graham loved his job. Perhaps even more than being a senator himself. He certainly had more power than many elected members of the Senate and the resources available to him exceeded what was available to all but a very few senior members of that august body. This was nearly entirely because of his full access to the resources of Compass Inc. He found it possible to augment his annual salary by accepting non-conflicting projects from the Compass Board of Directors. There was a fleet of executive jets available at his call and hotel suites were always available throughout the country. Spencer could also allocate these resources to other less fortunate but, nonetheless, deserving members of both houses. Needless to say Spencer made discreet use of such allocations to accumulate IOUs for his employer.

Because of the loyal bond between Spencer and the Senator the latter recognized the wisdom of having no secrets from his Chief of Staff who had also become a trusted friend after working together for ten years. For example,

74

Buck had immediately told Spencer about his indiscretion with the young intern and Spencer, while agreeing with the Senator's self-confession about his stupidity, made no moral judgements but immediately set about initiating measures to control potential damage. A quick visit to the family lakeside cottage, the site of the tryst, convinced Spencer that someone else also knew of the incident. There were obvious signs that the cottage had been wired and that the equipment had been hurriedly removed before Spencer's inspection. There would be audiotapes and, what would be much worse, pictures.

Spencer had come to a very rapid conclusion that the prime suspect was Pat. His only hope was that she had personally collected the evidence because his long experience in intelligence had taught him that risk and problems of control increased exponentially with the number of people in possession of sensitive information. His suspicions were immediately drawn to Pat because she was so obviously her father's daughter and Howard Conrad, Sr., was one mean son of a bitch whose rise to the top of a huge industrial empire could not be attributed in any great measure to a dedicated practice of Christian ethics.

Spencer had always prided himself on his ability to read people and while attending a fundraiser with the Senator and his wife the previous weekend Spencer became convinced that Pat knew something that she wasn't telling. Spencer had always liked Pat. She was an intelligent, beautiful woman; the ideal senator's wife and, for that matter, an ideal first lady. But he did not underestimate her. When her father had been obliged to step down she had stepped in as Chairman of the Board of Compass Inc. This was not one of those figurehead appointments. Pat took an active role in board meetings and had insisted that she be consulted in all major decisions.

Acting on what Spencer felt was a well-supported conclusion that Pat had collected the evidence at the cottage, he had immediately embarked upon a program of damage control. Spence had never before really made a conscious effort to gather information on the family but he had always readily accepted information coming his way and just filed in away for possible future reference. Somewhere along the way he had accumulated a few references that included Pat and the famous Italian concert pianist Umberto Fillini and suggested Pat and Umberto were a work in progress. Once again Spence was not judgmental but this was the type of information that should be filed away for possible future use. Some people might just describe this as an act of disloyalty in that he did not inform the Senator of his suspicions but Spencer's intelligence training had taught him to divide such information into "Passive" and "Active" files. Information such as Pat's extracurricular love life was classified as passive because its disclosure at the present time might raise problems that might be far more serious than it really deserved. Then there was the distinct probability that the full value of the information would be compromised by using it prematurely thus limiting its impact at a more opportune time.

Spencer quickly switched to his investigative mode and, without much difficulty, was able to trace the Umberto/Pat relationship back to the days when Umberto had been Pat's music teacher in the late 1930s. From there it was not that difficult to discover Umberto's reputation in Europe as an outstanding teacher of music and the seducer of many of his young female students. It became quite obvious that he had been the first to tune Pat's piano and Pat's confidential medical records revealed that medical intervention had interrupted their joint production of a never to be named composition. This was followed by an order from the Immigration Department that denied one Umberto Fillini future access to the United States on grounds of moral turpitude.

Spencer's research also took him to Pat's visit to Europe in 1948 as the chaperone for a group of graduates from the family sponsored Dallas School of Music, founded by Howard Conrad, Sr., where top members of the Graduating Class were rewarded with six weeks of advanced training in Europe. One of the instructors had been one Umberto Fillini and considering he had been recruited by Pat Buchalter, Spence found it very easy to assume that Pat's piano was again in need of tuning. He also did not fail to observe that Jason Buchalter had been born precisely eight months after Pat's return from her sojourn in Europe in a birth that her attending physician described as probably full term. Not conclusive but Spence was quite willing to come to a conclusion that would make his ammunition much more effective if he found it necessary to fire for effect.

The Senator returned to his office at about ten-thirty and Spence briefed him on what had happened in his absence. He was very interested in the call from his wife and the news of the arrival of the cassette. Of course, Jason's whereabouts was also no mystery to Buck Buchalter because Spence's sudden movement of Jason to Germany had been on his orders and facilitated by his old friend and West Point classmate Carl Reichold who was now a Lt Gen and an armoured formation corps commander in Germany.

The Senator called his wife and received a detailed report on this latest communication from their missing son. She was obviously very pleased to hear that Jason was continuing to work on his music but she was not happy to hear that he was now aiming at the Julliard semester commencing in January instead of the one commencing in September as originally scheduled. She urged him to redouble his efforts to find their son and he promised to do so. He told her that he would be picking her up in Columbus early in the afternoon on their way to the rallies and fundraisers in Illinois and Wisconsin.

The Senator gave his Chief of Staff a thumbs up signal to indicate that he had touched base with Pat and they turned to a sheaf of briefing notes that Spencer had placed on his desk.

77

The Senator was forty-eight years of age in 1968 and in the final year of his second six-year term in the Senate and facing little opposition in his run for his third term the current year. He was a tall man, just over six foot one inch with a very distinguished erect carriage so typical of all graduates of the Point. Women found him very attractive, his graying hair very distinguished and their maternal instincts were always aroused by the slight limp in his gait only partially corrected by the heavy cane he used while walking. For years he had insisted that the cane was unnecessary but Pat insisted that it continually reminded the voters of his war wounds and this conjured up the recognition of his Congressional Medal of Honor and other decorations. On this Spencer was in complete agreement with Pat so the cane had become a fixture.

With men Buck was also very popular. His reputation on the Hill was that of a straight shooter, someone who could always be depended upon to keep his promises. Again Buck would attribute this to his military training. Buck prized the quality of loyalty above all else but he would also agree that his enviable position of near unlimited resources made it just a little easier for him to conform to his personal code in the often cut throat environment of national politics. His prowess as a student athlete as a football first team All-American with honorable mentions in ice hockey, was also known and respected among his colleagues and found prominent mention in election material whenever elections came around.

Although the Senator was a contented man in most ways as he looked forward to easy re-election and the position of at least ranking minority member of the powerful Senate Armed Forces Committee, there were some days that he regretted the premature termination of his military career. On these occasions he envied his old friend and ice hockey linemate, Carl Reichold who was now a Lt Gen and commanding an armoured corps in Germany. But his gimpy leg meant restricted duty and a career behind a desk and that just did not appeal to him. Furthermore he reminded himself that he encountered more action nearly every day on the floor of the Senate and in committee dogfights than he would ever see in some obscure office in the Pentagon.

On this particular day in June, 1968, the only clouds on Buck's horizon were the stupid slip he had made with the little intern and Pat's concern about Jason who for Buck had always seemed to be a problem. The twins represented no problem. Patrick had graduated from the Point earlier in the month and had been posted to a regiment in Korea. He was engaged to a beautiful girl who was the sister of a classmate from the Point and from a very fine old family in Virginia. His mother had not been that fussy about his choice of a military career but was now resigned to it although a little apprehensive about the Viet Nam buildup. Carly, the other twin, who would be entering medical school in the fall, was engaged to another medical student a couple of years ahead of her and they had plans to establish their practice in Denver when they both completed their residencies.

But Jason was different. He was quite obviously very talented and although music was not really Buck's bag, Pat and his father-in-law both had a deep love of music and had been very proud of Jason's accomplishments from the time he was old enough to hold his own recital. Of course, Pat herself, encouraged by her father, had been a very accomplished concert pianist. She had actually played Carnegie Hall although skeptics pointed out that her father had paid all the expenses and even papered the hall. The same skeptics pointed out that the New York critics had not really been that kind in their reviews although there had been sufficient kind remarks that the old man had not purchased all the New York papers and fired all the critics. Pat and her father seemed convinced that Jason would be able to make that final big step to the top level of concert pianists.

However, the Senator found that for some reason that no matter how hard he tried, he and Jason just did not connect. There was no denying that he was very talented and also very handsome with the dark curly hair and good looks inherited from his mother's side of the family. The girls flocked to him in droves and Buck suspected that he was becoming a bit of a stud and even went to the extent of having one of those father to son, "the birds and the bees", talks with Jason at which he arrived at the conclusion that Jason should be lecturing him. He seemed to know more than Buck did on the subject. The only real satisfaction he gained from the session was the realization that his younger son appreciated the importance of safe sex. It did not do much for the Senator's ego that when he related this experience to his wife she laughed uproariously.

Jason had a preliminary audition by the Juliard School of Music and the results were highly encouraging. A second audition would be held about a month before the first day of the semester when Jason would actually enroll. There seemed very little doubt that he would be accepted but just to be sure they had arranged for him to spend a year in New York with a highly regarded music teacher. They made all the necessary arrangements for Jason's year in New York. He was given exclusive use of one of the luxury condominiums owned by Compass Inc. and normally used by corporation executives temporarily assigned to the city and a concert grand was installed in the condo. Pat was terrified of her youngest son being on his own in New York after the son of a friend had been kidnapped. On her insistence Spencer arranged with one of the security consultants with Compass Inc, for Jason to live in New York under a completely new identity. For the year he would be known under his new identity and to ensure his identity remained secret his mother and father were given the address of a mail drop and a telephone number that was really an answering service. His mother accepted these measures as necessary to provide protective cover for her son who was not only the son of a very important member of the US Senate and also the son of one of the richest women in the United States.

Another layer of security was added when the security consultant created two additional identities for Jason which were to be used only in the case of emergency. These identities were to be known only to Jason, Spencer and the consultant in observance of the "need to know" principle to be employed in security matters.

The plan had worked very well for the first five months into the year and there were highly favorable reports from the music teacher on Jason's progress under his guidance. However, unbeknownst to anyone including the music teacher and Spencer, young Jason had shacked up with a very attractive young aspiring actress. It is still uncertain whether the beautiful young thing was attracted more by Jason or his spacious luxurious condo. In the three months that the affair lasted Jason came to the point where he thought he was in love with the young starlet. Later he would realize that he had been in love with sex in which the young lady was a highly skilful practitioner.

Then the affair fell apart when the young lady saw a better future with a young actor coming off a Broadway hit and on his way to Hollywood under contract for a major role in a big budget production. Jason was very disappointed at this sudden disruption of his tail supply. After all he still thought he was in love. He took on one of the emergency identities and headed for Hollywood as Jason Creighton after making arrangements for continuing the transfer of funds to accounts under his new identity. When he arrived in California he found that his starlet and her new bedmate had moved on to a secret location in South America where the production would be involved in six months of filming on location. Jason was not long in California before he discovered exactly what he had been missing when he was recruited by the young lady with anti-war sentiments.

It had not taken Spence very long to catch up with Jason but it did take just a little longer to decide just what to do with him. Jason kept in touch with his mother who was willing - for at least the time being - to accept his story that he needed to get away from music for just a little while and that he just wanted to find his own space. So long as Pat was going along with this story Spence could see absolutely no urgency to tell Pat where Jason actually was but he made sure that the Senator was kept informed. Ironically the Senator, if he had been asked for an honest opinion, would have revealed that he couldn't care less where his younger son was. In fact the young bugger was just becoming a major pain in the ass to him.

The Senator and his wife spent the weekend meeting their commitments at the rallies and fundraisers in Illinois and Wisconsin. Spencer Graham was off for this weekend but would join the couple on future events scheduled for Oregon and Washington. The Senator used all of these events to consolidate his base in the political party. Assisting other members of both houses in their campaigns for re-election through personal appearances and fundraisers just established a few more IOUs that would be called at the appropriate time.

On the corporate jet Pat gave him all the latest details on Jason and even played the cassette that Jason had sent. It all sounded very good but Buck was just about tone deaf when it came to music, especially classical music. Before she played back Jason's recorded message she played back one section several times. This was the point at which Jason had just completed playing when a feminine voice could be heard saying "Oh, Jason, that was so beautiful."

"There" said Pat each time after replaying the clip. "That accent. It is not that clear but there is just a trace of an accent. Sometimes I think it's Spanish or even Italian or it could be central European. It's very difficult to identify."

After listening to the clip several times Buck admitted he couldn't help in identifying the accent. Pat put the tape away and settled back in her seat. The flight to Springfield would be about two hours and she settled back in her seat to try and catch a little sleep. They had several events scheduled during the next twelve hours in Illinois and they would be on stage for nearly the entire time.

Buck had never been able to sleep on planes so he opened his brief case and spent a few minutes reviewing Spence's briefing notes and quickly read over the biographical outlines that Spence had prepared on people he would be meeting during the weekend. The cassette from Jason had nothing new in information for Buck. He recognized the little touch of accent in the girl's voice as German but in the identification it helped to know where Jason actually was. He was completely satisfied with the present situation but he realized that it would not be long before Pat started putting the pressure on again.

The Senator looked very carefully at his wife reclining in the seat opposite him. She appeared to be sleeping as he admired her beauty now even more striking in repose. Beautiful and so very smart, Buck thought. Spence had told him his suspicions that Pat had collected the evidence of his stupid little fling with the intern. Spence was usually right and had assured him that damage control included a plan to neutralize any personal attack Pat might decide to mount. His first line of defence - if, indeed, Pat was actually the culprit - was that Pat's personal ambitions were very closely tied to his. Pat wanted to be First Lady and regarded the White House as a very likely future address. So if she took any action that would damage his career she would be, in effect, damaging her own. But then there was the problem of Jason and Buck was convinced that if it came to a choice between the White House and avenging any mistreatment of Jason she would opt for the latter.

The stupidity of the incident with the intern was that Buck had never been a womanizer. He had been totally faithful to Pat since their marriage despite many opportunities on the party circuit in Washington. His sex drive was very moderate and Pat had always been all the woman he needed. Thinking back now he just couldn't understand his sudden attraction to the very pretty and nubile young intern. There had been absolutely no doubt from the time her sponsor had brought her to his office that she was attracted to him and available. To make matters even worse she had just recently been married to a young marine officer who was currently serving in Viet Nam. He was now absolutely certain that the incident hadn't been worth the trouble or the possible future danger. The little intern did prove to be as hot as a firecracker with an appetite that vastly exceeded his. She proved to be just too much for him and a reminder that he was now in that age and physical category referred to as middle aged.

As Buck continued to study his wife his mind went back to earlier days. He had met Pat a number of times when she came to the Point to visit her brother and Buck's close friend and classmate Howard Conrad, Jr. She dated several of the cadets and Buck was very interested but they just ran out of weekends. The next time they had met was after tragedy struck the Conrad family when Major Howard Conrad, Jr., already a highly decorated veteran of the South Pacific, was killed in a training accident in California early in 1945. Howard Sr. was devastated at the loss of his only son and he asked Buck to take charge of the funeral arrangements at Arlington. Buck had been still on convalescence leave and receiving physio therapy at Walter Reid and he was only too happy to be able to help and this once again brought him into contact with the Conrad family which, of course, included Pat.

On the day after the funeral Howard Sr. came to see him to thank him profusely for the very professional manner in which he had handled the funeral arrangements. The old man was still in bad shape and he told him of the plans he had had for his son. Howard Jr, would have resigned his commission after the war and moved to Compass Inc. where he would have become his father's executive assistant. Howard Sr. was a very strong supporter of the Republican Party and he planned a political career for his son with the ultimate objective of challenging for the presidency some day. Buck had no doubts that Howard Jr, with his outstanding ability and supported by the huge resources of his father and Compass Inc., would have gone a long way towards this lofty objective.

Before that meeting had concluded Buck recalled what he could only describe as the most bizarre development of his life. Howard Sr told him that he was one of Pat's favourite people and then, in effect, as Buck later described it to Carl Reichold, he proposed to him on behalf of his daughter. At least he impressed upon Buck just how much Pat liked him and how much Howard Jr. had respected him and that he would like to consider him as being very much the same as the son he had lost. He had also told Buck that should he ever decide to leave the armed forces the same job that had been reserved for Howard, Jr, Executive Assistant to the CEO, would be open to him. Buck had always been attracted to the beautiful Pat but she had always been so in demand at those weekends at the Point that he had never managed even a date with her. Now, just like magic. Pat became very available to Buck and they were married later in the year.

The union proved fruitful nearly immediately and the twins had been born in 1946 nearly exactly nine months later. The twins, Patrick and Carla (named after his other great friend Carl Reichold) appeared to satisfy both their family needs but the best laid plans..........and Jason had been born in 1949 and when he showed early musical aptitude, Jason became Pat's personal project with the full support of her father who had always been so supportive of her own musical aspirations.

Buck had stayed with his military career, despite a gimpy leg, until just after the Korean war. He had served as a regimental commander in Korea, picked up a Distinguished Service Cross, a Bronze Star and another Purple Heart to go along with his Congressional Medal and Silver Star and had made the list for promotion to full colonel when even as much as Buck loved the service, the writing on the wall was quite obvious. His lowered medical classification meant severe limitations on future employment and the prospect of riding a desk until retirement. Buck had very reluctantly resigned his commission and accepted the position as Executive Assistant to the CEO of Compass Inc. The following year, with his father-in-law's encouragement and support, Buck took advantage of an open congressional seat in Ohio and the war hero holder of the Congressional Medal of honor and several other awards for gallantry, the former all state athlete, football All-America at West Point, won the election in a walk. Two years later a senate seat opened up and, again with his father-in-law's encouragement and support, Buck angered many of the party faithful by jumping the queue. He won a very tough primary fight and the subsequent election. One year later his father-in-law was nearly totally incapacitated by a serious stroke and, based on the old man's written instructions, Mrs. Patricia Buchalter stepped in as CEO of Compass Inc and her father remained as a non participating Chairman of the Board, Emeritus. Buck had retained his position as Executive Assistant to the CEO together with all of the perks that such a position entailed. The following year the Senator made the smartest move of his life when he appointed Lt-Col (Ret) Spencer Graham as his Chief of Staff.

Late Sunday evening, after their very successful junket to Illinois and Wisconsin, Pat dropped the Senator off in Washington and carried on to Dallas to visit Daddy and at-

86

tend a regularly scheduled Compass Inc board meeting on Tuesday, June 11th.

Dallas really had always been home to Pat. Both she and her brother had been born there and remained there under the watchful eyes of nannies, housekeepers and security guards after Howard Sr decided that their mother, a former Hollywood star, did not come up to his standard of family values, and divorced her. Pat had inherited her mother's raven haired beauty and found that her life went on without much disturbance when the news came that her mother had died in the crash of a light plane in Los Angeles.

Pat had demonstrated significant musical talent at an early age. She was quite competent on the piano at age six and her father, also a lover of classical music, spared absolutely no expense in developing her talent. Even before she was twelve Pat had been participating in piano recitals in Dallas, Houston and Austin. Indeed, as related earlier, Pat, at barely sixteen, played Carnegie Hall. Following the mixed reviews of the New York critics Pat's father made a determined effort to find the very best teacher of concert pianists in the world. Europe seemed closed to him by the gathering war clouds but he discovered that one candidate near the top of his list was available. This was Umberto Fillini, a well known, although youthful concert pianist, who although Italian was living in Argentina and taking advantage of dual citizenship acquired from his Argentinian mother. Despite his youth, Fillini was a concert pianist of the first rank and already a teacher with a growing reputation for success with young aspiring concert pianists. Fillini was very receptive to the idea of becoming Pat's private tutor and Howard Sr was very impressed with some of his recordings and his curriculum vitae.

Umberto Fillini was hired under an exclusive contract to Howard Conrad, Sr. under which he would be able to accept occasional concert engagements in both North and South

America. In his final selection of Umberto, Pat's father did not carry out his usual careful check of other facets of the talented young maestro's character. In all fairness this could probably be attributed to the problems that the war was imposing on personnel research in Europe. If he could have conducted his usual painstaking background search the father would have discovered that while young Fillini had enjoyed outstanding success as tutor to ten young aspiring female concert pianists all between the ages of 16 and 19, he would have found that Fillini had amassed a record of eight to two in his success in deflowering his charges. He had only missed out on the Spanish twins who were always accompanied by their rather fierce looking chaperone and her even more formidable husband.

Pat remembered how excited she had been when she had met Umberto for the first time. He was so handsome and really so young to have attained the level of renown he enjoyed on the recital circuit. And, of course, he was very talented. To her father's delight Pat made great progress during her first year under Umberto's tutelege. He had gone so far as reserving another date at Carnegie Hall.

Pat was sure that if Umberto had been asked to explain his sexual conquests of his piano students he would have rationalized that a virgin could never attain the degree of emotional intensity so necessary to achieve the optimum level of artistic expression.

About three months after Pat's seventeenth birthday Umberto decided that it was time for her transition to womanhood as the final step in her artistic development and he found that Pat was ready, oh so ready, for the maestro, as he euphemistically put it, to tune her piano. What Pat lacked in experience she made up for in enthusiasm and these supplementary lessons continued for more than two months when Umberto had to leave Dallas for a series of recitals in Brazil and Argentina. When Pat appeared for her annual medical the dear old family doctor had some interesting news for her. While she was obviously in excellent health she was also very definitely pregnant. Pat knew that there was absolutely no way the kindly old doctor would not inform her father when he returned to Dallas a week later, so she tried desperately to reach Umberto by phone but that being nearly impossible in 1940 she had a trusted friend send him a cablegram. His answering message provided only one very definite piece of information. Umberto's return to the US would be delayed indefinitely. From his hotel suite in Buenos Aires Umberto undoubtedly heard the explosion all the way from Dallas when Howard Sr was informed of Pat's condition. This confirmed the wisdom of his decision to remain in South America.

Although Umberto was beyond his reach Howard Sr inflicted his wrath on his household in Dallas and a number of heads rolled. Sound legal advice and the rather vague age of consent laws in Texas stopped the very angry father from attempting to pursue statutory rape charges and he had to settle for having the Department of Immigration issue an order barring Umberto from reentering the US by having him declared persona non grata on the grounds of moral turpitude. In later years Umberto incurred major legal expenses and had to call upon the support of a number of famous musicians before the noted concert pianist was allowed to return to the concert circuit in the United States. Even then it was only possible by travelling on a diplomatic passport provided by a grateful Italian government for their world famous musician.

Her father used money and influence to arrange for Pat to have an abortion but only over her protest of undying love for the missing Umberto. By this time it had become obvious even to her father that Pat was doomed to the ranks of the also rans as a concert pianist but she had retained her love for music and her support for the Texas music programs funded by Howard Sr and some other rich music lovers. By now the wife of Lt-Col Richard (Buck) Buchalter, Pat was appointed to a number of scholarship boards that selected the most promising of program participants for advanced training. In 1948 Pat escorted a group of such students to Europe for six weeks to enjoy the benefits of instruction by some of Europe's finest music teachers. One of the really big names who had been recruited for the symposium was Umberto Fillini. They soon realized that the fires were still burning and Pat recognized that her piano was badly in need of tuning. Their six-week affair combined with Umberto's continuing disdain for safe sex had the predictable result. Pat arrived back in New York with the strong suspicion that Umberto had struck again and only a couple more weeks were needed for proof positive that she was indeed pregnant. But this time Pat resolved that the baby would be a keeper and the relatively brief period between the "Bon Voyage Party" in New York and the "Welcome Home Party" six weeks later was short enough that Buck, although just a bit surprised by the news of the imminent family addition after their mutual agreement that two was enough, should have every reason to believe that he had participated in the conception. So much for safe sex, Jason was born almost exactly nine months after her departure for Europe and while in no way resembling his brother and sister was said by all to strongly resemble his mother.

When the Compass Executive Jet landed and taxied up to the Corporation hangar in Dallas late Sunday evening a limousine was waiting to take her to Howard Sr's Dallas mansion. The nurse on duty that night informed her that her father was sleeping but he had been having a few good days and was looking forward to her visit. When she visited him in the morning she played the tape from Jason after erasing Jason's personal remarks to her. Her father had not been told of Jason's decision to seek out his own space because there was really no need to increase the load on his already confused mind. He enjoyed the tape very much and asked her to leave it with him. She promised to send it back to him but told him that there was still one person she would like to play it for but, for very obvious reasons, avoiding the mention of Umberto. Her father looked reasonably well and the medical staff were quite obviously taking good care of him. However, he was only a shadow of his former self. Pat remembered him when he was known as the meanest, toughest bastard in the American World of Business, but not now.

Pat met Umberto in Chicago the following week but he could offer little help in identifying just where the concert grand was located and where Jason had recorded the cassette. Umberto was very impressed with Jason's playing of Chopin even with the loss of quality attributable to the recording equipment but all he could say about the piano was that it was quite obviously a magnificent instrument made by one of the famous piano makers who had long since gone out of business. Most of the models that had existed before the war had been destroyed during the war and the few that were left were probably in old family homes. They spent the night in her hotel suite and Umberto again reminded her just how well he knew all of her tunes and he played several of them during the night. She considered that her sessions with Umberto would always keep her one up on Buck and the intern. Her father had taught her to always stay one up on the opposition and that in the existing cut throat world the opposition included everyone. In other words the philosophy he passed on to her was: "Don't get mad, get even!"

Spencer Graham made it a point of knowing everything of importance that happened in the family. This included the actions of the Senator's wife and this area of intelligence had become particularly important since the incident with the intern. In his broad ranging intelligence gathering activities he had enlisted the services of a highly trained operative, his wife Jessica, whom he had first met when she had joined an intelligence staff he had headed early in the war. Jessica's background had been similar to his except her parents had been missionaries in the Far East with many years divided between Formosa and mainland China. She was fluent in Mandarin and after their marriage she continued to assist

Spence in his various intelligence duties in addition to raising two very successful children. She continued as his most loyal and trusted aid when he served in Congress and the Senate and now in his role as Chief of Staff to Buck Buchalter.

Jessica had become a very good friend of Pat Buchalter but she never confused the lines of loyalty which were always centered on Buck. When Spence informed her of Buck's little indiscretion with the intern he also told her of his cover plan. Jessica, being a very observant person with extensive training in the art of observing human behavior, had always suspected that Pat had a secret love and, now, Spencer's briefing just focussed her on the identity of the lover. One of her tasks was to follow the travels of the Senator's wife and, with the aid of an insider in the corporate transportation nerve Centre, this was really a simple task. She would also follow the travels of Umberto Fillini and make careful note of the points at which the travel lines merged or actually met. Then their insider at Compass Inc could easily identify the hotel and actual suite number occupied by their CEO who nearly always took advantage of those suites for which senior Compass corporate executives had first call. The Chicago meeting of Pat and Umberto had been a very easy fix. Jessica knew that Pat had taken one of the executive jets from Dallas to Chicago and that Umberto was currently on a concert tour that included a recital in Chicago the day following Pat's visit with the previous day being an open date on his schedule. Jessica had always been taught to look for what was identified in intelligence and legal circles as "opportunity and proximity". In applying these principles it was reasonable to assume that they had met in Chicago. Although there was no evidence as to what they may have done when they met, those lurid details were of little interest to Jessica and she just made suitable notes in the confidential log that she and Spencer reviewed from time to time.

CHAPTER VII

JASON AND SANDY - THE MUSIC CONTINUES

At about seven p.m. on Thursday, June 6th, Jason arrived at the main entrance to the Mansion. He had been waiting for this opportunity eagerly since he and Sandy were together the previous Friday. This time it was Sandy herself who answered the door and, for just a moment, Jason thought he detected just a touch of coolness in her greeting as she led him through the drawing room and through the heavy glass doors of the music room. She sat at the piano still unsmiling and Jason noted an additional sheaf of sheet music on the top of the piano. He hesitated in joining her on the piano bench waiting for her to speak.

"I have been speaking to Gerda and Woody," she opened with. "They told me all about Saturday night at the gasthause. How you had many dances with that very pretty girl. That is not really fair while I was studying for my exams. Well, tell me, did you take her home, did you ….her. Oops, that word again and I promised. But I was angry at hearing about you dancing all evening with that girl. After all, you really broke your promise to me."

"What are you talking about?" Jason asked. "I danced with that girl twice and no I did not take her home and I certainly did not do with her what you suggest using that very bad word again. I'm quite sure that I could have but I could only think of you. And what is this promise you talk about? I don't remember making promises."

"Yes you did when you kissed me. I took that as a promise."

"Wait just a minute, I didn't kiss you, you kissed me and then jumped away when I tried to return your kiss."

"To me your response to that kiss was the same as a promise and I have a witness."

"Witness, what witness? There was no one else there."

"Oh, yes," she was just starting to bubble now, "My friend Plato was there!"

At the mention of her dog Jason knew she was pulling his leg and she now broke out in a sustained giggle. As he sat beside her at the piano she gave him a quick peck on the cheek. "Please Jason, don't be angry, I'm just having a little fun with you. But I don't like it when you dance with those pretty girls particularly when they ask you to dance."

"Now you will have to admit that it would not be very gentlemanly of me to refuse when a lady asked me to dance, would it?"

"I don't think that girl was a lady," was Sandy's quick retort.
"Well, at least she talked like a lady and she never used that word you say so often" was Jason's rejoinder.

Recognizing that she was cornered, Sandy changed the topic and, suddenly, she was bubbling again. "Oh, Jason, the girls were just thrilled with the cassettes and we played them over and over on the weekend and at school during the week. They are so impressed with you. I think some of them are even in love with you but I warned them that they must keep their hands off, that you are my friend. And my music teacher also heard your cassettes and she had the highest praise for your.....what is the word musicist or something like that, of, yes, your musicianship. Yes that is the word I was looking for. She also played the Chopin pieces, both yours and mine and really loved them. She gave me some more Chopin sheet music and the sheet music for that other composer you played, Tchaikovsky I think it was. She gave me the sheet music for his Piano Concerto. It's so lovely and now you must teach me to play it."

Sandy was now just bubbling with enthusiasm, Jason had never met anyone quite like her. All her reactions were so natural and obviously genuine. She appeared so completely innocent yet capable of using words that might be common place in the barracks but not coming from a young lady from an exclusive girls' school. And she did so with absolutely no indication of even the slightest embarrassment. Jason was becoming convinced that nothing would embarrass this bewitching and thoroughly genuine, beautiful young girl.

He set up the Tchaikovsky sheet music and played through the piano concerto. This was another piece that he had played so often that he could almost play it from memory. It was one of his grandfather's great favourites but it was quite a while since he had played it so he welcomed the sheet music to follow this time. They noticed that the old General's study door opened nearly as soon as Jason commenced playing and they knew he was standing in the doorway. They had left the heavy glass doors to the music room ajar for precisely this reason. As Jason finished Sandy clapped involuntarily and they heard the old General's voice.

"Ah, that was that other composer, Tchaikovsky I think you said. "That was very beautiful. Was that you playing Sandra?"

"Oh, no, grandfather. That was my friend Jason but now that I have the sheet music he will teach me to play it and I'll be able to play it for you."

They watched the study door slowly closing shut and Sandy turned Jason's attention to the cassettes. He told her that he had managed to get some more cassettes through the Base Exchange but they were still quite new on the market and in short supply. They were available in some of the larger electronic stores in Frankfort but much more expensive than in the Base Exchange."

"Jason, some of my very best friends at school would just love to have copies of some of these cassettes. They will pay for them. Could you make them?"

"Yes, but I will not be able to make copies until I get a second recording deck next week. I have it on order at the Base Exchange. Then we will be able to make as many copies as we like. Be sure your friends have players that will play the cassettes. Cassette players are quite new and very expensive."

Sandy was thrilled all over again. "Just tell me what it will cost. Remember these girls have lots of money and I'll make sure they pay me and thanks to you, I'm the most popular girl in the whole school. There are even two of the teachers who have asked for copies and that includes our music teacher."

They spent nearly two hours playing Chopin from the sheet music and Sandy improved dramatically each time through. She needed very little in the way of corrections and she had nearly mastered the light touch demanded by the Chopin technique. They noticed that the old General's door had opened again and it remained open as Sandy played through Tchaikovsky's piano concerto for the first time. At this point Mannheim appeared with a tray bearing the old General's late snack and indicated to them that Gerda was waiting for them in the kitchen.

Once again Gerda had prepared a delicious snack for them and Plato was there ready to make his rounds of the table starting from a position close to Jason whom he had identified as the softest touch from the previous evenings.

Woody was also there and before starting to eat Jason told Woody and Gerda that he had a bone to pick with them. He accused them of telling tales out of school when they had given Sandy highly misleading information about his activities at the gasthause the previous Saturday evening. They immediately protested their innocence and out of the corner of his eye Jason could see Sandy, very red faced, as she attempted to stifle her laughter.

"And just what has that naughty girl been telling you? All we told her was the absolute truth, that you had been the perfect gentleman in the face of very strong temptation. That very pretty girl - I think her name was Tina - was determined to take Jason home with her. Isn't that right Woody?"

"Yes " agreed Woody. "And that Tina was really something. I almost went with herself myself!" Then Woody ducked as Gerda made a threatening gesture with her ever-present long serving ladle.

Sandy was now laughing merrily. "Oh, Jason, I had you going. Don't blame them if I was just a little jealous. There I was studying for my exams and you were dancing with a pretty girl. But I forgive you this time."

Jason just rolled his eyes and stretched out his arms. "I'm forgiven, but for what, pray tell?"

Sandy spoke up. "Perhaps it is for what you were thinking when you danced with that girl."

"Now I'm guilty for thinking. Tell me, what kind of justice is that?" He appealed to Gerda, Woody, Mannheim and, of course, Plato. He received sympathetic support from all but Sandy's friend Plato.

As they walked across the lawn to the dam accompanied, of course, by Plato, Sandy took Jason's arm. "Jason, you are so good to me and believe me, you are my very best friend in the whole world. But I have one more favor to ask you." She looked up into his face with a near pleading look in her eyes. "You know that our graduation at school is at the end of the month. The girls, all my friends asked me to ask you if you will play at out graduation party that evening during the orchestra breaks. Jacob Wiseman, Helga's very good friend, has agreed to hire an orchestra and has made available the ballroom of the hotel where Helga has her condominium. It would be so wonderful if you would play for us. The girls are just crazy about your music. Helga and Jacob will be there. My escort will be my good friend's brother. This was arranged a long time ago when my friend was worried that I would not have an escort for our prom. He's very handsome but don't worry he's decidedly gay and he just might try to take you away from me. It's on a Friday night, June 28th, and the school dance committee will arrange for a room for you at the hotel."

"Sandy," replied Jason as they sat down on the wicker bench by the dam, "you certainly know by this time that I just can't say no to you. I will have to arrange to get the afternoon off because I would like to check out the piano in the ballroom. I'm sure that the hotel keeps the instrument tuned but I'd just like to try it out. It's too bad we can't take our piano with us."

"Oh thank you, Jason, thank you, thank you! You are so kind to me."

Jason just sat there. He recalled the wonderful rewards he had received on previous evenings just for some cassettes. He thrilled in anticipation at what he might receive as a reward for accepting an unpaid professional gig. He felt her hand touch his shoulder very lightly and heard her whisper.

"Jason please close your eyes and again promise me that there will be no hands. Really, I trust you but I'm not that sure that I trust myself. I have beautiful dreams about you and I'd tell you what we were doing except you don't want me to use that word. Now, close your eyes and remember, no hands." But Jason noticed that she did not take the precaution of pinning his hands between his body and the back of the bench.

And now he felt her lips close on his and this time he felt near full body contact as her full breasts pressed against his chest. Again, her tongue flickered through his half open mouth and made contact with his tongue. This time Jason just couldn't help himself as he enclosed her in his arms and he felt her response as she tried to get even closer to him. And then she was gone and as he opened his eyes she was standing there just beyond his reach and the look on her face was not the same impish grin he had seen on the previous two evenings.

'Oh, Jason, I'm so sorry. But I told you that I'm not sure that I even trust myself."

"Sandy I'm not sure just what you think I'm made of but, please, I'm just human. But don't worry you'll be safe with me. I love you and I'll never hurt you. You must know by now just how much I want you but nothing will happen until you are sure you are ready. And, as for you, Plato, just keep your mouth shut."

He heard her giggle and as he started across the dam he was thinking that another session like this one and he'd be able to pole vault across the stream.

Hank was still awake when he got back to their room and, quite obviously, he was expecting a detailed report on Jason's activity for the night. When nothing was forthcoming Hank went back to what had become a familiar theme.

"My girlfriend called and her friend Tina has been giving her a hard time and it's all about you. That girl really has the hots for you. Perhaps it's just her female pride but now she's suggesting that because you have no interest in humping her beautiful body you might just be gay. Tell me old buddy should I be sleeping with my back to the wall?"

Jason was standing just a few feet from Hank's reclining figure on his bed and he was only wearing a bath towel wrapped around his waist to cover the huge erection that was still present from the session with Sandy down by the stream. He dropped the towel revealing his full state of arousal and took a step toward Hank. "Yes now the secret is known and you are really my secret love. I must have you Hank my love."

Hank made a hurried move to get his back against the wall. "Just stay away from me you crazy son-of-a-bitch or I swear I'll amputate that hunk of salami and feed it to you. I know you're not gay but what kind of a girl leaves a guy in that condition at the end of the evening. If that is a product of just playing the piano I'm going to start taking music lessons."

"I'll tell you the kind of a girl she is; she's a nice girl and I'm hopelessly in love with her."

When Jason called at the Mansion on Friday it was Helga who answered the door. She allayed any fears he might have with a very friendly smile. "Good evening, Sandra will be right down. She has been practicing all day and the General is very pleased with the new scope of her music. She played that piano concerto through for me and I think she did it beautifully. I had forgotten the promise she showed in music when she was just a little girl. It appears that you have inspired her and I guess that is the secret of a good teacher. She also tells me that you have agreed to play for the girls during the orchestra breaks at their graduation ball.

100

Their Prom as I believe you would call it. My condominium is one of the dozen or so located directly above the hotel. The chairman of our board, Jacob Wiseman, has very generously agreed to sponsor their Prom and has arranged for a good orchestra. With your agreement to play during the three orchestra breaks it should be a perfect fit. The girls just love your music and the breaks may very well outshine the orchestra and they will be very good. The Chairman and I are guests of honor for the prom and we will ensure that there is a room reserved for you at the hotel."

At this point a bundle of blonde enthusiasm arrived and completely took over the situation.

"Did Helga tell you, did she, did she? I phoned the chairman of our Prom committee and she nearly freaked out when I told her that you would play during the orchestra breaks. She asked me to arrange your program with you. She called the other members of the committee and they are all thrilled with the news and their only requests are the Beatle tunes we recorded on the cassettes. Will that be all right with you?"

"Yes, Helga told me most of the news and, yes, that will be all right with me. You know by now that I just cannot say no to you." He was glad to note a smile of approval from Helga on hearing his words.

"Well," said Helga, "It sounds as if you will have abeautiful evening. And now I'll just leave you to your practising." With that she disappeared down the hall.

For two hours Jason had Sandy practise the Chopin pieces and her improvement was nothing short of remarkable. "I have been practising." The old General's approval was obvious very early in their session as they saw his study door open and remain open. Once he actually appeared at the door and when he realized that Sandy was playing he congratulated her by telling her how much he enjoyed the music.

Jason told Sandy that there was no rush in preparing their program for the Prom with three weeks to go. Sandy reminded him that she would be studying with her friends again this weekend but her exams would start on Wednesday June 12th and they would be finished the following Wednesday. He told her that he would prepare a suggested program for each fifteen minute break and they could review each mini-program when they next met on Thursday the 20th.

Mannheim appeared with the old General's tray indicating that Gerda wanted them in the kitchen. Gerda and Woody again invited Jason to join them at the gasthause on Saturday evening and they talked about just what they would do. Woody had a very pleasant baritone voice and suggested that they might do a duet on a Presley number. Jason knew the number and would have no difficulty in at least chording accompaniment. Sandy reminded Jason that he was not to spend the whole evening dancing with that very pretty girl named Tina while she was working hard at her studies.

As they walked across the lawn and sat on the wicker bench Sandy was talking excitedly about the Prom. "The girls are so excited that you will play for them. There won't be much time for requests but we must include "Hey, Jude" and there are four girls who have been practicing the vocal and they would like to accompany you on that number. They are all juniors so they would be able to meet you while the graduation ceremonies are in progress during the afternoon when you are checking out the piano and run through a practice. Please, Jason, they are very good and so keen about singing with you."

"OK, OK, it's your Prom and I'll do what you like. Besides I just know that you have told the girls already that it will be OK. Sandy, you take advantage of me."

Sandy immediately broke out in that infectious giggle that always amounted to a confession when he caught her out on something. She moved quickly and now she was on his lap and her lips had closed on his. No talk of restricting his hand movements and no efforts to pin his hands between his back and the back of the bench, just a long lingering kiss. Again her tongue was active as he lifted her so she was now astride his legs and he reached down to lift her closer against his body and his hands came in contact with the silky warm skin of the backs of her legs. His fingers touched the narrow band of her panties and she moaned and returned to her kiss. "Oh, Jason, it's so wonderful."

Now she clung to him as he moved forward on the bench so he could get closer to her. Her head now moved side to side and then back to his lips as her breathing deepened. Her moaning started now higher pitched and then it was happening. He tried to control the movement of her hips but the movement increased in tempo, until she moaned again and with a heavy sigh she collapsed against him. Now he felt her tears on his cheek and her body was shaking with sobs. He tried to look into her eyes but she again glued her lips to his.

Her sobs had attracted Plato's attention and he was now standing with his front paws up on the bench. Then she spoke in a low hoarse whisper "Oh, Jason, it happened. I'm not sure I wanted it to happen but I just couldn't stop myself. I told you I didn't trust myself." She now reached out and patted Plato on the head saying in soft German "It's all right boy get down now. "Then she was rearranging her clothing and she kissed Jason again. "Now I do think I love you and I think I know what love means. I'm still not sure that I really wanted this to happen but perhaps it's all right if we are really in love."

"Oh, Sandy, I really do love you and I'm sorry it happened. I didn't want it to happen until we got married but now it's happened and there's really nothing we can do about it." He returned her kiss and now she stood up.

"I'll be away now until June 20th but I'll be thinking about you all the time. I know that you will go to the gasthause tomorrow night but only to play for Woody and Gerda not to dance with Tina. You're mine now." She kissed him again lightly and moved up the path to the house accompanied by Plato.

As he watched her climb up the steps to the rear entrance Jason remained seated collecting his thoughts. He had really meant it when he had told her that he had not wanted it to happen but he now realized that it had been inevitable; that there had been absolutely nothing either of them could have done to prevent it from happening. When he stood up he found his knees had turned to jelly and he made his way back to the barracks on very wobbly legs.

When he got back to his room he found that Hank had put a line on the floor using toilet paper about three feet from his bed. Hank was in his bed with his back securely against the wall. "Don't you dare come closer than that line. I warn you, I'm armed," he revealed a big bit of two by four.

"Jason, I know you're not really gay but when I see the condition you come back in every evening you spend with Sandy, I'm just not taking any chances. Now, stay your distance!"

Tonight Jason offered no comment and just collapsed on his bed.

"Hey, man, just what does this mean? Don't you love me any more? Or has the beautiful blonde finally disarmed you.

Jesus Christ, that's it, the music man finally scored." But even with his continued probing for details Jason remained silent.

The following day Jason sent another cassette to his mother. The music on this one was Tchaikovsky's piano concerto, another favourite of hers and also a favourite of her father. In the commentary he added that morning in his room, he told her that he had met the most wonderful girl in the world and that he was deeply in love. He added that when they were married he would continue his music studies.

CHAPTER VIII

BACK IN THE STATES - THE PLOT THICKENS

Jason's mother received Jason's second cassette on Thursday June 13th. Pat was thrilled with the quality of the music but very angry on listening to Jason's protestations of love for the mystery girl and his plans to marry her. She had been unsuccessful in her efforts to identify the grand piano that Jason was using when Umberto told her that such an identification would be nearly impossible but she had more success with the make and lot number of the cassette and the second cassette reflected the same lot number. She had put the investigative power of her corporation to work and discovered that the Japanese manufacturer of the cassette could testify that the cassettes had been manufactured for one of their major customers who sold these cassettes all over the world.

Then Pat contacted the distributor and the information she received from the distributor had her detecting the distinct smell of a rat. All cassettes bearing this lot number had been shipped to the American Armed Forces distribution center in Frankfurt, Germany, which supplied all the Base Exchanges that were operated by the US Army in Germany. Pat immediately concluded that if Jason was in Germany, and in the armed forces, then she knew who had put him there.

Pat checked with Compass Inc's transportation coordinator and found that there was a corporate jet sitting in Cleveland that would be available that afternoon. She then called the Senator and told him that she would be in Washington that evening and she wanted to see him at her hotel and added that the Senator should bring that son-of-a-bitch Spencer Graham with him. At shortly after six that evening Pat was in her Washington hotel suite and had set up the equipment required to make her presentation starring the Senator and the intern.

For the Senator and his Chief of Staff all the red warning flags were at full staff. Pat had quite obviously learned something about Jason and his carefully arranged recent movements. How, they did not know, but they knew that somehow or other Pat had additional, and possibly, incriminating evidence. The summons to the neutral grounds afforded by the hotel suite plus her rather unkind reference to Spencer were the clinchers. The Senator had a very spacious condominium in Washington and any meetings with his wife were usually held there. The ominous message was obvious; Pat was ready to unload.

The Senator and Spence arrived at the hotel shortly before seven p.m. and were ushered up to Pat's suite. She met them at the door. The greeting was very friendly but Spence was glad he had brought along the file on Pat and her piano tuner in his brief case.

Pat wasted absolutely no time in putting the show on the road. She started by playing the second cassette she had received from Jason but stopped right after the music.

"That was beautiful wasn't it. I am relieved that he keeps up with his music and that is a tribute to the measure of his talent." She then played the message that Jason had recorded at the end of the tape. "And now boys, let's hear it. Why have you been holding out on me? I still don't know exactly where Jason is but I know he is in Germany and probably in the armed forces and I had to do some detective work to find that out for myself. But I have no doubts that both of you know exactly where he is over there and you also know just how he got there." She paused for a moment to let her words sink in and then continued. "What I don't understand is just why I was kept out of the loop. Don't I have the right security clearance? After all who has a better right to know? I am his mother. And now he's in love and wants to marry some girl and we have no idea who that girl is. Correction, I don't know who the girl is. It's quite possible that you both know and may have even set this up."

Buck now indicated that he wanted to speak. "Well darling it would appear that apologies may be in order but I can assure you that there was a very good reason for everything that has occurred. Perhaps you should have been kept informed but the first principle of security is always the "need to know" principle. With every person you add to what you have referred to as the loop the problems of security increase exponentially." Pat started to speak but Buck quieted her with an outstretched hand. "I know, dear, just exactly what you were about to say and can sympathize with your position that no such principle should take precedence over a mother's right to know."

Spence watched with great interest this collision between two very strong people. He had witnessed this before and Pat usually got her way but he suspected that, in this case, the Senator knew he was right and he was prepared to hold his ground at all costs.

"Pat, first let us identify our objectives in this matter. First, of course, is Jason's security. Second is Jason's continued progress in his studies of music and we will agree that that is dependant upon his enrolment in the special course at the Julliard School of Music and preferably in the semester that starts in September. As for that first condition, we can all rest assured that Jason is absolutely safe where he is right now. Second, he is obviously continuing his music studies. Until this message the only potential problem facing us was the enrolment date - one more audition is required - but now we have the problem of this new love in his life."

"First, Pat, let me digress just for a moment but only because I realize that you deserve an explanation on just how

Jason arrived in his present location. It all started about six months ago in New York where we had placed him to study with a very fine music teacher. Everything appeared to be going along very well but then, unbeknownst to us, Jason became seriously attracted to a very beautiful young aspiring actress who moved into his luxury condominium and proceeded to teach Jason things other than music." Again the Senator raised his hand as Pat appeared about to speak. "Excuse me for approaching what you call coarse but I think it reasonable to assume that this twenty something year old lady of the theatre was attracted more to the very luxurious condominium than an eighteen year old music student. I think we are very fortunate that we had certain security measures in place because if she had known Jason's real identity I have absolutely no doubt that we would already have a daughter-in-law and, probably, at least one grandchild."

"The depth of the attraction of the young actress for Jason became obvious when her regular boyfriend, an actor in a play on Broadway, landed a major role in a large budget Hollywood production and they both took off for Hollywood leaving a very angry, jealous, and frustrated Jason. That was the point at which he first disappeared. Where did he go? You guessed it, he took off chasing his true love to Hollywood. By the time he traced her in Hollywood the production had relocated - on location - to an undisclosed location in South America and by this time Jason had realized that he was missing the sex more than the starlet." Again, the Senator's hand went up; "Sorry again, dear, but it does appear that our dear son has developed into a bit of a stud. In California, Jason became involved with a very pretty little anti-war activist who reserved her favors only for those who shared her anti-war sentiments. After sampling her goodies Jason joined the anti-war movement but he soon lost interest in walking around carrying placards bearing anti-war slogans. However, because he was still enjoying the favors of the young lady, he joined a group of his new found friends in a scheme to slow the war effort.

"Nearly all of the young men in this group were highly vulnerable to the draft so they came up with a plan. Instead of skipping off to Canada before they were drafted they would volunteer and as volunteers they would be given a choice on trades training to which they would be allocated when they completed their basic training. Then, just as they were completing their trades training, and probably on draft for Viet Nam, they would take off for Canada. The failure to deliver qualified tradesmen that were in short reply would be much more serious to the overall war effort than a dozen potential draftees taking off to Canada. Someone, supposedly in the know, told them that there was a severe shortage of communication specialists so they all opted for training as communications' specialists.

"That is where we caught up to Jason. You will recall that we provided him with three separate and fully docu-mented identities as a security cover while he was in New York because of the fear of kidnapping. Spence suspected that when he disappeared he was using one of the other identities we had provided and, as usual, Spence was right. It was then a relatively simple matter to locate him but he had completed his basic training and he was already two weeks into a twelve-week trades training course and still enjoying the favors of the little anti-war supporter. However, what he and his co-conspirators did not realize was that they would have very little chance of slipping off to Canada at the con-clusion of their course because the final two weeks of the course would be held in Japan and then they wouldn't need a posting to Nam because they would be well on their way to Viet Nam already. To complete the security arrangements for the Viet Nam buildup, all the drop outs from trades training courses were to be remustered immediately as Infantrymen 1st Grade and would be shipped to Viet Nam immediately.

"So you can see that we had a problem, and Jason had a problem that he didn't even know about. One way or the other he was heading for Viet Nam where his lack of sex just might be the least of his worries. Something had to be done but it had to be handled with great delicacy. Many otherwise highly patriotic families were looking for ways of keeping their sons out of Viet Nam. Political influence in career changes for individual soldiers could have very serious consequences. What we had to arrange was for a reinforcement demand from a front line regiment in Germany because they were the only units whose priority in demand for reinforcements was equal to the demand of the Viet Nam buildup and that parity would not last for long. So what we arranged was for a very old friend in Germany to request reinforcements with a priority on communication specialists and partially trained specialists would be accepted to participate in an "in job" training program that they already had in place in Germany. Jason didn't even know what hit him; he was in Germany within seventy-two hours. Oh, yes, I know what you are going to ask. Why didn't we just get Jason out of the Army. This is not as easy as it sounds even when dealing with a volunteer. In times of conscription much care must be exercised to avoid the potentially dangerous paper trail that might expose someone to charges of exercising political influence. The method we used in Jason's case achieved our primary objective of keeping him out of Viet Nam and left no paper trail. This also relieved all the pressure in our efforts to achieve the other objectives relating to Jason's future. We now had time to work on the other solutions."

Spencer Graham was thinking that this was the Buck he had seen at work in committee meetings of the Senate and at important party strategy meetings. He was cool, logical and very convincing in defending what had originally appeared to be an untenable position. Pat really had them by the short hairs. How do you go about telling a mother that the location of her favourite son was really none of her business? He could see that Pat was still angry but he also knew that she was her father's daughter and Howard Sr was tough and mean but always logical. And Buck was succeeding in putting everything in its proper perspective and reminding Pat that they all had a stake in this matter that just might be more important than Jason's short term inconvenience.

Buck continued. "The arrival of the girl on the scene does introduce a problem. I can only wish that I had had that "birds and bees" talk with Jason earlier and more often. He just can't seem to keep his zipper zipped up. He is safe and in Germany and as long as he is there with what is classified as a front line unit he will not wind up on a Viet Nam draft. If he comes back to the States, unless on a specific assignment, he will become available for Viet Nam. We must still be concerned with the avoidance of any paper trail and the best way to do that is get him to make a voluntary application for transfer to the non-effective list to attend university. I can assure you that any such application will be immediately approved but, first, he must make the application. Once back in the States he would be on unpaid leave of absence until his umiversity class graduates and this Viet Nam mess should be over. With official student status he will not be available for service in Viet Nam."

Buck looked to both Spencer and Pat as though expecting questions. There being none, he continued. "While we are working on this plan we must be very careful not to rock the boat. Too many cooks might spoil the broth, etc., etc. We have some well-positioned friends ready to help us in this matter but we must be very careful to avoid the slightest hint of political influence for reasons I have already explained. We do not want to put any speed bumps in the careers of our friends. Just keep our objectives in mind. Jason is safe and I can make an unequivocal promise that Jason will enroll at Julliard no later than the commencement of the January 1969 semester." Buck paused again.

And now Buck skated out on some thin ice. He continued. "All three of us have vested interest in the primary aim of seeking the Republican nomination when Richard Nixon completes his second term in 1976. As of this date we are right on course. We have identified the possible opposition and we have the resources to develop the required support by helping the right people in both this general election and the general election in 1972 as well as the congressional elections in both 1970 and 1974. But remember, once we are identified as the front runners, we will also become the prime target for the opposition in our own party leading up to the primaries. They will be looking for anything that can be filed away as potential ammunition that might be used against us. If we mishandle the matter relating to Jason or we allow any hint of scandal to arise from any source they will jump on it like a pack of hungry dogs. We are fortunate in having so many friends in the party and we will be gaining more if we continue in our discreet allocation of resources to our friends. But political friendship is a very delicate thing and it can be blown away by the first whiff of scandal."

Buck sat back and studied the other two. Pat spoke but her tone had changed significantly from that of her opening remarks. "Buck, now I think I understand just why I was left out of the loop when you stepped in to remove Jason from the threat of going to Viet Nam. But I still do not agree with your decision to eliminate me from the loop and now it appears that I'm still not to know just exactly where my son is in Germany."

"Unfortunately, Pat, that's right. And please try to understand. It is not that we don't trust you. Just try to understand the position of other important people who will be involved in our plan. They are also vulnerable and any slip up could effect their careers. Please, just be patient. You have my promise that Jason will be in the school of music no later than January, 1969. Tell me, have I ever failed to keep a promise to you?"

113

"No, but then you've never held out on me before. Well all right, but I'll keep on top of this matter and I give you fair warning, don't cross me up again or there will be real hell to pay!"

Spencer Graham was greatly relieved that the file Jessica had developed could remain in his brief case. A very nasty showdown had been averted. Buck had handled the matter extremely well but Pat had a short fuse and they would have to keep her informed as the case developed.

Pat was also relieved that she had been spared the presentation she had been prepared to give starring Buck and the intern. But all the material remained locked in one of her travel bags and it would be used if they screwed her around again. However, her trust in her husband would not be a blind trust. Pat resolved to extend her own detective work that had been so rewarding so far and, this time, she would hire the security consultant who had completed the installations at the cottage and removed them after Pat had collected all the evidence. She knew that this consultant would be only too anxious to help because his company had been an unsuccessful bidder for a large block of Compass Inc's security business and, quite obviously, intended to bid again when the lucrative contract reopened for bidding.

Buck stayed the night with Pat and they had a very pleasant late dinner in the suite, some good wine and while Buck was no Umberto in the sack, Pat was still a very healthy woman with appetites that were not always that difficult to satisfy.

In the morning they had breakfast and Buck went straight to his office and Pat advised the captain of the corporate jet that she would be departing at about noon. She then contacted the security consultant that she planned to employ

114

and asked him to meet her at her home in Columbus that evening.

Pat also remembered that Spencer had located Jason in California by reaching the very logical conclusion that Jason was using another of the two additional identities they had provided him with to meet any emergency in New York. Pat had not been provided with any details on those additional identities but she knew who had them. She called the head of the security firm which had designed the security plan for Jason and with a few very explicit threats on the future of Compass Inc's security contracts, she not only received the information she needed but also a promise that neither her husband or Spencer Graham would be advised that she had acquired this information.

That evening the representative of the other security organization - First American Security Team Inc (FAST) - arrived at her Columbus home and Pat briefed him very carefully. She provided him with the two identities that she suspected Jason would be using and instructed the representative that she would require all details on her son's location in Germany, the name of the girl with whom he had become involved in Germany and all available details about the girl including her employment, family, details on other family members and everything that could be gleaned about her general character. She then offered the words that security consultants love to hear as she told him that speed was essential and expense would be no object. There would also be a handsome bonus for fast thorough work. The security official promised that an experienced team of operatives would be assigned to this case and that this team consisting of at least three operatives would leave for Germany within forty-eight hours.

CHAPTER IX

JULES, HELGA AND THE OLD GENERAL

On Saturday, June 8th, and Sunday, June 9th, Jules spent about six hours participating in highly competitive chess matches with the old General. It had been a few years since Jules had played so often against this caliber of competition and he found he was playing much better chess because of this competition. But the old General was also improving and this was on top of the fact that he was already a fierce competitor.

Jules was still winning most of the matches on a ratio of about three to one and the sequence was always the same. When the old General lost he would finally concede when all hope was lost. He would stand up and bow to Jules and then extend his hand to Jules and congratulate him on his play. He would then offer what was supposed to be a smile but came out more like a grimace. This was a very tough loser. And then he would sit back in his chair and close his eyes and remain motionless for several minutes. While he said nothing Jules was convinced that he was reviewing every move he had made in the previous game and Jules was also convinced that with his powerful intellect he was capable of total recall.

When the old General emerged from the match victorious the situation was completely different. He would clap his hands with delight always commenting on what a good game that had been and pointing out to Jules moves he could have made to avoid defeat. This reaction to victory would have been highly irritating with just about any other opponent but Jules felt no such annoyance. He now realized just how much these victories meant to the old General. In his total withdrawal the game of chess had become his only outlet and the only way in which he could focus this powerful intellect on problems in competition with another person

Jules would then stand up and bow to the old General and reach out his hand which the old man would grasp and shake vigorously.

At these points the old General appeared to become much more expansive and prepared to engage Jules in far ranging discussions on any subject that Jules would choose. Here, as he had already related to Lt Gen Reichold, he encountered that other facet of the old man's powerful intellect. For all of those years leading up to 1938 he had total recall. He spoke about his teachers, the instructors at Heidleburg, the officers he had served under and with, the philosophers such as Nietzschke, Hagel and Schopenhauer whose ideas had contributed to the rise of Germany.

The old General was not really very impressed with the philosophers or "the thinkers" as he called them. He was more impressed by people such as Metternich and Bismarck or, as he referred to them, "the doers". He also talked at length about members of the royal families of several states, the nobility and senior military leaders who provided such vital role models for young Germans. The key words that recurred again and again in his conversation were honor, duty, responsibility and the social evolution of leadership.

During each of the two afternoons Jules was able to tape nearly two hours of the old man's conversation and was delighted at the manner in which he could lead his dissertations into areas that included topics in which Jules was interested.

On Sunday afternoon, again after one of the old General's wins, Jules was able to encourage him to return to his theme of social evolution. Here the old man actually drew a parallel between Darwin's theory of evolution through the process of natural selection and his belief in social evolution and the gradual development of leadership through an evolutionary process that could span generations. Revolutionary

117

forces always disrupted this orderly progress and accelerated the emergence of leaders who had not been conditioned by time and, thus, did not possess those qualities that are essential to leadership. They assumed privilege without responsibilities and were motivated into actions without any true understanding of duty, patriotism and honor.

He also talked about his family including both ancestors and his sons and daughters. There was always a heavy responsibility on parents to instill an understanding of those qualities that were so important for young people as they matured into leadership roles. The development of these qualities were always the responsibility of the family even when the children were in full time attendance at school. While an appreciation of the importance of discipline and group loyalty could be developed in an academic environment, most of the qualities of leadership required the emotional bonds of the family as if, the old General said, permanently linked by a perpetual umbilical chord.

The old General had only limited respect for those whose qualifications were limited to academic fields. At one point he made this very obvious when he offered the opinion that he had only encountered two groups of people who were impressed by academic qualifications. First were those people who didn't have any and, in the second group, were those people who had nothing else.

The old man spoke at some length of the many weekends he had spent as a boy at the family hunting lodge with his brother and cousins and reminisced warmly about the male bonding that he had experienced and to which he had exposed his own sons in later years.

During his more expansive moods the old General was never averse to stating very strong opinions and at least some of these, especially when they expressed Ayrian or Teutonic superiority, could have produced a strong argument from

Jules. But Jules was impressed with the old man's apparent convictions and he decided to withhold his comments at this stage. He would have ample opportunity to make his comments in his discussions with General Reichold and he also intended to include a commentary with the English translation of the tapes if the tapes were accepted in support of his thesis.

When Jules left the Mansion Sunday evening the old General was in a very happy frame of mind after winning their final match of the day. Helga accompanied him to the door and she was delighted by the transformation of her grandfather and very grateful to Jules. Jules waved off her expressions of gratitude by pointing out how much he was enjoying the games and the conversations. He did, however, arrange to have dinner with her on Monday evening following a unit commanders' conference in Frankfort. He told her about her grandfather's description of the family hunting lodge and was surprised to learn that the lodge was still in the family and one of the conditions of the lease of the family's hunting preserve to NATO and the American Armed Forces decreed that strict security measures would be enforced so that the lodge was retained intact. Helga told him that she and Sandra went up there at least once a month just to get away from the traffic and the lodge was in excellent condition.

Because of the length of the tapes and considering that there would be additional tapes from the following week before his next scheduled meeting with General Reichold, Jules called the General and suggested that he might drop off the current tapes when he was at the commanders' conference the following day. This would give the General the opportunity to listen to at least part of them prior to their meeting. The General agreed.

He had a very pleasant dinner with Helga at the hotel which occupied the first twenty floors of the building in which her condominium was located. She insisted that the bill be charged to her condominium pointing out that the hotel might prove just a little expensive for a soldier. Besides she explained that all such charges were billed to her public relations budget. Jules found it very difficult to argue with this beautiful young woman. She was dressed casually but elegantly and once again he had noticed heads turning as they made their way to their table. She was obviously very well known to the maitre d'hotel and their service was outstanding. The wine was coming from what the sommelier referred to as the Chairman's Cellar and she explained that this was a separate wine cellar maintained especially for her boss Jacob Wiseman, the Chairman of the Board of the Rhine Group which had its head office in the next building.

Jules remarked on the beautiful view of the valley that was framed by the huge windows of the hotel dining room and Helga told him that this was nothing compared to the view from the penthouse level. She promised that she would give him the opportunity to see it while they had liquors and coffee in her suite.

When they went upstairs for liquors and coffee he found the view to be all that she had promised but her suite was much more that he had expected. As far as he could see this was not a penthouse suite it was the penthouse. They had their coffee and drinks on a balcony that opened off a huge living room. A trip to one of the bathrooms indicated that there were at least three bedrooms and a master bedroom.

"Pretty impressive, isn't it? She asked when he returned to the balcony.

"The answer is WOW! I don't know just how that translates. If this is an example of employee benefits then I'm in the wrong business."

"Not all employees enjoy such a benefit. Please remember I am the Vice President of Public Relations and I sit on the Group Management Board. It also helps that the Chairman of the Board, Jacob Wiseman is a very good friend of mine and he's a very sweet man. I really hope that I have not shocked you but I am under the impression that Americans are just a little narrow minded about such relationships."

"Please do not include me in that group of Americans to which you refer. I may be many things but I am not judgmental." My God, Jules was thinking she is so beautiful so self confident, so refreshingly honest.

"There, so now you know." Jules now realized that she was just a little tipsy. "The General's granddaughter is also the mistress of the Chairman of the Board. The Jewish Chairman of the Board. I'm sure that the irony will not escape you. But it's really much more than that. Jacob is a very sweet, very mature, widower and I am very fond of him. Also you should remember that I am a German woman and Germans, women included, are very practical. Our arrangement, that is Jacob's and mine, is very satisfactory to all and very practical."

She suddenly changed the subject. "Last Sunday I recall we were talking about the family hunting lodge. I am planning to go up there this coming Sunday and I thought you would like to join me. I'm sure that you would find it very interesting."

"Yes," Jules replied. "I'd love to go with you. I'll ask your grandfather to play on Friday evening instead of Sunday and that will enable me to accompany you."

At the door, as he was leaving, Jules thanked Helga for a very pleasant evening. She was standing very close and her perfume was nearly intoxicating. The kiss seemed to be perfectly natural and her lips were warm and responsive. She

121

drew away with a broad smile. "And now Colonel it's not very gallant to make passes at another man's mistress."

"That's not a pass, it's just my mark of admiration for a very beautiful and practical woman."

"Thank you for the kind words Colonel but we must remember that you just can't afford me and what is more important, I can't afford you." The door closed and the vision was gone.

The old General was only too happy to rearrange their schedule and play Friday evening instead of Sunday afternoon for this week and Jules decided that he would ask the old man on Friday if he would like to extend their competition to include a two hour session each Friday. Jules had no doubt that the old general would welcome such an arrangement and Jules' only concern was the capacity of his tapes. When he succeeded in getting the old man talking on a subject he could carry on for an extended period especially if this followed one of his victories.

Jules was now totally caught up in his project. He spent hours reviewing the existing tapes and made a note of those points where he would like to lead the old General to expanding on his comments. The more Jules listened to the old man the greater his admiration grew for this amazing intellect. Jules spot-checked on some of the events described by the old General, about people, places and dates and all the old man's accounts checked out right down to the smallest details. Jules was pleased to note that once the old General got started on a subject he appeared to actually enjoy the opportunity to explain his interpretation of events and when it came to expressing opinions there was never any reluctance to give his impression of the relative merits of the people who had been involved.

Jules was determined to try and lead the old General back to the subject of the German school of philosophy which he had touched on during their previous session. The old man had also been exposed to earlier European philosophers and Plato and Socrates of the Greek golden period.

On Friday evening the old General welcomed Jules warmly. He pointed out that he had not arranged for his personal servant, Mannheimm, to be present that evening and this could be attributed entirely to Jules' completely honorable approach to competition. The old man complimented Jules on his competitive spirit and his total honesty. In such spirited competition it would be so easy for a sighted player to take advantage of a sightless player and the old man was so pleased that there had never been the slightest hint of an improper move. Thus Mannheim would be no longer required to make the old General's moves; he would ask Jules to act on his instructions in placing the pieces.

Jules assured the old man that the thought had never even occurred to him and this was principally because he was convinced that no one could cheat a player who had such a complete grasp of board layouts as the old General. He loved the game so much that he could never bring himself to cheat but the General would be aware of any improper move immediately: so nothing would be gained.

"Thank you for your very kind complement, Colonel, but people will often seek to exercise their advantage. I have encountered several such people in games I have engaged in by phone or mail but I have always discontinued any such competition when the honor of my opponent came under question. You may have noted by now that honor is very important to me and that is why I enjoy our matches so much even when I lose although not as much as when I win. You are quite obviously a man of honor Colonel who possesses a superior intellect. You must come from a very superior background and offer such a good example of what I was talking about the other evening, the social evolution of leadership. You will recall that I made certain disparaging remarks about Americans when we first met. I withdraw those remarks. It now becomes obvious that such a young country as the United States is making rapid strides in developing those qualities that are essential in the evolution of leadership. This is all the more remarkable when we consider the serious disadvantage imposed on such progress by such a large block of intellectually inferior citizens as the blacks who are in that state largely because of the disruption of their own natural development caused by the slave trade."

Jules just clenched his teeth. Again a retort was on the tip of his tongue but he knew he would have ample opportunity to comment on such remarks in his discussion with General Reichold and in his translation of his cassettes for the final presentation to the Doctoral Studies Board of Supervision.

Perhaps spurred by the old General's remark about blacks in America Jules made quite short work of the old man in their first match that evening. His aggressive moves did not escape the attention of his opponent.

"Aha Colonel, "the old man commented, "you are very aggressive tonight. You really had me on the defensive in that game. But that is all very good and now I must be ready for such an offensive. Chess is so much like waging war in many ways as we plan our strategies and employ our tactics. And all without casualties except for the occasional bruise to our egos."

Their second match that evening was lengthy and fiercely contested and they were finally obliged to accept a draw. In their third match the old General struck quickly to gain the advantage and, eventually, Jules was obliged to concede. As usual the old man was jubilant and he obviously savored this victory even more after his decisive loss in the first game. He clapped his hands excitedly pronouncing, "Those were very good games, Colonel, perhaps the best we have played. It is really wonderful to play against an opponent who is so obviously my equal in every respect. We are so well matched."

Mannheim arrived with a late snack for them both and, as he poured the coffee, the old man was still savoring his win. Now Jules saw the opportunity to lead him into a discussion of the influence of philosophers on German ascendancy in the one hundred years leading up to World War I.

The discussion went on for at least an hour and a half and ranged from Nietzsche all the way back to Plato. Again the old man indicated that he was not overly impressed by those he referred to as "the thinkers" except that they provided ideas that helped to explain the relative success of various societies. He kept coming back to what he regarded as the essential qualities of those societies that enjoyed the greatest success. The qualities of honor, responsibility, duty were attributed to England's success until their upper classes were decimated by World War I and castrated by creeping socialism. He had nothing but disdain for socialism, which he pointed out, was based upon the false premise that people are equal. "No!" He exploded, "people are not equal, they are the product of their social evolution." and then he came back to his basic theory of social evolution.

He also had some interesting comments on morality. He went back to the Golden Age of Greece where he pointed out the importance and honor of citizenship as it was conferred on only those who had been proven worthy through their contributions to the state. He reminded Jules of the true meaning of virtue and lamented that in modern days virtue had become synonymous with chastity.

He then spoke about how socialism had created unreasonable expectations that people just could not realize and this, inevitably, led to dissention. This combined with the decline of morality allowed advertisers, even in the 1920s and early 1930s to aim their appeal at individual's baser instincts. How else, he asked, could the act of procreation be converted to a principal form of recreation?

Jules was very pleased with the evening sessions. Helga came in just before he left and she remarked again on her grandfather's transformation as they walked to the front door. "He's just a different man. Everyone notices it. Poor Mannheim just cannot understand what has happened because he always took the brunt of the General's anger. And now he has not been verbally assaulted in ages. We are so grateful for what you are doing."

"Please, "Jules answered. "No one is getting more out of this than I am." He indicated his cassettes. "But I also enjoy the chess and he's getting tougher all the time. I know that I have never encountered a mind like that of your grandfather. He would have been a formidable opponent in battle. I still find some of his ideas very difficult to accept but I'm following your advice and trying to keep everything in perspective."

"Yes I have been doing that for years but it's easier for me because in spite of everything I guess I do still love him even though it is very difficult at times. Now, I won't be here tomorrow but I'll be back Sunday morning. Gerda will be putting together a lunch for us and I'll pick you up at about eleven at the garage at the side of the Mansion. You can park your vehicle there."

Jules agreed with the meeting arrangements. He was up very early on Saturday morning to review the tapes. Once again he was very pleased with what he had captured during the previous evening.

On Sunday morning Jules parked his car beside the utility building used as a garage. The very sporty little Mercedes-Benz two seater that he assumed was Helga's was already there. As he walked around the front of his car he saw Helga approaching followed by Mannheim carrying two large baskets.

"We'll take my car," said Helga as she popped the trunk to enable Mannheim to load the baskets. "Gerda, as usual, has provided a care package for us and I assure you that no one under Gerda's care ever goes hungry or thirsty. I prefer always to drive. I do not think men are very good drivers and Americans are probably no exception."

Jules offered no argument. She was much too beautiful to argue with. It was a lovely early summer day and she was dressed in a form fitting blouse and medium length shorts that revealed more of her beautifully shaped legs than they concealed.

As she moved the little car smoothly onto the highway she revealed a fairly heavy foot but complete control.

Jules could not withhold a comment about the beautiful little car. "And fair lady, is this another of your employment benefits? Its really a magnificent little machine."

"Yes, " she replied, "all our vice-presidents have access to their choice of Mercedes models. Of course we are the company's banker and that certainly, makes things much easier to get the models we want." She glanced over at him and she was smiling. "No, it's not what you are thinking. It's not a gift from my lover." Now she was reading his thoughts because that is exactly what he was thinking.

"I hope that you will meet Jacob soon. I think you will like him. Everyone is very impressed with Jacob; he's a brilliant man. In fact, he is in Brussels today at your NATO

127

Headquarters. He is an advisor to NATO on the economic problems facing the European Community. He has also been asked to conduct briefings of the Commander of NATO.'

She continued to talk while driving smoothly through the beautiful countryside. "It is ironic that Jacob is held in such high regard by the heads of many European governments but he still has problems with leaders of the German Jewish community. The problem is that he holds dual citizenship, German and Swiss, and he moved to Switzerland with his family just before the war. It was really his father's decision. He was also a very successful banker but could see the direction in which Hitler was going. The Wiseman family did very well in Switzerland and made a determined effort to protect the assets that had been transferred to Swiss banks by German Jews who remained in Germany. But the Wisemans and other Jewish families who relocated in Switzerland escaped the death camps and gas chambers. Then, after the war, those families who had relocated in Switzerland and other countries were ostracized by the families that had remained in Germany and who had suffered so much. Jacob is very bitter and says that he does not get respect because he did not suffer enough and many of those who had remained in Germany had taken a calculated risk and some had achieved significant short term gains by supporting the German military buildup."

"That seems to be just a bit unfair." Jules observed. "Surely he gets some credit for his work with NATO and European security."

"Not that much. He does many other things for Jewish groups. He is very popular in Israel where he makes really major contributions and is the best salesman of their bonds. He also acts as an economic advisor to their Cabinet. But it just doesn't do much for him with the German Jewish leaders. He gets really frustrated at times and he told me that this is one reason why he prizes our friendship. He says that by

128

having me on his arm or at his side helps because while he still does not receive the respect he thinks he deserves he might just make up for it through the envy he sees in the eyes of Jewish men when we are together."

"He's right there. I'll bet their tongues are actually hanging out every time they see you." And Jules, now watching this beautiful woman through his sunglasses thought, as they drove along, that this was merely the truth and not just flattery.

"Oh, kind sir," she replied, "Go easy on the flattery because I give you fair warning, flattery will get you everywhere."

About forty minutes after leaving the Mansion they were on the heath and from rises in the road Jules could see the trails crisscrossing the heath where the armored vehicles, including those from his own regiment, conducted their training. The training area was not large enough for live firing of tank primary weapons but he knew that there were several areas in which troops could be exercised in using small arms. Helga slowed down as she came to the top of a rise in the road from which they could see most of the training area and turned into a side road. About fifty meters along this road they encountered a heavy gate. There were numerous signs on the gate and on each side of the road announcing that this was private property and the signs were in both German and English. In an arc across the top of the gate were the words "von Freiderhoff Lodge" in large gold letters.

Helga handed Jules a set of keys indicating that the largest one was for the gate. Jules unlocked the gate and then closed it and locked it again after Helga had driven in. It was only another fifty meters to the lodge and Jules was surprised at the size of the building. It was much bigger than he had expected and its sighting on the forward slope of the hill gave it excellent command of the training area. As they got out of the car each took one of Gerda's baskets and Helga asked Jules for the ring of keys. Just outside the main entrance to the lodge Helga opened a metal box telling Jules that she was disarming the very sensitive security system which was linked to the control center that was responsible for thetraining area and lodge security. They crossed a wide deck that extended the full length of the lodge and Helga opened the main door.

When Helga turned on the lights Jules was surprised to find that the lodge appeared to be fully furnished and tastefully decorated. Helga touched a button and the heavy solid wood covers on the big picture windows opened and the bright midday sun light bathed the room. The hillside positioning of the lodge gave them a view of much of the training area.

The furnishing was much more than Jules had expected. Chairs and tables were of heavy oak and at least one of the tables appeared to be mahogany. The walls were covered with many paintings and many of these were of hunting and military scenes. In what appeared to be a dining hall the only paintings were of a series of very distinguished-looking individuals.

"This is the family gallery," announced Helga. "All of the Barons von Freiderhoff from one to eight starting just behind the head of the table. You can see there is room for just one more and it has been painted but Grandfather refuses to be hung before he joins his ancestors wherever they have gone."

"I'm impressed. These are beautiful paintings and would produce some highly spirited bidding at any art auction. And they have been well cared for. Some of them must be close to two hundred years old. They must have been restored."

"No, Jules. First they are not for sale and, second, they have not been restored but they have been carefully maintained. Mannheim loves this place and he spends several days up here each month taking care of maintenance. Once or twice a year we provide him with a work crew. Grandfather comes up here nearly once a month. Even now that his sight has gone he loves it up here. Most of the time he just sits there in the dining hall and I know he is just thinking of all the memories he has of this place going all the way back to his boyhood. I guess we could think of this place as a shrine for male bonding. Come with me; I want to show you something." She entered one of the many rooms opening off the dining hall. When she turned on the light Jules could see that the walls were covered with photographs. She drew his attention to one picture of a teenage boy standing over what appeared to be the body of a very large wild boar. Standing beside the boy was, unmistakably, the old General at a much younger age, his hand extended to the boy quite obviously in congratulations for the kill.

"That is my father enjoying one of his proudest moments in the presence of the man he admired more than any other man in the world. I wonder if he was that proud the day I was born. But, then, we'll never know because the day I was born he was on patrol in the North Atlantic.

"But there can be no doubt that this is a very important place for my grandfather. For at least five generations the men of this family received their basic family training on this heath. All of those highly valued characteristics were instilled or acquired here at the knees of successive generations of fathers. Honor, duty, courage, responsibility, patriotism, you name it this is where they got it. All of these qualities contributed to the code they lived by and I just might be excused if I add that this was the code they died by. It was here and places like this that they learned how to live but they also learned how to die." Her voice broke just a little bit and Jules put his arm around her shoulders. She refused to look

131

at him but he knew there were tears in her eyes." Really, it's all so useless." She turned off the light and he followed her out of the room.

"I have thought of selling this place many times but my grandfather was absolutely adamant. There were too many memories wrapped up in this place for him to ever agree to sell it. I have power of attorney and could have acted on my own but I just couldn't bring myself to selling it. But, then, the NATO lease is very good and it will come up for renewal next year and then I'll ask Jacob to negotiate the new lease for me. He is a very good negotiator and now he has many friends at NATO."

Helga decided to set up for lunch and Jules put Gerda's big baskets on the heavy table in the dining hall. As she set out the plates and the food Jules wandered around the various rooms and found that there was much more space than he would have imagined. Some of the rooms were large enough that they could have been used as conference and lecture rooms. Jules was convinced that hunting lodges such as this had been used by the old General and members of his "action group" after World War I for their meetings and discussions in their effort to lead Germany back from the humiliation of the Treaty of Versailles.

He could easily visualize many of these rooms set up for map and sand table exercises where future commanders were introduced in the all-important skills of battle procedure.

When he returned to the dining hall Helga had completed setting up one end of the table and Jules could easily see that Gerda had lived up to her reputation. There was enough food for at least eight people and there was a huge bottle of white wine. "How can we possibly get through all of this?" he demanded.

"Don't worry, there is a refrigerator in one of the rooms over there. What is left we will leave there. Mannheim is coming up with a work party next week and they can finish it off."

They had a long leisurely lunch and Helga told him more of the history of her family. Then she talked for a little while about Sandra. She told him of finding the baby on the Mansion grounds after following the directions slid under the Mansion door by a desperate mother. Then they had adopted the little girl when they could not find the mother., Gerda had wanted to adopt Sandra but her nationality had not been established at that time so Helga had proceeded with the adoption and was successful largely because of the family name even though she was only twelve years old and had to wait until her eighteenth birthday before the adoption became official. Her grandfather had attempted to dissuade her protesting that the baby was probably just another product of the irresponsible sub culture that was pulling Germany down to their level. However, Helga stuck to her guns and never really had any regrets. Sandra quickly became the joy of the household as her antics and general zest for life brought smiles to the faces of everyone including the old General.

Sandra, now known by most as Sandy, had been named for Gerda's younger sister who had not survived the Displaced Persons Camps. Since age eight she had been enrolled in a fairly exclusive girls' boarding school in Frankfurt. Helga told Jules about the young American soldier that had restored Sandy's interest in music a subject in which she had shown early promise. The young soldier seemed to be a very nice young man and was very talented. He was teaching Sandy how to play Chopin's compositions for piano and the old General had been very impressed when Sandy played a piece that his wife had played for him many years ago and had played it so well. Helga was trying to get Sandy accepted at her university in Switzerland but some of Sandy's marks were a bit low. If unsuccessful there Helga would try to gain her admission to a junior college in Frankfurt and come and live with her. Other members of the household were not that fussy about either of these ideas because Sandy's cheerful presence would be missed around the Mansion.

When they finished their lunch they moved into the main hall with the remainder of the wine and the thermos of coffee and sat on the broad leather upholstered sofa in front of the big picture windows that gave such a good view of the training area. Jules commented on the wine and checked the label to identify its origin. He was surprised to note that the label bore the von Freiderberg coat of arms and Helga explained that it came from their own cellars. That at one time her Grandfather had accumulated one of the finest collections of wine in Germany. The Mansion cellars occupied the climate controlled basement that extended the full length of the original Mansion and still contained about 25,000 bottles of the finest vinteges. Her grandfather had always been a connoisseur of wines and had acquired his collection during the 1920s and 1930s when prices were very reasonable.

"Mannheim looks after the cellars now but we had an old family retainer until he died a few years ago and his sole responsibility was the wine cellars and he taught Mannheim how to look after the wine."

Jules took the two picnic baskets into the room where the refrigerator was located and stored the remainder of the food in the freezer section. When he came back to the main hall Helga had closed the big picture windows and was sitting on the sofa after pouring the rest of the wine into their large glasses. They drained their coffee cups and sipped from their wine glasses. He put his arm around her and drew her towards him and the kiss just seemed to be the logical extension of that kiss at the door to her condo but now there was total response as her armed circled his neck. "Oh, Jules Pelladeau, "he heard her sigh. "I knew that I would not be able to resist you for long."

Their clothes were off in a matter of seconds and they both were so ready. Their lovemaking was slow and deliberate and her response was as active as his firm grip on her hips would allow. Towards the end she became very vocal in a mixed stream of German and English words that would only cross her lips at a time of uncontrollable emotional response. As he slumped towards her she turned his head and kissed him warmly on his lips. "Oh, Jules, I knew that you would be dangerous from that first time we met. You are so beautiful. I am a practical woman but nevertheless a woman and I just cannot resist anyone who is so beautiful. And now look what you have done. Taken advantage of a poor defenceless woman when her lover is away. Aren't you ashamed of yourself?"

He looked down into her beautiful blue eyes and noted the little smile that was flickering across her face. "Not a bit. What happened was because we both wanted it to happen. You're such a beautiful woman; how would you expect a strong, young, red blooded American man to resist especially a black man. Surely you know about the stories of our abnormal sexual prowess. I give you fair warning that you are about to receive further proof of that prowess."

"Promises, promises, nothing but promises" and her voice trailed away with a gasp as he started again and her long legs, again in a near involuntary response, wrapped themselves around him.

Later they sat together in the dim light of the main hall. Her head was on his shoulder and at times her lips would brush against his velvety black skin. "Enough, enough. Pelladeau, you have made a believer of me and no more proof is necessary. You're just so beautiful it's almost unfair to poor defenceless women. But now we should pack up and head back and, I almost forgot, we should dress."

When they reached the car Helga gave Jules the car keyes. "You drive, "she said. "I'm a little sleepy. Afternoons in the country always do this to me." As he took the keys from her fingers he thought he detected just a little smile spreading across her face.

They arrived back at the Mansion early in the evening and he had to resist the temptation to kiss her because there were possibly many inquisitive eyes on the handsome black American officer and the beautiful lady. He pulled the car up to an entrance at the end of the building thinking that this would be the most convenient for her. She waved him on telling him that this was the entrance to the old General's living quarters which were located just behind his study. She pointed to another wide door and told him that that one led to the wine cellars. He asked her to be sure to thank Gerda for the wonderful lunch and their fingers lingered for just a moment when they touched.

CHAPTER X

Lt Gen REICHOLD AND THE TAPES

At shortly before 3 p.m. on Tuesday, June 18th. Jules arrived at General Reichold's office and he was met by the same aide who had met him two weeks earlier.

"Yes, Colonel Pelladeau. The General will be with you in a few minutes. He asked me to give you this preliminary outline for the presentation we will be making at the NATO conference in August. You will note that your name has been pencilled in for the parts of the program in which you will be involved. He thought that you might like to browse through this paper while you are waiting for him."

Jules glanced through the paper and put it in his briefcase. The General came out to greet him after about ten minutes. The General told his aid to hold all calls with the exception of those with a specific priority code and ushered Jules into his office. "Well, I spent about three or four hours listening to these cassettes over the weekend. They were like one of those very good novels you pick up from time to time and just hate to put it down. I was fascinated by just how successful you were in leading the old General into your specific areas of interest. That was really an excellent idea to give me the cassettes in advance because now we will not have to spend all our time listening to the tapes and devote that time to discussing the very interesting comments contained on the tapes. As you tried to impress upon me, this is a very interesting man and the more I listen the more I am coming to agree with you on the power of his intellect."

"It may not be always possible for me to get all the current cassettes to you in advance but I will whenever possible. If you have time to review them it will give us time during our sessions to review the contents of the cassettes and discuss possible directions in which to lead the General in future sessions."

"On Sunday I spend a very interesting day at what is called "The Lodge von Freiderhoff" which is the family hunting lodge at the edge of our training area and what was the family's private hunting preserve in the old days. They have kept this part of the property in the family because the old General does not want to part with it. He spends about a day each month up there and my guide, that is his granddaughter, told me that he spends hours just sitting there in the great hall going over all the memories that the place must bring back to him."

Jules went into great detail in his description of the hunting lodge. He told him of the huge dining hall with the paintings of all the first eight Barons von Freiderhoff, of the rooms with walls lined with photographs of memorable family events. He also told the General of his conclusion that it was in locations such as this hunting lodge that German officers like the old General had met after World War I to plan for Germany's recovery from the humiliation of the Treaty of Versailles. He told the General of how surprised he was at the excellent condition and the size of the old building with the key being the old General's insistence that terms of the NATO lease ensure that the lodge be off limits to all troops and training area staff. He told the General that the general's granddaughter had power of attorney and could have sold this property but did not have the heart to dispose of it so long as the Old General was still alive. For obvious reasons Jules' very detailed briefing of General Reichold on the physical characteristics of the hunting lodge did not include any account of the recreational activities that Jules had enjoyed that Sunday afternoon.

"As I was listening to the cassettes," General Reichold interjected, "I found myself coming back again and again to your impression in regards to the old man's intellect. Colonel

138

Pelladeau your conclusions in this regard, after a relative brief exposure to the old man, is a tribute to your powers of perception. I have now had the advantage of nearly seven hours of tapes and have reached the same conclusion but I doubt if I could have made that assessment after the first chess matches you played with him."

"Do you play chess, General?" Jules asked.

"Just a little," replied the General. "Both my father and grandfather were devotees to the game and played for hours. "I played with them occasionally and they tried their very best to teach me the game but they whipped me so easily and I'm not a good loser. Besides there were hockey practices games and tournaments that were of much greater interest to me."

"Yes, that is very easy to understand. My grandfather played with me for hours on end on Martinique when I spent the summers there and he insisted that I learn to play the game seriously. What he really succeeded in doing was hooking me on the game and I guess that was his objective right from the start. He was a legitimate Chess Master and I'll never forget the first time I beat him. He was not a very good loser but I'm sure that he was very proud of me for a legitimate win at twelve years of age. But I have always found that a serious game of chess offers a very good insight and understanding as to just how your opponent's mind works. Weaknesses become immediately obvious and this is particularly true in the capacity of the mind to collate information and store moves that can be subjected to immediate recall as needed. As a match progresses into critical stages the mind's capacity for discipline becomes obvious as the patience of the experienced player will contribute to success. All of these mental qualities became obvious in my very first chess match with the old General and they have remained constant factors in all the matches we have played since.

Thus the chess matches gave me the insight that you have gained in the hours you have spent in reviewing the tapes."

"I think I know exactly what you mean." Said the General. "While I'm not much of a chess player, I am an ardent bridge player and while I would hesitate to put bridge in the same category as chess, much of what you have said also applies to bridge. I have played in competition at the national level and found the full mental capacity of opponents becomes obvious very early in a match."

After a short pause, the General continued. "The other conclusion I came to in listening to the tapes in addition to reviewing our introductory session is what a truly amazing opportunity we have been presented with through your meeting with the old General. I did a little research on Baron von Freiderhoff and, as I had suspected, this man was a very important figure who ranked right up there with Hindenburg but had not been exposed to having his reputation subjected to attack because of political activities. Somehow or other he managed to keep himself clean. He always presented himself as just a soldier and a proud patriot. His name did become connected with Hitler's cabal but the word kept coming out that other people such as Goebels, von Ribbentrop, Hess and the others had Hitler's ear and he did not listen to von Freiderhoff. And then one day he just walked, or drove, away from Hitler's HQ and went home. He survived this apparent reckless move only because of his reputation and popularity with the German officer class. Goebels attributed his departure to a mental breakdown and beyond asking him to compensate for the staff car he drove away in, they just let him go. The post war "War Crimes Commission" cleared the old General of all war crimes charges although the Russians made a determined effort to have him cited as a war criminal but all of their charges were based upon some very outspoken anti-Communists articles he had written in the early 1930s but they really couldn't make anything stick."

The General stopped and handed some papers over to Jules. "These are my notes from that little bit of research I did on the old General. They may just be of some use to you. Let's just stop for a minute and think of what we really have here. First, we have a very important German Field Marshall, the most decorated German veteran of World War I, and certainly the most respected of any German general officer at the end of that war. Laterhe was at least an associate of Adolph Hitler but whose advice Hitler disregarded. Then one day in 1938, the same day that Hitler met with Mussolini at the Brenner Pass in the Alps, Field Marshall Erich von Freiderhoff reached the state of total frustration and just walked out of Hitler's HQ, got into his staff car and drove himself home to that Mansion so appropriately named "The Enclave". He just dropped out. The expression that you used in our introductory session was "Stop the world, I want to get off". It's as if he said it and did it, got off, I mean."

"That's is exactly what happened, "commented Jules. "That is the expression that his granddaughter used that first day we met. And I have told you about that remarkable thing that I noticed about his library. I have yet to find any books in there that were published after 1938. In all of our discussions he had indicated little or no knowledge of what has happened since the war or, for that matter, since 1938. Certainly, he knows that Germany lost World War II and it seems that he could foresee no other outcome after Hitler had made so many mistakes up to and including the alliance with Mussolini. But equally as remarkable is his total recall of everything that happened before 1938 and that goes all the way back to the days of his youth. You are absolutely right in recognizing the tremendous opportunity that has been presented to us and possibly one of the most important factors is that the old General did drop out completely. His impressions of the period of our primary interest - from World War I to World War II - have totally escaped the contamination of the views of all those "talking heads" who, even with the help of history, still have great difficulty in describing what really happened."

The General had also made extensive notes as he had listened to the cassettes that Jules had given to him in advance of their meeting. He noted the repeated references the old General had made to what he called social evolution which he theorized was very similar to the biological evolution that had been such an important part of Darwin's theories. He emphasized that time was such an important factor in both social and biological evolution and that the parallel could be extended to the process of natural selection. He repeatedly came back to those qualities of leadership consisting of loyalty, honor, patriotism, citizenship, responsibility and how their product leadership had evolved through generations.

General Reichold introduced his own family experience in support of the old man's ideas His great-grandfather had emigrated to America at a time when their Catholic communities had come under some stress from the predominantly Lutheran majority. The family had been upper middle class with ties to the business community instead of the military class. While discriminated against to a certain extent, the Reichold family was deeply imbued with those qualities of loyalty, responsibility and patriotism of which the old General spoke. In fact, even after three generations in the United States they remained very proud of their German background and continued to embrace many of the German customs and practices they imported to their new communities.

Reichold attributed the strong moral fibre of the German/American communities of the midwest to the same high standard of morals that the old General identified as the strength of the German character and maintained only through family role models.

General Reichold's notes also commented on what Jules had identified as the old man's near total recall of nearly a lifetime of participation in that level of German society that was totally involved in preparation for and involvement in war. He continually amazed Reichold with his detailed accounts of meetings, the names of those participating, dates, places and the debates and the decisions that were made. As he told Jules the possibilities of further discussions were mind boggling if only for the verification of history they would provide. Jules' final thesis would be undoubtedly one of the most imaginative and most important in the university's doctoral program.

It was early evening before they sent down for coffee and their session was nearly over. Jules noted that a local newsletter was open on the General's desk and the article it was open to described how S/Sgt Mombirkett of his unit had successfully defended his regional heavyweight boxing title. The General noted his interest and told him that he had meant to ask about S/Sgt Mombirkett. The General had had a top sergeant by that name in Korea who also had been a boxer and the third in four generations of career army men from the same family. He asked Jules if he knew Mombirkett and Jules told him that he was his Non Com in charge of communications specialists. In fact he was ramrodding the in-job training program that the General had set up a couple of months earlier. He described the S/Sgt to the General as a big red head. Apparently he was a good soldier but a "redneck" in the "good ole boy Bubba" tradition. "That must be him," replied the General, "The fourth generation of Mombirketts. But you're right, another "redneck" in the "good ole boy" tradition."

Jules was very pleased with his second session with General Reichold. They agreed that they would meet again on July 2nd and that Jules would review the paper on the proposed NATO presentation and they could discuss that program at their next meeting.

Leaving the General's building Jules stood for a moment looking over towards the penthouse where Helga had her condominium. A thought crossed his mind but he permitted it to pass. She was very tempting but the possibility of meeting Jacob Wiseman at this point was really not that appealing.

CHAPTER XI

JASON, SANDY AND THE PROM

Sandy completed her exams on Wednesday June 19th and spent that night with Helga. She tried to persuade Helga to take her back to the Mansion on Thursday but Helga was busy in the morning and suggested that they should celebrate with a day of shopping. They were still awaiting final word from Helga's alma mater in Switzerland but Sandy had been accepted for the fall term at a good college in the Frankfurt area. Sandy reluctantly agreed. She was anxious to see Jason and start working on their program for the orchestra breaks at the Prom. What had happened that final night down by the stream was still very fresh in her mind and she was determined to tell Jason that they must not do that again no matter what word she was allowed to use to describe what they had done. What finally decided in favor of the shopping expedition was the promise of a very special dress for graduation and a gown for the Prom. The shopping was successful and Sandy was just thrilled when she returned to the condo and tried on each outfit several times.

Early in the evening Jacob Wiseman arrived after spending two weeks between NATO and the UN. He was also highly complimentary on her choice of dresses and Sandy was thrilled all over again. She had always liked Jacob as he had always been so kind to her. He was very handsome in a very distinguished, mature way and Sandy had often thought of how proud she would have been if Helga and Jacob had been the mother and father she had never known.

Jacob, of course, spent the night and Sandy knew that, as usual, Helga had joined him in the master bedroom. During the night Sandy was still so excited that she couldn't sleep. She went to the kitchen for a cold drink and then brought her drink back to the living room and sat by the huge

145

picture window. She was suddenly aware of muffled sounds coming from the master bedroom and she knew, immediately, what was happening. By listening intently she could hear heavy breathing and Helga's voice softly crying out the words "Oh, yes,yes,yes!" as the sounds faded away and the heavy breathing subsided. Helga and Jacob were doing what Helga had told her that she must not do. But Sandy knew that Helga was right in what she had told her but this did not prevent her from thinking back to what had happened that last night with Jason as her body responded with a surge of excitement.

When she returned to her bed she still had difficulty in sleeping and her mind turned to other things. Last weekend she had spent with her very best friend Meta studying for their final three exams. She and Meta always told each other everything they did. Meta had told her when she had done it for the first time last year with the tennis pro at her club. Meta had also told her about an experiment with another girl at school that had not been very successful. So Sandy made her tearful confession to Meta when they went to bed that Saturday night and Meta had comforted her. She told Sandy that she should not worry that these things happened when people were in love. She reminded Sandy that she had done it with the tennis pro more out of curiosity than love and she wasn't shedding any tears about it. Sandy asked Meta what she would do if she was pregnant and Meta answered with all of the wisdom of a recently deflowered virgin that she should not worry because a girl just didn't get pregnant the first time.

Jacob was gone by the time Helga and Sandy had breakfast together the next morning and the latter's excitement about her new dresses and the Prom had returned and by the time they loaded Helga's car Sandy was bubbling again. When they arrived back at the Mansion Mannheim was waiting to help them with Sandy's luggage. When Mannheim had taken everything to her room Sandy noticed that he

146

seemed to be preoccupied and she did what she always tried to do, that is, to make him smile but, this time, without success.

"What is the matter Mannheim,?"she asked.

"Oh, nothing really, I'm just a little down." He replied. But he continued. "Sandy you know I love you and I would never do anything to hurt you, you know that, don't you? And the same for all the other members of our household including the old General. You know that also, don't you?

"Oh, yes, Mannheim and we all love you because you are always so good to us." Answered Sandy. "What is the matter with you. Mannheim?"

"Oh nothing really; it's just that I do stupid things and say stupid things sometimes and I really don't mean them." With that Mannheim left her room and she heard his door close behind him.

Sandy then went downstairs with her arms full of more sheet music. She hugged and kissed Gerda and talked excitedly about her new dresses for graduation and the Prom promising to model her new outfits for her the following morning. The old General was in his study and she entered unceremoniously and gave him a hug and a kiss on the cheek. "Grandfather, I have some more Chopin sheet music and sheet music for other composers. I will practise and play for you. My good friend Jason will help me."

She spent the rest of the day practising on some of the Chopin sheet music. She also played back some of the Beatle music on the cassettes and practised playing these melodies by ear. She was quite pleased with the results. She then turned to all the requests she had received from the girls at school and there were far too many to be included in the three orchestra breaks even when she reduced it to requests from the graduating class. Finally she drafted mini-programs that included the requests that had been made the most often and decided that she and Jason could start from there. When her thoughts turned to Jason she also started to plan what she would tell him. She would be very firm with him they should not do it again. Sure, Helga and Jacob do it and Gerda and Woody do it, but that's different. She and Jason must not do it. Sandy was totally unprepared to deal with the logic, or illogic, of the situation but just resolved that she would be very firm with Jason. At the same time, thinking again of what had actually happened, Sandy was far from convinced that she had the will power to effectively resist.

When she went out to the kitchen for supper Woody had arrived and as she entered Gerda was asking Woody about Mannheim. "It's not like him. He is usually very happy but he has been very sad these past few days. I saw him in a car with a man and when I asked him about it he was evasive as though he had something to hide and that is also not like him. I hope he will not get involved with those people who say they can smuggle people into Canada or the United States. They are criminals and very dangerous."

Sandy told them that she had found Mannheim down-cast when he helped her with her luggage earlier in the day and she told them of what Mannheim had said about saying stupid things. "But who has he been talking to?" she asked.

"There's something strange going on," offered Woody. "There were a couple of strangers in the gasthouse last weekend asking questions. I think they were Americans and one way to get in trouble around here is to ask questions. We are always being warned to be on the lookout for curious strangers. One of them spoke to Jason's roommate Hank and he reported it immediately to his section chief. I don't know who they are. They're not Russians because that's not the way they operate but they appear to have lots of money and are always ready to buy drinks."

"Well, " said Gerda. "Perhaps they are spies but what would they want from poor Mannheim? Woody and I and Jason will take them prisoner tomorrow night at the gasthause and collect a big reward."

Jason arrived shortly after seven and was greeted by Helga who told him that Sandy would be there in a few minutes. She told him how excited Sandy was about the Prom and that she would want to show him her Prom dress and the outfit they had bought for her graduation ceremony. She also told him that Sandy would be receiving a very special award for her progress in music and much of that had been in the last few weeks. Her music teacher at the school had been so impressed and wanted to pass her congratulations on to Jason. Then, suddenly, as she always seemed to arrive, Sandy was there nearly bursting with excitement.

"Oh, Helga, Jason, I have prepared a suggested program for the orchestra breaks. There were too many requests, even for members of the graduating class so I selected the most popular ones." She was still babbling away when they arrived in the music room.

On the following day Saturday June 22nd, Sandy modeled her graduation and Prom gowns for Gerda, Mannheim and Woody and then there was a repeat performance for Jason when he arrived later in the morning. They were all impressed and Helga was pleased. Sandy and Jason spent the rest of the day recording the other two orchestra break miniprograms and played them over for Gerda, Woody, Mannheim and Helga. Everyone was in agreement that the breaks would be even bigger hits than the professional orchestra that Jacob Wiseman had hired. Sandy acted as Master of Ceremonies and she and Jason filled in for the four girls who had agreed to provide the vocal backups for the Beatle numbers.

In the evening Gerda, Woody and Jason left for an evening at the gasthause after Sandy appealed unsuccessfully to

Helga for permission to accompany them arguing that, after all, she was now a high school graduate and all she wanted was to listen to the music. Helga reminded her that, first, she was too young and, second, she was not quite a high school graduate. Sandy argued that lots of girls went to the gasthause at eighteen years of age and she would most definitely be eighteen on September 12th because Helga had found her on that date in 1950 and she had been at least six months old when they found her. She persisted until Helga promised to reconsider after her graduation the following week. As they left Sandy was sitting on the rear steps, looking a little sad but being comforted by her friend Plato.

The evening was a great success as Jason, Gerda and Woody were called back for encores each time they filled in for the orchestra. Tina was there but she was accompanied by the marine captain. Hank and his girlfriend joined them but only after Jason had taken him aside and asked him not to mention that the strangers' questions had been focussed, in part at least, on him. Near the end of the evening "Red" Mombirkett stopped by the table and told them their keyboard player had been posted and asked Jason to consider joining the group starting in two weeks. Jason agreed to consider the offer and promised to let Mombirkett know of his decision the following week.

The following week Jason was on duty two evenings but the other three were spent with Sandy reviewing their miniprograms and practicing the piano pieces for which Sandy had brought home the sheet music. She had not been told of the special music award she would receive at her graduation ceremonies but Jason was very pleased with the exceptional progress she was making. The continuing approval of the old General was obvious as they observed his study door remaining open most of the time that she was practising.

Sandy was delighted to hear that Tina was back with her marine captain. She had mixed feelings about Jason joining the combo at the bar but Jason assured her that it would consist mostly of the Saturday night gigs and just maybe Helga might agree that she could join the group to assist with setting up for any gigs at which Jason would play. She was excited with this prospect and was busy in plotting her strategies in the effort to convince Helga that such employment would be suitable for a high school graduate who already had experience as a Master of Ceremonies.

Sandy continued to resist the temptation of remaining too close to Jason for too long each night when they parted down by the stream but the length of the "no hands" kisses became just a little longer each evening. Jason managed to control his temptation to wrap this beautiful young body in his arms but it was becoming very difficult. He had been successful in his application for a weekend pass from Friday morning until Sunday evening and Helga advised him that they would arrange to have him picked up at about noon on Friday. She and Sandy would have to leave early in the morning to get ready for the afternoon graduation ceremonies.

At about Friday noon the Military Policeman on duty at the barracks front gate called Jason's barrack block to tell him that there was a vehicle waiting for him at the front gate. At the gate Jason found one of the biggest stretch limousines he had ever seen and a very impressed Military Policeman.

The limousine transported Jason to the hotel and at the hotel he found that he had been pre-registered. The room key had been picked up by the person completing his registration but a second key was quickly provided. The limousine driver told Jason that he had been instructed to pick him up at the hotel at 2 p.m. on Saturday to transport him hack to his barracks.

After a quick lunch in the hotel dining room Jason visited the ballroom to check out the piano and found it perfectly in tune. At about 2.30 the four girls who had volunteered to provide vocal backup for the Beatle numbers arrived and for two hours Jason was totally caught up in the contagious enthusiasm of four talented, attractive and energetic sixteen year olds who were already highly accomplished flirts and teases. They spoke mostly in German but Jason's rapidly improving German and certain passages that were thrown around in English convinced him that he was the near continual target of highly suggestive innuendo. Now he knew where Sandy had picked up many of the words in her vocabulary that she was never reluctant to use However, despite their professed designs on Jason, they went through several successful rehearsals and left only after each had rewarded Jason with long kisses that told Jason just where Sandy had developed her proficiency.

The Prom, actually a dinner dance, was held in the hotel ballroom starting at seven-thirty and Jason was seated at a table with the patrons of the Prom, Jacob and Helga, the headmistress of the school and her husband and Sandy and her escort, Karl who was the brother of Sandy's best friend, Meta. As usual Sandy was bubbling with excitement even heightened somewhat by the special music award she had received during the graduation ceremonies during the afternoon. She insisted that Jason accompany her from table to table where he was introduced to all of the other girls and the teachers. When he showed initial reluctance for this tour Sandy pleaded with him that she had promised all her friends that they would meet Jason and some had even been promised a dance with him. He accused her of being a procurer hesitating to use the shorter equivalent because he wasn't completely certain if there was a feminine form for "pimp".

The evening was a total success and the three orchestra breaks were smash hits; so much so that they had great difficulty in getting off the stage when the orchestra returned. The orchestra leader congratulated Jason and told him that he would be adding some Beatle numbers to the orchestra's program if he could get the permission of the Beatle's publisher. Sandy carried out her MC Duties with her typical bubbling enthusiasm. It was late in the evening before Jason got the chance to dance with her after completing all but one of her dancing assignations with the other girls. It was a waltz and Sandy pressed herself very close to him and whispered in his ear her thanks for the very best day of her life. At the end of the dance she kissed him passionately before running back to the table. The kiss left Jason in a predictable condition and the friend of Sandy who had the next dance with him was fully aware of his arousal as she pressed very closely against him throughout the dance with considerable giggling.

Jacob and Helga left before midnight because they were leaving for Paris at 6 a.m. where they would be attending a weekend meeting of Rhine Group(International). The girls were breaking up into smaller party groups at about one-thirty when Jason made his way to his room. It had been a wonderful evening and the constant contact with those nubile young bodies had left him in a state of semi-arousal. A quick cold shower seem to be the answer and, after a brisk rub-down with the heavy bath towel, he just collapsed totally naked in the middle of the huge bed and was asleep before his head hit the plush duvet.

His sleep was that of a newborn baby except his dreams consisted of substantially more mature topics as all of those beautiful young bodies that pressed against him throughout the evening returned to his mind all bearing promises of pleasures young ladies should not even know about. But it was Sandy who kept recurring in his dream as he saw her again as he had seen her that first day at the stream and the feel of her body on the special night by the dam.

He slept until nearly eight o'clock and in the final dream just before waking up Sandy was wrapped in his arms wearing nothing but that infectious smile of hers. As he reluctantly opened his eyes he found himself looking directly into

153

the most beautiful blue eyes in the world and to the sound of bubbling laughter. His first reaction was to reach for the hem of the duvet hanging over the side of the bed and pull it around his naked body but she moved against him with the result that they were both under the duvet.

"How did you get in? What are you doing here?" He asked her.

"Remember, I registered you so they gave me a key to your room. I was very lonely up in the condo because Helga and Jacob left at about five o'clock. When they left I came down here and I have been just lying here watching you sleep. You must have been having some very nice dreams because that thing of yours became very big and hard. Who were you dreaming about, I hope it was not Tina." She was very close to him under the duvet and he was becoming increasingly aware that she was not wearing much under her white bathrobe. He kissed her and she responded warmly and that darting tongue of hers flickered against his.

"Oh, Sandy, this is so unfair. How am I supposed to resist?" She didn't answer but just resumed her kiss. He threw off the duvet and put his hands on her. He had been right, there was nothing under that robe but a baby doll sleep set. The bras slipped off easily and as his fingers touched the flimsy panties she moved and they disappeared. He felt her moving against him and they heard her whispering breathlessly in his ear. "Jason, will you use this. I don't want to have a baby." And he realized that she was pressing a little package into the hand that was caressing her thighs.

"What the hell," he started to say as, anticipating his question. she told him "Meta gave me some of them because she is my friend and does not want me to get in trouble."

It was over in a matter of minutes. He tried vainly to control the movements of her legs and hips as she became

154

more and more vocal crying out his name as he finally collapsed against her. He looked down into her face and she seemed to have fallen asleep in the afterglow but then her eyes opened and a lovely smile spread across her face. "Oh, Jason that was so beautiful! You are so wonderful! I'm so lucky to have you for my lover. Now I'm really hungry. Let's call for room service." She ordered a huge breakfast for two and hid in the bathroom when the waiter arrived. Jason signed the voucher noting that the bill would have taken a large bite out of his monthly pay and was very grateful to Jacob and Helga for their hospitality.

After they finished breakfast Sandy accepted his invitation to join him in the shower and after a long leisurely shower they found use for another of Meta's little gifts.

They then went up to Helga's condo and Jason helped Sandy to pack her belongings. She showed him the beautiful, very expensive engraving that she had received at the graduation for her outstanding progress in music. She said that it should really be Jason's but she was going to keep it because this was the first award of any kind she had ever won.

The limousine arrived at 2 p.m. and the driver came up to help them carry down their baggage. As they drove back to the barracks Jason couldn't help but notice men's heads turning as they drove through the streets and they were probably wondering who that lucky guy was in the back seat of the luxurious limousine with that gorgeous young blonde. Sandy aided the illusion by keeping her head on his shoulder and kissing him from time to time. When they arrived at the main gate to the barracks the driver drove into the gate so he could turn the long car around by backing out. Jason noticed that the same Military Policeman was on duty as had been there the previous day. As he was getting out of the car Sandy reached out and pulled him back and wrapped her arms around his neck and closed her lips on his in an embrace that could be measured in minutes. The driver had set Jason's bags on the sidewalk beside the entrance to the guardroom. Jason realized that the MP was a very interested observer of everything that had happened and as Jason signed in and gave him his pass he heard the MP mutter "Things just get better and better don't they? I know what they say and it's true. Some guys have got it and some guys ain't. Soldier, I don't know who you are but you've sure got it!"

Hank appeared to be still asleep when he got to their room and Jason just stretched out on his bed to relax to savor a beautiful night. His reverie was interrupted by a barrage of questions. "Hey, buddy, I want all the facts. What gives with the stretch limousine? I suppose they drove you back too with that delicious little blonde in the back seat with you?" The barrage just went on and on.

Finally, just seeking a bit of peace, Jason told nearly everything. He didn't mention waking up naked with Sandy in his bed but he did tell Hank all about his session with the four sixteen year olds providing the vocal backup. He also told about the great success of their orchestra breaks and all the beautiful young things with whom he had danced with only a slight exaggeration of the promises that their nubile young bodies seemed to be making. By the time he finished, Hank was very nearly climbing the walls and bewailing "My Dad taught me baseball and football, why oh why couldn't it have been music?"

CHAPTER XII

JULES AND Lt Gen REICHOLD - 3rd MEETING

Between his meeting with General Reichold on June 18th and his next meeting two weeks later on July 2nd, Jules recorded nearly five hours of his discussions with the old General on five separate cassettes. He had delivered all of the cassettes to General Reichold having the final two cassettes delivered on the previous day. He had reviewed each cassette and added his own comments on the contents of each suggesting just how they would be used in supporting his thesis.

During the four sessions that the taping took place Jules and the old General had engaged in twelve chess matches. The old man had discontinued all the other matches he had been playing by either phone or by mail to concentrate on the matches he was having with Jules and Jules was finding it even more difficult to maintain the slight edge he had been enjoying. The net result was that after throwing out two very hard fought draws, Jules enjoyed a six to four advantage on the games that went to a final decision. The old man was absolutely delighted with his improved performance and for Jules the old man's reaction was just a little bit contagious. While he was determined never to let up in his efforts to win, Jules greatly enjoyed the increased competition and the improvement in the old man's disposition.

With the competition between them now even closer the reaction of the old man when he emerged victorious was elevated to an even higher level of satisfaction and even in defeat he remained quite amenable to Jules' very subtle guidance in the direction followed by the discussions that occurred between the games. There were still specific areas in which Jules was anxious to hear the old General's opinion of the policies and strategies that Adolph Hitler chose to follow in his master plan for the rehabilitation of Germany. In gen-

157

eral these areas could be classified as demographic and military.

The most important consideration on the demographic side was the treatment of minorities and, in particular, the Jews of Germany and adjoining countries. The old General was not in the least reticent in expressing his opinion of the Jews. It was never a matter of hatred but a distrust of them based upon his opinion that Zionism and Jewish traditions, culture and language represented more of a nationality than a religion and patriotism could have but one focus.

In his commentary on this cassette Jules pointed out several of the old General's comments that suggested a degree of admiration for the German Jews and what they had accomplished in widely diverse areas of human endeavor from business to science and the arts. He suggested that their accomplishments could be attributed to a large extent to the vitality they derived from a combination of religion, culture and language. It was also his opinion that another source of their strength came directly from the necessity of closing ranks in the face of ever present anti-semitism.

Jules' commentary also underlined the major error Hitler made when he selected the European Jews as a target. The old General's recommendation was to encourage acceleration in the establishment of the State of Israel as envisioned by the British Foreign Secretary Hoare-Belisha after World War I. The establishment of their own national state would give European Jews an alternative and if they decided to remain in Europe it would then be reasonable to expect them to commit themselves to a patriotic focus on the country in which they had made their decision to reside.

In the opinion of the old General Hitler made the mistake of deciding that the envy many Europeans felt about the relative success of the Jews could be used as a building block in the renewal of German nationalism. His theory was that a degree of unity could be achieved if everyone joined in dislike or hatred of the same minority group. The envy of the Jewish people that was already present promised to be an excellent starting point and to this could be added the spectre of communism and creeping socialism that had undermined the German war effort in the latter stages of World War I. Hitler and his advisers through their very effective propaganda machine found it relatively easy to divert the attention of German working people to people such as the Jews who appeared to be enjoying a life style superior to theirs.

In all of the mistakes that Hitler had made there was one common factor identified by the old General. Hitler did not appreciate the importance of time in the achievement of Germany's recovery. He was in much too much of a hurry. Whereas the members of old General's "action group" that had formed just after World War I were willing to accept gradual progress over their lifetimes, Hitler was measuring his plan in years or, at most, a decade. To accomplish his objective within this time frame Adolph Hitler was willing to use any expedient available to him regardless of the long term consequences that might result. This carefully nurtured hatred of the Jews appeared to achieve some advantages in the short run but contributed in a major way to his eventual downfall.

As early as the mid-thirties the old General could see that Hitler was heading towards alliances that made neither strategic or national sense. Hitler refused to recognize the importance of France and Great Britain to German security when he pursued the settlement of that issue of minor importance represented by Alsace Lorrain and by joining with Italy in supporting General Franco in Spain.

The old General had continually advised Hitler that the real threat to Germany was from the East where the Communist threat would only increase with time. Instead of threatening those states such as Poland, Czechoslovakia and an already sympathetic Austria, states that were acting as a buffer between Germany and the real threat posed by Russia, the old General advised Hitler to negotiate defensive alliances with these countries by proposing measures that would guarantee their Eastern borders. This approach would be much more productive than any alliance with Italy which had a rather undistinguished record in North Africa since 1919 and in 1936 was embarking upon another adventure in Ethiopia for which an objective was not clearly identifiable except for that very limited reward to be gained through revenge.

When Jules arrived at General Reichold's office shortly before three o'clock on Tuesday, July 2nd, he was very pleased to find that the General had listened to the cassettes including Jules' commentaries. The General expressed his complete approval of the direction that Jules was following in his discussions. Much of what the old General had covered in these last four cassettes approached the material that General Reichold had focussed on in his own thesis a few years earlier. He was very pleased to find that the old General's assessment of the early decisions made by Hitler was very similar to the conclusions he had arrived at without the benefit of this incredible "inside man" now available to Jules.

One of their main topics of conversation during this session was their consideration of the position in which the old General found himself on that day in 1938 when he just drove away from Hitler's HQ. At that point he could see that everything he had worked for was collapsing and Germany was again on a path to disaster. Hitler, through his short sighted policies was isolating Germany from potentially active or neutral allies and approaching alliances with countries such as Italy which would be able to offer very little in effective military support. On that day in 1938 the old General must have reached the depths of despair, his eyesight was failing and he no longer had any influence on members of Hitler's group of advisers. He had been used by Hitler to at-

160

tract the support of German's officer class and Hitler, always the supreme demagogue, now had their loyalty through extravagant nationalistic promises that would be impossible to keep. From the perspective of 30 years later it was quite easy to understand just why the old General had just walked out to his staff car and drove himself home.

General Reichold suggested that after he had completed and presented his thesis Jules should consider a book that would tell the story of Germany from about 1910 to the end of World War II that would be largely through the highly accurate reminiscences of the old General.

They scheduled their next meeting for Tuesday, July 16th and at least half of that meeting would be devoted to their preparations for the NATO presentation. The General's staff had put some ideas on paper and he gave Jules a folder containing details on this preliminary work so he could prepare for the next meeting.

While they were drinking their coffee Jules told the General about the minor security flap that had occurred in his area when several strangers - all apparently Americans - had been asking questions about personnel in his unit and their friends. They appeared to have left the area and had not been active for several days. They seemed to be well funded but his security people could not discover just what they were looking for.

The General confirmed that the matter had been reported to him with the suggestion that the Russians might be involved but this was waived off when it became obvious that the methods being used lacked the sophistication of the Soviets. The General was highly amused by a report that the actions of this as yet unidentified group was causing some annoyance to the Russians who thought they were being set up.

On the Sunday following General Reichold's third meeting with Jules the General received a call from Senator Buck Buchalter on a secure "scrambled" line that explained the presence of the group of Americans who had been asking the questions. The Senator was very apologetic when he told the General of how his wife, acting completely on her own, had retained the services of First American Security Team Inc (FAST) to find their youngest son and all relevant details about the young German girl with whom he had become involved. His Chief of Staff, Spencer Graham, whom Reichold knew very well, had obtained a copy of the FAST Inc report which would not be given to the Senator's wife until Tuesday, July 9th. The report was so amateurish that it should be an embarrassment to FAST Inc and he would send Reichold a copy of the report by courier.

General Reichold knew the Senator's wife very well from her visits to spend special weekends at the Point with her brother Howard Conrad, Jr. In fact he had actually dated her one weekend but while he found this young lady highly intelligent and very attractive she was just a little too self centered for him. However, he could easily understand Patricia Buchalter doing just what the Senator had ascribed to her.

The General realized that any security threat was now past with the group of operatives now back in the States and the only apparent damage done was stirring up the Russians who were still looking for the hook. The Senator assured him that he had the matter under control and he would have a face to face with Pat in Washington the following Wednesday. He implied that the group he referred to as the Keystone Kops may have created some problems through their ham-handed actions and this meant the solution to the Senator's problem just might need one more favor from the General. He had made a promise to Pat earlier that their son would be back in the States in time to enroll no later than the Julliard semester commencing in January, 1969, but preferably the semester commencing in September, 1968. If he needed this one additional favor the Senator would brief the General when he attended the NATO conference in August.

General Reichold had always preached preparedness as one of the first requirements of commanding officers and he also identified anticipation as a vital component of preparedness. After his long telephone call with his old Point classmate, Senator Buchalter, he realized that the favor that the Senator would be asking would have to do with getting the boy back to the States in time for college enrolment and the movement must be achieved without a trace of a paper trail. One solution, and possibly the easiest to achieve, would be an application for voluntary transfer to the non-effective list to enroll in college. The General decided to put the pieces of his plan together immediately and the first step had been taken with his inquiries about S/Sgt "Red" Mombirkett when he and Jules had met for the second time. Subsequent discreet inquiries had determined that this man was actually the son of the top sergeant who had worked with him during the War in Korea.

CHAPTER XIII

FIRST AMERICAN SECURITY TEAM Inc

ALIAS

THE KEYSTONE KOPS

At 10 a.m. on Tuesday, July 9th, Pat Buchalter received a call from First American Security Team Inc (FAST Inc), the security group that she had given her instructions relating to Jason, his location, the identity of his love interest and all relevant details relating to the young lady. The report would be available that day and Pat agreed to meet their representatives at her home at 2 o'clock that afternoon.

When the two men arrived Pat took the report to her small office asking them to allow her half an hour to run through the details as they waited in the library. Her initial reaction to the report was complete satisfaction. The report appeared to be very thorough and pretty well what she expected. It included photographs of all the principals and several of the rather pretty young girl identified as Sandra. Also included was a full account of all expenses and details of the hours spent by members of the team on surveillance.

When she returned to the library she expressed her satisfaction with the report and thanked them for providing two additional copies. From all appearances this report was the product of a highly professional organization and Pat wrote a personal cheque in the amount of $162,578.25 and the voucher was endorsed as paid in full. Business cards were exchanged and the organization identified as First American Security Team Inc. (FAST) advised that members of their surveillance team would be available should any questions arise.

Pat spent the remainder of the day pouring over the report and planning her next move. She also tried to reach Umberto Fillini who would be starting a North American Tour of about a dozen cities in a few days and he had told her that he would be in Los Angeles early on this date. His hotel advised Pat that he had registered the previous day but there was no answer from his room.

The following morning, Wednesday, July 10th, she tried again to reach Umberto with similar results and she decided to try again later in the day. At about 10.30 a.m. her phone rang and it was her husband calling from Washington. Something had come up and he wanted her in Washington that afternoon. A Compass Inc. corporate jet would be arriving at Columbus Airport at 1 p.m. to pick her up. He and Spence would meet her at his condo at about 4.30 p.m It was rather short notice but Pat decided that this would be an opportunity to give Buck and Spence copies of her report, just watch for their reactions and accept their apologies. She packed quickly ensuring what she referred to as the "intern package" was included together with the three copies of the FAST Inc report she had received the previous day. She arrived at the Washington City Airport at between three and three-thirty and the waiting limousine whisked her to the modern luxury condominium where Buck had his apartment.

Buck and Spence arrived at about four o'clock. Buck commenced with what could only be described as a shock tactic.

"I believe you are familiar with this report" and then, to Pat's surprise, held up a copy of the FAST Inc report she had received the previous day. "We have had this report for about three days and probably received our copies before you received yours. Have you had an opportunity to review this report.?"

Pat was struck dumb by this development and all she could do was nod.

Buck continued. "I believe it would be appropriate but completely unnecessary to tell you just how disappointed I am that after your promise to trust me, to leave things in my hands, you retained the services of a "fast buck" security outfit that very same day." When Pat indicated that she was about to break into the conversation Buck held up his hand. "Just keep quiet, Pat. You'll have your chance to speak but by then I hope that you will have some understanding of what you have actually done. And yes, I assure you we have all the required electronic equipment to enable you to make that little presentation on my indiscretion that you have been planning for so long " Pat's jaw dropped. The pre-emptive strike scored a direct hit.

"I realize your first question will be on just how we came into possession of your supposedly exclusive report. But you tend to forget that Spence has been very active in the intelligence and security community for many years and nothing really happens in that area without his knowing about it. Your initial problem was in your selection of the security agency known as FAST Inc. You should have remembered that this is the same company that your board at Compass Inc. refused do business with despite a significantly lower bid than that of the corporation that currently provides us with security services. I will ask Spence to introduce us to the company known as First American Security Team or FAST Inc."

"Thank you Senator. This new company came upon the scene about five years ago and the original executive and Board of Directors consisted of a number of former FBI and CIA agents and senior administrators, retired high ranking representatives of various police organizations and several prominent members of the bar. Initial funding of the corporation was provided by two major banks from Texas and

California. The primary aim of this corporation was to move aggressively to establish its presence in the area of providing security services to major corporations through personal contacts of well known members of the board and low balling bids on security contracts opening for competitive bids. Their targets were, for the most part, major corporations currently served by "in-house" security departments and with particular emphasis on corporations who had never been major consumers in the security field. In business such a business plan is often referred to as "cherry picking" and using this tactic, FAST Inc. sought to build up its cash flow and quickly go public with an IPO in the next couple of years. With an attractive, although possibly short lived, cash flow, the initial share price would quite easily double or even triple very quickly enabling the original founders to get rich through cashing in on their stock options."

Spence took a moment to study his notes before continuing. "When we review the names appearing on the original Board of Directors and the Executive Officers appointed by the Board we cannot help but be very impressed by many of the names because they represent nearly a Who's Who" of the entire security industry over the past twenty-five years. But while the corporate masthead reflected a great deal of experience, there was really nothing very much in the lower echelons that would be required to do the work. They had recruited some FBI, CIA and Secret Service retirees but many of these came from long term employment in senior administrative appointments. The considerable success enjoyed by FAST Inc can be attributed nearly entirely to its strategy of "cherry picking" and its limited exposure to real security problems. The intelligence community has been watching the development of FAST Inc but is unanimous in its opinion that its success will be limited unless it can add significant experience to the rank and file by whom the work must be done. That's the picture on FAST Inc., Senator."

Pat again tried to make a contribution to the very one-sided discussion but Buck again demanded that she desist. "You'll have your chance, Pat, and I once again ask that you keep quiet until we have completed our presentation. You will notice, Pat, that I have not told you to shut up but those words have been on the tip of my tongue each time you have attempted to speak. After over twenty years, Pat, you must recognize by this time those signs that indicate just how angry I am right now. I am approaching that point at which I will not be responsible for what I say. So, just be quiet."

"Next, let us review the FAST Inc. report starting with the tasks you charged them with. You instructed them, first and foremost, to locate our son although I suspect you applied a little pressure to another security agency and were really able to give your agents a pretty good fix on his location in Germany and the identity he was using. Your major assignment was to obtain complete information on the German girl with whom Jason had become involved and most of this information would only be accumulated after breaches of privacy that could lead to criminal charges if they occurred here in the States."

The Senator paused to study his notes before continuing. "The greatest problems arise from the methods that your group of Keystone Kops resorted to in gathering their information. Think for a moment about just where they were carrying out their supposed investigation. This is the area where NATO troops are only minutes away from first line Russian troops and where all aspects of security are a constant challenge to both sides. In come the Keystone Kops asking their questions. And just how did they do this? They started at one of the local bars or gasthauses. Then they quite openly questioned Jason's roommate who is an experienced Communications Specialist whose training includes extensive heightening of sensitivity to possible enemy approaches on security matters. Just imagine for a moment the immediate consequences. The Russians heard the questions in the bar and they alerted their security people. The roommate immediately reported the approaches to him to our security people and the result there was a brief state of panic on both sides. Our security people quickly stood down on the problem when they realized that this was much too amateurish for the Russians but the Russians hung in for a while because they suspected they were being set up. This was mostly because the Russians were so impressed by the amount of money that seemed to be involved. The Keystone Kops were staying in one of Frankfurt's finest hotels, they were each driving a Mercedes, they had arrived in Frankfurt on first class return tickets, they dined in the very best restaurants and dining rooms and were always very quick to pick up the tab at all the watering holes in what they would explain as continued efforts to loosen tongues. Fortunately the whole situation was well below the radar screens of both sides because what honest to goodness security professional would think that all this money and effort were being expended just to get Mummy's little boy back to Mummy before he became totally addicted to a lovely little German piece of ass that just might result in amnesia on the subject of music."

Buck was just shaking his head at the thought of the antics of what he had identified as the Keystone Cops. "Sorry Pat, there I go being coarse again. But I'm angry and probably angrier than I have been in years. Nothing angers me more than stupidity and just wait, I haven't really got started yet. After the bar and the roommate our skilled investigators turned their attention to a building that they refer to as an old mansion in advanced stages of disrepair. Following one of the first principles of effective security action they looked for a soft spot and it seemed that they struck pay dirt immediately when they identified not only what they were convinced was a soft spot but also someone on the inside. However, in selecting a soft spot the experienced operative knows very well that the softness extends to both sides. Our agents target was Mannheim Hillstrom a pale inoffensive little man who was the nephew of the Mansion housekeeper, Gerda

Hillstrom. Manny - we'll just call him Manny - had one consuming weakness. He wanted desperately to become an American citizen, so much, in fact, that he had never met an American that he didn't like, no, change that, worship. They gave him the impression that they were very impressed with Manny when he demonstrated his command of English including lots of American slang, his ability to recite the Pledge of Allegiance and the Gettysberg Address and to participate in detailed discussions on a wide variety of topics from American history. He explained to them that he was making full use of American dietary supplements, using American patent medicine and a wide variety of American exercising equipment to ensure that he would pass the next immigration medical he would be taking next year."

The Senator was shaking his head again trying unsuccessfully to suppress a smile. "And now just try and put yourself in poor Manny's shoes. He would do anything for his newfound friends. He not only answered their questions but measured each answer to ensure that he was saying what these fine Americans wanted to hear. Let's just review the invaluable information they obtained from Manny. First the old General who Manny was really quite willing to agree was crazy; he was always very angry with Manny but he had been much easier to get along with in recent weeks. He was blind but insisted on riding in the back seat of the old Mercedes staff car with the top down and that Manny wear his chauffeur's uniform as they drove through the countryside. In recent weeks the old General had been playing chess with a black American officer. Manny became convinced under skillfully directed questioning, that the chess matches were really only a front for the American officer's real objective of investigating the old General's participation in possible war crimes."

"And now let us turn our attention to what Manny had to offer on other members of the household again under the skillful questioning of our security experts. On the subject of

170

his aunt, Gerda Hillstrom, who had protected him and kept him alive through all of those Displaced Person Camps, Manny was willing to admit that Gerda had been very good to him but just a little additional questioning had him admitting that her generosity had extended to many men over the years until she had met her current boyfriend and fiance' Woody Washington. The other permanent member of the household was, of course, Sandra or Sandy as she was known by most people these days. Sandy was Manny's favorite in the household. He remembered the day that Helga, only 12 years of age herself at the time, had found the baby Sandy on the Mansion grounds after following the written instructions provided by the baby's mother. Helga had finally got approval for Sandy's adoption but she was away most of the time so much of the responsibility for raising the little girl fell to Gerda. For some strange reason there was no mention of the very good girls' boarding school where Sandy spent at least four days a week since she was nine years old. Sandy had been spending a lot of time recently with Jason an American soldier who was teaching her to play pieces by Chopin on the piano. Turning to Helga, the old General's granddaughter, Manny recognizes her as the manager of the household and his boss. She was very nice but could be very demanding and had a very sharp tongue when she was displeased. When they questioned him about Helga's friends Manny revealed that she really lived with her boss in Frankfurt who was a Jewish banker. Recently, Manny thought that she had met a few times with the American officer who was investigating the old General."

The Senator now paused but did not invite any questions. "Let's just sum up at this point and summarize what the FAST Inc. report really says. Manny has told us that the old General is really a crazy, blind old man who is suspected by the Americans of war crimes. Gerda is a loose woman who has had a large share in the responsibility of raising Sandy over the years but now appears to have a stable relationship with an American Army cook, Sgt Woodrow Wilson Washington, to whom she is now engaged. The girl known as Sandy was actually a foundling who lacked a continuing firm hand in her upbringing. The General's granddaughter managed the household largely in absentia as she lived in Franfurt with her boss the Jewish banker. It was also quite possible - as Manny had been induced to admit - that she was sharing her favors with the American officer who was investigating her grandfather. That is the summary offered by our expert observers but this is a classical example of people believing what they want to believe and taking pains to ensure that their final summary will meet with the approval of the employer. So, what is the real truth? While we have not had the time on the ground that our Keystone Kops had I'm willing to bet that my summary is one hell of a lot closer to the truth than the summary we have just heard. Another very important factor is that in our summary we will point out the damage that our Keystone Kops have done and indicate the first steps to be taken in damage control."

Buck paused for a minute to collect his thoughts. "Let's start with the old General. Manny was led up to the opinion that the old man is crazy. There is absolutely no evidence to support that opinion. Admittedly, he is a perfectionist and Manny has taken the sharp edge of his tongue from time to time. But crazy? Decidedly not! He's just a very old man who is now very sad about his life and what has happened to the country he loves. Under investigation for war crimes? Definitely not. The old man has channeled all of his frustrations and energies into the game of chess. The American colonel is a very good chess player and they play a couple of times a week with reportedly highly beneficial effects on the old man's outlook on life. Please remember there is ample evidence that not only was Baron Field Marshall Erich von Freiderhoff one of Germany's most decorated soldiers in World War I he was also a leading force in the attempts to lead Germany back after the Treaty of Versailles. He walked or drove away from Hitler's HQ in 1938 when he gave up in near total frustration. But regardless, this is a brilliant man who has the capacity of total recall of the period of Germany and Europe through nearly the first forty years of this century. The black American officer, Lt Col Jules Pelladeau, is not investigating him for evidence on war crimes but using the old General's vast knowledge as a resource vehicle in his Doctoral Studies in the extension department of a leading American University. The suggestion of a possible romantic link between the Colonel and the old General's granddaughter is spurious and potentially dangerous."

Buck paused again but seemed to be quite satisfied with the progress he was making. "And now let us turn to Gerda who has had such a tough life. Manny was just a little too anxious to please his newfound friends and his comments could only be described as approaching disloyalty. Gerda had, in fact, saved Manny's life by protecting him through those years of disrupted lives in the DP Camps. It is very unfair to mark her with a scarlet letter when many of her lovers could have represented the only means of guaranteeing food for the table. Remember she joined this household staff as a chambermaid and has worked her way up to housekeeper. This is a good woman who is finally enjoying a measure of stability with Sgt Woodrow Washington after so many tough years. There also can be little doubt that in her joint guardianship of the young girl Sandy, Gerda has provided both love and meaningful direction. In fact when just a very little girl Gerda suggested that she be named Sandra in memory of her own younger sister who had died in one of the DP Camps."

"And now let's turn to the old General's granddaughter Helga who just might suffer the most from the antics of our Keystone Kops. The FAST Inc report mentions that Helga von Freiderhoff lives with her boss in Frankfurt and just mentions that he is a Jewish banker. In other words they want us to believe that she is just another German girl who becomes the mistress of a wealthy Jew. Just a touch of anti-Semitism, perhaps? What their summary does not explain is

173

that Helga's lover is not just any Jewish banker. Her lover is Jacob Wiseman, Chairman of the Rhine Group and one of the most important bankers in Europe if not in the world. He is a special adviser to NATO, the World Bank and the IMF. He is a bachelor widower and she is just not his mistress but she is also the Vice President of Public Relations for the Rhine Group and we are assured that the success she has enjoyed in her career has not been in any way because of her personal relationship with the Chairman of the Board. This is a very bright young lady and a very capable executive.

"You will recall that in my opening remarks I spoke of the actions of our Keystone Kops attracting the attention of both the Russian and American security organizations. Well, there was a third security agency and a more dangerous one that was also involved. When your very amateurish sleuths started asking questions about Jacob Wiseman, their CEO, the Rhine Group became involved and their security forces would be equal to those of a small country. When people start asking questions about Jacob Wiseman or his "great and good" friend Helga von Freiderhoff, the security forces of the Rhine Group immediately think of kidnapping, blackmail and/or extortion. It should be also remembered that these security agents are highly professional and totally ruthless. Actually I am rather surprised that our fearless threesome escaped Europe unscathed. I can only suspect that this is only because the Rhine Group's security people had a sense of humor and quickly recognized that the Keystone Kops were only a threat to themselves. But it's still not clear that the beautiful Helga will escape unscathed. There is little doubt that the Rhine Group security agency has also received a copy of the FAST Inc. report. You know that report might just turn out to be a best seller. The only question remains is whether, as Manny was led to suggest, the suggestion that Helga might be sharing her favors with Colonel Pelladeau would be relayed to Jacob Wiseman and just what his reaction might be. Just think for a moment of what would happen if the black Colonel and the lady did not exercise safe sex. A black baby would be very difficult to explain unless Jacob

Wiseman might be persuaded that such an offspring could be explained by some connection to one of the five lost tribes of Israel."

By this stage it was quite obvious that Pat understood the danger of what she had done. Seeing that Pat was no longer anxious to speak Buck returned to the plan for damage control. He offered no details and Pat didn't ask for any. Buck repeated the promise that he had made at the previous meeting. He assured Pat that Jason would be safe and that he would enroll at Julliard no later than the semester commencing in January 1969. Pat accepted this promise without comment.

"There's just one other point, Pat, and please don't get me wrong. It may seem that I'm piling on but you will find out and I think the sooner you know the better. You recall that we met "Big Jim" Taylor at that fund raiser in Harris County, Texas, about a year and a half ago? Remember, he had those three strappng big sons and the one very attractive teenage daughter. They were all so proud of that little girl because she was so talented and they wanted her to achieve her ambition of becoming a concert pianist. He knew about Jason and his music and he also knew that you had been a concert pianist in the Dallas area and he asked if you could advise him on a special music teacher for his daughter and you recommended that Italian maestro Umberto Fillini. Well he told me that this worked out just fine and his daughter was making remarkable progress. But then when the Maestro went back to Europe for a concert tour "Big Jim" discovered that his daughter, who had just turned seventeen, was pregnant. The whole matter was hushed up but when Fillini returned to the States the other day "Big Jim" and his three sons met Fillini at his hotel in Los Angeles, loaded him into their executive jet and took him back to their ranch in Harris County in Texas. Therethey had him charged with statutory rape but the Italian Ambassador got into the act with counter charges of kidnapping and wrongful confinement and managed to have Umberto released on bail.

Then just as the Ambassador had a jet standing by to take Umberto back to Washington he disappeared and the Ambassador claimed he had been kidnapped again. One Dallas newspaper investigated and discovered that the flight plan filed by the Captain of the Italian jet was not for a flight to Washington but for a flight to Rome via Gander, Newfoundland. It appears that Umberto was prepared to forfeit his bail rather than take a chance on Harris County Justice. They found Umberto a few days later when an ambulance was called to a rural motel in Harris County. Umberto had been subjected to a very severe act of Texas justice which when applied to cattle is referred to as being gelded or, as we would call it, castrated.

Fillini is still down there in hospital screaming blue murder as well as from a bit of pain. Fillini and the Italian Ambassador are demanding that criminal charges be laid but "Big Jim" and his sons apparently have solid alibis. The Harris County District Attorney has announced that the statutory rape charges against Fillini will be withdrawn and he is free to leave the country but a part - or parts - of him will always remain "deep in the heart of Texas". The Italian Ambassador continues to demand that charges be laid against "Big Jim" and members of his family but the District Attorney claims that they have cast iron alibis and that a conviction under such circumstances would be absolutely impossible to attain. The Judge in the Harris County Court also attracted the anger of the Italian Ambassador because when he dismissed the charges of statutory rape against Fillini he reminded Fillini that there was, at least, a bright side that the maestro should recognize. This had been the second time Fillini had been accused of statutory rape in Texas but he now had the ultimate defence against any such charges in the future

Pat, please excuse me for seeming to make light of the rather harsh treatment of your old mentor but the "good ole boys" have their own ways of applying what they would call justice. I decided you should know about this because we have another fund raiser in that area next month and while I'm sure that "Big Jim" realizes that you would not have known about the maestro's penchant for deflowering his students, I just thought that you should know just in case we run into "Big Jim" when we go down there."

Spence watched as the color drained from Pat's face. He reviewed with admiration the Senator's performance and thought of this just another reflection of the Senator's recognition of the importance of the principles of war even when applied far from the battlefield. First had come the Senator's application of the principle of surprise in his preemptive strike on the matter relating to the intern; second was the application of the principle of concentration of force as he described the potential consequence of her actions and the final stroke in the little story he told about Umberto Fillini. Spence left them together in the condo and, as he left the building, he was convinced that he had seen a future president at work.

Back in the condo Pat had broken down in tears and Buck was comforting her. "Oh, Buck, I made such a balls of it. I should have trusted you and I really do now. After making a mistake like that perhaps I should resign from the board of Compass Inc."

"There'll be no more talk like that. Just put it down as a mistake and we all make mistakes. You remember that you rejected FAST Inc. in their bid for Compass Inc. business even though their bid was much lower. You acted on the advice of your advisors and that's the secret here.

"You're statement about making a balls of things brings my mind back to Fillini. He's going to find it very difficult to get justice in Harris County. That seems to have put an end to the maestro's piano tuning!"

CHAPTER XIV

S/SGT BILLIEBOB "RED" MOMBIRKETT

The Staff Sergeant had joined up at age eighteen and represented the fourth generation of his family that was "Army". He would often brag that when he was cut he bled khaki. His father who had retired as a Master Sergeant had taken "Red" to the recruiting centre on his eighteenth birthday and repeated this visit with each of "Red's" four younger brothers one of whom had disgraced the family by joining the Air Force.

"Red" was a "Redneck" of the "Good Ole Boy Bubba" tradition and was proud of it. Despite limited education "Red" had worked his way up to his present rank through establishing a reputation as a good soldier and a "hard ass" non com. He had qualified as a communication specialist and could be depended upon to run his section with efficiency and a minimum of disciplinary problems. The latter was achieved through a combination of maintaining a high standard in his own trades proficiency and a rather threatening physical presence. As regional heavyweight boxing champion "Red" was quite capable of handling his own discipline problems as word got around very quickly that you just didn't cross "Red" Mombirkett.

The S/Sgt showed his rural Alabama roots in his general dislike for minorities but he was careful to ensure that his dislike for African Americans did not interfere with the admininstration of his section which included a number of African American soldiers. He also did not like "college boy" junior officers but succeeded in getting his way with most of these by just "knowing the ropes". His fitness reports had consistently classified him as a good soldier who could always be depended on to turn out a section on formation parades that maintained a very high standard of appearance.

His greatest hatred was reserved for Communists or "Commies" as he referred to them with deep disdain.

"Red's" hobby, aside from boxing, was music. He was attracted to the guitar by an uncle back home and while he had never really mastered the reading of music, he had an excellent ear and could pick up new numbers very quickly. Since basic training "Red" had always been a member of a small musical combo and was currently leader of the local group under the name of "The Chastity Belts" that consisted of five enlisted men from units in the area. The group had become quite popular in the gasthauses in the region and usually played two or three gigs a week for audiences that preferred volume over quality in their music.

His annual fitness reports also indicated that while "Red" was married with four children he was unaccompanied by his family on this and previous postings and this was based upon his own personal preference. His wife was a school teacher in North Carolina and, when questioned, "Red" always stated that she had her own career and had no wish to accompany him to areas where accommodation would be either very expensive and/ or of doubtful quality.

"Red" had met his wife, Allison, about seven years earlier when he had been posted as an instructor in a training centre in North Carolina. She was a sophomore at a major university and "Red" was playing his guitar with a small combo from his base that had little difficulty in lining up as many gigs as they wanted with fraternities, sororities and local taverns that catered to the college crowds. "Red" had already established himself as a "stud" and welcomed these forays onto campuses in what he described as his personal quest for "educated pussy".

Unfortunately Allison Magioli, a very pretty nineteen year old third generation red blooded girl of Italian extraction, was attracted to the big, handsome, wild redheaded

179

guitar player with the combo that played one night at a bash at her sorority. After a number of beers at an after hours establishment Allison became just a little tipsy and in an incident that really approached "date rape" gave in to feelings she had never experienced before and "Red's" superior strength. It was always "Red's" avowed opinion that "safe sex" was for faggots and eunuchs as he asserted that when the old redhead nailed them they stayed nailed. "Red" enjoyed the experience and Allison, until she realized that she was pregnant, had found the session not that unpleasant and far more satisfying than her two sessions with equally inexperienced freshmen the previous year. Red and Allison continued to meet and Red continued to regard her as his personal "educated pussy" until Allison expressed her concern to Red that she just might be pregnant. At this point Red found it convenient to take some accumulated leave and seek a posting to some unit as far away from North Carolina as possible. Before his leave was finished Red found himself posted to Germany and, breathing a large sigh of relief, departed for Germany without a thought in his head except for those pictures of tall cool blondes he had seen in recruiting brochures.

Unfortunately for Red, Allison's inexperience led her to procrastinate until it was really too late for an abortion even if she could have convinced her very strong Roman Catholic parents to take that route. It was also unfortunate for Red that Allison's father was a circuit judge in North Carolina who had some old fashioned ideas about parenthood and the responsibilities of fathers. The Judge called in a few political IOUs and Red found himself back in North Carolina as the unwilling participant in what came as close to a "shotgun wedding" as he could get.

Allison's father was a tough old bastard and he had seen people like Red in his courtroom too often to be that happy about his new son in law and Red was not permitted any meaningful contributions to the family's discussion on the future of either Allison or the baby now due in a matter of weeks. However, looking back later, Red decided that he had come out of the situation in pretty good shape. Allison wanted to complete university and her mother agreed to look after the baby until she graduated. Red would return to his new unit in Germany with visiting privileges. He would come back to his wife and family on leave and therein lay the weakness of the agreement. When he came back on leave he and Allison were back in bed together with predictable results. It was only when Allison was carrying their fourth child that she and her mother decided to turn their backs on their strict Roman Catholic upbringing and resort to the pill.

In fact Red found, as things worked out, he now had the best of two worlds. First, he was classified as married as far as career moves were concerned and this, plus his rapidly increasing family, protected him from some of the less attractive postings such as to Viet Nam. Second, Allison was now fully employed as a teacher as her ever supportive mother looked after the kids. With her father's support Allison was able to put a significant down payment on a nice family home close to her parents and added Red's name to the title as co-owner all without Red putting up as much as a penny. Red was still not that popular with Allison's parents but they were strong believers in the sanctity of marriage and he found himself accepted so long as he kept the exposure to a minimum. Although Allison was not deeply in love with Red she did find his near insatiable sexual appetite very rewarding during his periods home on leave especially now that the pill had put an end to the constant threat of pregnancy posed by Red's unquestioned virility.

While Red firmly resisted all efforts by Allison and her family to domesticate him, he found it convenient to have a home base to operate from while he was home on leave. Having Allison ready and willing to meet his sexual needs meant he could conserve his energies and resources from the constant chase. Red had always been a devout believer in the old saying that it wasn't the sex that would kill you but it was the running after it.

It wasn't that Red didn't like his children. He really loved them but only for about three days at a time. Red was not completely to blame for this attitude because this is how the three "Army" generations of his family before him had treated their families. In the rural South society was largely matriarchal. The families were generally large and under the mother's plus grandmother's care in many cases while the soldiers traveled the world. They came home on leave just often enough to meet new additions and to exercise those conjugal rights that would ensure that family expansion would continue. Pat recalled his father's answer when someone asked him how he could be sure that his wife wouldn't be sharing her bed while he was away. Red's father quoted the old philosophy of the hills "Just keep them barefoot and pregnant and they won't run the roads."

Jason's roommate Hank had reported immediately to Red the presence of the three American strangers in the local bars who had been asking some questions about military personnel, namely his roommate and other local people and Red had immediately passed this information on up the security organization chain. As the senior non com in the communications section Red had immediate access to a contact at the next level. Because of the importance of security in an area of constant contact with Russian forces selected personnel in the security network with each unit were given special code names and monthly authenticating codes to facilitate the speedy passage of instructions relating to security matters. Red had this code name for his unit but the instructions were very clear that no one was to initiate action without receiving very specific instructions. After reporting the presence of the very inquisitive group of Americans, Red fully expected to receive detailed instructions within days. In fact Red was just a little disappointed when he found that the suspicious group had apparently left the area before he had received any instructions on how he should deal with them.

On Wednesday, July 19th, Red received the Intelligence Alert call identifying him by his code name and including the authentication code for the month of July. He was advised to stand by between 2 and 4 p.m. the following day at which time he would receive his initial briefing on a security assignment and that was it. Red cursed softly. "Now the silly bastards are going to give me instructions and already it's too late. Those guys are long gone."

The promised call came the following day and Red found that he had jumped the gun in assuming that there was a connection between this assignment and the three Americans who had been asking the questions between two and three weeks earlier. There was no direct connection but the briefing did bring up the name of Jason Creighton once more. It also brought up the name of Sandra von Freiderhoff or, at least, that was the name by which she was known in the community. Red's only task at this point was to observe the pair, get to know as much as he could about them but to do absolutely nothing more until he received very specific instructions from the caller. Red could expect his next call on Wednesday, July 26th, again between 2 and 4 p.m.

This would work out perfectly for Red because Jason had just joined his combo to replace the keyboard player who had been posted. To make things even better Jason had told him that Sandy, or whatever her real name was, now had permission to accompany Jason, Gerda and Woody for two gigs a week to help with the set ups and just sit with the others at a table right beside the combo and look pretty. Red knew that the latter would not be difficult because Sandy, or whoever she was, was a real dish and the most beautiful girl Red had seen in Germany, or anywhere else for that matter. He hoped that he would be able to persuade Jason to share.

The permission from Helga for Sandy to accompany Jason to the pubs for two gigs a week had come after a determined campaign by Sandy aided by Gerda and Woody after they succumbed to Sandy's pleading. They finally persuaded Helga that Sandy was now a high school graduate and, at least, eighteen years of age, and Gerda and Woody would be with her every evening. Later in the summer Sandy might even fill in on the keyboard or piano if the pub had a piano available. Helga agreed that it was, after all, Sandy's summer holidays and she had been putting in hours practicing on their own piano every day and being helped by Jason each evening. There were very specific instructions about drinking and dancing. Absolutely no drinking and dancing only with Jason or Woody. The drinking did not pose a problem although Jason was discovering that Sandy loved wine and, especially, champagne. Because of her naturally exuberant nature, Jason found it very difficult to tell when she was getting just a little tipsy but suspected that her capacity for champagne was very limited. He had also noticed that she became very romantic after a few drinks but Jason was really not prepared to complain about this latter facet of her personality.

Joining the combo gave Jason and Sandy a few chances to meet outside the Mansion in addition to when they were together on actual gigs. These meetings were justified on the grounds that rehearsals were required. Helga had been away traveling with Jacob for the most part of the month of July and Jason found Gerda easier to convince than Helga. Jason had become a great favorite of both Woody and Gerda and she had no desire to limit the pleasure the young people found in each others' company. Most of these rehearsals were held in a small cottage Jason had rented just on the outskirts of Freiderberg and they spent several hours a week just making love. Now that Sandy had been introduced to those little packets Meta had given her the fear of pregnancy was gone and she became an enthusiastic partner and, sometimes, the leader in their love making so much so that Jason found it difficult to understand just how quickly she had progressed from a sweet innocent young girl to such an accomplished lover. His suspicions went back to her earlier brief little references to activities of the girls at her school. When he pursued his natural curiosity further she always had the same cryptic answer "Men just brag - girls talk."

Red used all of his wiles to get closer to Jason and Sandy. Jason found this arrangement to his advantage because Red set the duty schedule for all the communications specialists in the squadron. This ensured that Jason's weekend duties were kept to an absolute minimum so he could participate in the regular weekend gigs scheduled for the group known as the Chastity Belts. The combo was becoming more popular with the addition of Jason, Gerda and Woody and further enhanced on most nights by the presence of the beautiful Sandy. Sandy was just a little uneasy with Red because he was always trying to rub against her and had initiated group hugs and kisses at the start of each program.

There was a very awkward incident one evening during a gig for which Sandy was present. A group of American soldiers became quite drunk and took exception to the music the group was playing. When Jason declined to do encores of rock and roll numbers because the other members of the combo had not had a chance to rehearse them, he became the target of the group. They caught Jason outside during one of the combo's breaks and were just starting to give him a serious beating when Red intervened and kept Jason's injuries to nothing more than a black eye and a few scrapes and bruises. Woody then arrived on the scene and he and Red put the run to the trouble makers. Sandy had been nearly frantic as she clung to Gerda throughout the ruckus. She was so grateful to Red that she rewarded him with one of her very special kisses and accepted Jason's designation of Red as their very best friend. It was decided that there would be really no need to inform Helga about this incident.

By the time Red received his next anonymous but fully authenticated phone call on July 26th he had firmly established himself as the young couple's best friend and protector. This latest call instructed Red to maintain his surveillance and suggested that the ultimate action plan might be just to split the pair up and probably the easiest way to achieve this would be a application for voluntary transfer from Jason to the non-effective list in the United States for the purpose of either enrolling or returning to college. Red was instructed to take absolutely no action at this time but to give considerations of ways and means that the split up could be achieved preferably within existing provisions for personnel management.

So Red followed his instructions very carefully. He collected all the intelligence that might be useful in implementing the final plan. He had become very close to both Jason and Sandy as the latter realized just how important his presence was at some of the rougher pubs where they were engaged to play their gigs. Red had noted that Sandy really loved a few glasses of champagne and, as Jason had already discovered, she became very amorous when she got a little tipsy. He had received one invitation to join them for a picnic at their cottage and the bottle of champagne that Red had taken to the picnic had the desired effect as Sandy became very kissable. Any reservations that Sandy might have had were quickly overcome by a combination of the champagne and Jason's insistence that it was OK to give old Red a kiss because he was their very best friend and people should always do nice things for their very best friends.

The next of the anonymous phone calls came on Tuesday, August 6th and warned Red that he should anticipate that the next call on Tuesday, August 13th would be either an instruction to stand down and disengage or it would merely consist of the instruction "Act Now!" In the case of the latter Red would immediately implement the plan to separate these two people through an application for voluntary transfer from Jason to be posted to the non-effective list in the States for the purpose of enrolling in college.

CHAPTER XV

THE NATO CONFERENCE

The 1968 NATO Annual Summer Conference was scheduled for Brussels during the week from Monday, August 12th to Friday, August 16th. The American contingent including Senator Buck Buchalter and Spencer Graham had arrived by private jet on Sunday, August 11th. As ranking minority member of the Senate Armed Forces Committee Buck Buchalter had been asked by the committee chairman to head the delegation because the chairman was going to be tied up in preparing for the Democratic National Convention.

Buck and Spence had come to Brussels directly from the Republican Convention at which Richard Nixon had been officially nominated as the Republican Candidate for President and at which Buck had delivered a highly acclaimed keynote speech. During a brief stop over in London the Senator had been in touch with his old friend Lt Gen Carl Reichold and told the latter that he would probably need that favor he had mentioned in their earlier telephone conversation. They arranged to meet for both lunch and dinner on Monday. Reichold advised him that his team would be first up with their demonstration for the delegates on Monday morning. This would leave the General pretty well free for the remainder of the week and he assured the Senator that there was a plan in place that would achieve the desired objective.

On Monday morning the Senator and his contingent attended an outstanding presentation on the characteristics of the latest armored equipment and tactics. His old friend General Reichold directed the presentation with an impressively smooth combination of multi-media techniques that included some very dramatic visuals of the potential use of tactical nuclear weapons. The General's group were all very professional and the Senator's attention was particularly drawn to a very impressive young African American officer who took the role of a regimental commander in the presentation.

Every country in NATO was represented at the conference and at lunch in the special dining room set up for delegates at a nearby hotel, just about everyone on the political scene in Europe was there. The Senatorand Spencer Graham found their reserved table in what amounted to something that resembled an inner sanctum where adjoining tables contained the leaders of the more important delegations. They were joined in a few moments by General Reichold. No introductions were required because the General and Spencer had met before on numerous occasions. As the General took his seat he drew the Senator's attention to a very distinguished looking gentleman accompanied by an absolutely stunning blonde who were just taking their seats at the table reserved for the NATO General-Secretary. "Buck, that gentleman is no other than Jacob Wiseman who is one of the top advisors to the NATO Executive Council on economic matters and that very beautiful woman with him is Helga von Freiderhoff and I'm sure that both of you will recognize that name."

"My God!" exclaimed the Senator, "She's really a beauty. If she is any indication of Mr. Riseman's judgement the General-Secretary has an excellent economic advisor." Spence was still staring at Helga and could only nod in agreement until he finally found his tongue. "Yes Senator, that is a very beautiful lady and we might just see her again later. Mr Wiseman will be giving delegation leaders a formal presentation on the many economic factors that will be of concern to NATO as the European members move closer to European Union."

"Now there's someone I want you to meet. "The General was busily trying to catch the attention of the young African American officer who had participated in his morning presentation and was just now taking a seat with some other officers on the other side of the room. He succeeded in catching the attention of this very impressive looking young black officer who came over to their table.

The General handled the introductions. "Senator, Spencer, this is Lt Col Jules Pelladeau one of our unit commanders who participated in our presentation this morning. You might also remember him from those Army/Navy games we attended some years ago."

"Yes, certainly, I'll never forget those touchdown passes you caught. You certainly had some great games and made All America as I recall. I never really had an opportunity to thank you for beating those swabbies."

"Thank you, thank you." Replied Jules. "That's a real compliment coming from someone like yourself. Your picture from your playing days was always there in our locker room at the Point and the coach would point to it when he wanted to inspire us."

"Well, Carl, all I can say is that you sure teach these young commanders the right things to say to us old retreads. That is very kind of you to recall for me those wonderful days when the General Reichold and I were at the Point"

After Jules returned to his table the General added another bit of highly pertinent information. "The Colonel is also your son's commanding officer."

"So that is the man you told us about and you suggested that he might just be sharing the beautiful blonde with the banker?"

"That comes under the heading of idle gossip and the source of that juicy tid bit is none other than First American Security Team Inc hardly a reliable source but, nevertheless, very interesting."

Throughout lunch the principal topic of information was the FAST Inc report which they had all read by this time. The security problems raised by the Keystone Kops was now history although the Russians had not yet stood down on the flap. They were still convinced that there might be a hook in the situation for them and they were determined not to bite. The unknown quantity in the entire situation continued to be the reaction of the Rhine Group security staff and just what they would be reporting to their CEO and when they would be telling him.

"Carl, I hardly need to tell you that as my Chief of Staff, Spence, is kept fully informed on everything that could possibly concern me and that extends to matters relating to family. In fact, I have recently become convinced that good Chiefs of Staff always are a step ahead of the Senators who employ them and this certainly applies to Spence. His background at the Point and in the military made him uniquely qualified to become a Chief of Staff. There should be absolutely no hesitation in sharing any information with Spence no matter how personal that information might seem. In all important areas I have no doubt that Spence knows more than I do and I have found that I can rely on his judgement to ensure that I am informed at the appropriate time."

"Thank you Buck, that clears the air. Spence will be informed on all matters that arise relating to you and your family in addition to those largely military matters on which I should keep you informed because of your responsibilities as a senior member of the Senate Armed Forces Committee. The matter we discussed on the phone is well in hand and the most convenient solution will be implemented just as soon as either of you gives me the "go ahead." I see that you have a full program for the afternoon but I'm not certain that you will be seeing the beautiful blonde again. Perhaps that will be all for the best and you will be able to give Jacob Wiseman's presentation your full attention without the presence of such an attractive diversion." The General concluded with his promise to join them for dinner in their suite at their hotel at seven p.m.

Jules Pelladeau found a small envelope in his mail box containing a note from Helga. All it said was that Jacob Wiseman had to fly to London that evening. She was not that fussy about London and had decided to remain in Brussels for a couple of days before meeting Jacob in Paris at the end of the week. She advised him that she knew the Brussels area very well and could recommend a couple of very fine dining rooms in small hotels a short drive from Brussels. Unless she heard differently from him she would pick him up at his hotel when she came back from the airport at about seven p.m. There could be no doubt that this was the best offer Jules had received that day and he was waiting when she arrived shortly after seven. It was pure coincidence - Spencer Graham after so many years of dealing with intelligence matters always professed that he did not believe in coincidences. The Senator's Chief of Staff just happened to be in the Catering Manager's Office just off the lobby and observed the couple departing in what appeared to be a luxury rental car well beyond the means of an American Lieutenant Colonel. Coincidence or not this little gem of information was relayed to the Senator and Lt Gen Reichold at the appropriate time. The waiter had served brandy and coffee when Spence advised the other two that the beautiful lady who had graced the Secretary-General's table at lunch had left the building and not alone. Having caught their interest he added that she had not been accompanied her luncheon partner, Jacob Wiseman. He let them dangle for just a moment before he added that her companion was a very handsome young African-American officer whom they had all met earlier in the day.

The reputation of intelligence officers is always enhanced by acquiring such little gems that Spence had just dropped on the Senator and the General. He waited a few seconds for the impact to sink in and observed "It just goes

191

to prove that even First American Security Team Inc gets things right some of the time."

There was silence in the suite for several minutes before being broken by the Senator. "Well I'm not sure whether it reflects our age or our maturity but I didn't hear a single voice say "well, that lucky son of a bitch or words to that effect.""

"No, "was the General's comment. "But you can bet your last dollar that that's what we were all thinking."

It was a very pleasant evening and just before breaking up the Senator informed the General that he and his Chief of Staff had discussed the General's plan that would ensure that the Senator's promise to his wife was kept and his request to the General was that he should proceed immediately.

Jules spent a very pleasant two days with Helga at a small hotel just outside Brussels. His obligatory part of the program was over and he had packed up his luggage the evening before leaving the hotel. The following morning he had called the hotel advising that he would be checking out as of that day and asking that his luggage be stored in the baggage room and he would pick it up later in the day. He then contacted General Reichold's Chief of Staff and advised him that he would be taking a couple of days for sight seeing in the Brussels area but would be in touch with both the Chief of Staff and his unit back in Germany. He provided a number at which he could be reached during the next two days.

Helga shrugged off any suggestion that she was being unfaithful to Jacob with a nearly convincing rationalization of her relationship with her boss. He used her much like an exotic addition to his watch chain. For him she would never be anything more than a beautiful companion that would make him at least the subject of the envy of male leaders of the European Jewish Community when the respect he sincerely believed he deserved continued to be withheld because his family had not suffered enough during the war. She liked Jacob and respected him but had nearly convinced herself that she was just being used and had absolutely no compunction about following her interests elsewhere. She was not and had never been promiscuous. She thoroughly enjoyed sex and loved beautiful things. To her well developed eye Jules was beautiful. She would never forget that beautifully sculpted, black velvet body she had been introduced to at the Lodge that day and the powerful responses he had evoked from her.

One of the principal areas of resentment in her relationship with Jacob arose through their professional dealings and not on the personal side. Helga pointed out that she was a Vice-President on the Rhine Group Board and directly responsible for all Public Relations and Policy with a staff of over two hundred reporting to her. She always made her reports to Board Meetings and received directions and recommendations from other members of the Board. What she found very annoying was that other board members seemed to assume that because of her relationship with the CEO her reports carried additional weight and any questions would be regarded as the same as questions to the CEO. Helga regarded herself as an experienced executive and expected to be treated as such and she was giving careful consideration to a career change.

The small luxury hotel where Jules and Helga spent the two days was very small and very exclusive. There were no more than ten suites, a swimming pool, tennis courts and access to a championship golf course. The star attraction was the hotel dining room which would be the equivalent to a Michelin three star establishment.

Jules had returned to his original hotel late on that first afternoon to pick up his luggage. He had checked in with his Second In Command (2IC) at his unit back in Germany and the unit was heavily involved in preparing for the major training exercise commencing the following week. He advised his 2IC that he would join the unit at their allocated position early the following Monday.

At dinner that evening he found Helga a little preoccupied. He finally got her to admit that she was feeling just a little guilty but not because of stealing a couple of days with Jules. Her feeling of guilt came from her failure to return to the Mansion before joining Jacob in Paris. She had been speaking to Gerda on the phone and it seemed that the young American soldier, Jason Creighton, was spending a lot of time with Sandra and she was beginning to suspect that he might be teaching Sandra more than just music. Jason was a great favorite of Gerda's but now that Jason had joined a musical combo the leader of that combo had become involved and he just happened to be Jason's section chief. In addition to the two engagements the combo played each week they also had two rehearsals. They tried one rehearsal at the Mansion but the old General was not very happy with the type of music they were playing.

Gerda had also informed her that Mannheim was still very discouraged about the American strangers who had been in Freiderberg a few weeks earlier and who had been so nice to him with their promises to help him get to the States. Now he had not seen them for weeks and he was coming to the conclusion that they had been using him and led him to say many things about people that he really didn't mean because that is what they wanted him to say.

Helga had instructed Gerda to keep a close eye on Sandra and told her to try and limit her exposure to the Americans. She was just too young and innocent for this additional exposure to temptation. Helga told Gerda that she realized that she had made certain promises to Sandra but Sandra must not take advantage of the situation. Gerda assured Helga that Sandra was continuing to practise using the sheet music she had brought home from school and that Jason continued to help her. There were indications that the old General was enjoying these practices.

That evening Jules noted that Helga's attention had been attracted by a folio of family pictures that was lying on top of his open suitcase. She picked it up quickly and darted into the bathroom before he could reclaim his property. The bathroom door locked behind her and she ignored his insistent knocking.

"Helga, that's not fair. Those are just family photos. Bring them out here. "Jules tried to give the impression that he was annoyed without much success

"Yes," she replied through the door. "It is fair. I know absolutely nothing about you and you know nearly everything about me. Are these pictures of your mother and father?" No answer was forthcoming so she proceeded with her commentary. "Your father is so handsome and your mother is very pretty. But who is this gorgeous black girl?"

He finally gave in. "OK, OK, sure my father and mother are very good looking, how else could you explain me being so handsome? The girl is an old friend of mine Malina Mislara. I met her in Oxford and she is the Assistant Headmistress at the girl's school where my mother is the Headmistress. If you must really know we are engaged and plan to marry in December."

"But she's so beautiful. Have you slept with her?" The voice from the other side of the door was now attempting to tease Jules.

"That is none of your Goddam business! Now get out here this minute or I'll take you over my knee when you do come out!"

"Promises, promises, promises!" came the voice from the other side of the door and then, suddenly, the bathroom door flew open and a completely naked Helga dashed toward the bed tossing the folio to him as she flashed by.

Now she was just lying there on the bed with that beautiful body completely exposed. "And now, what about that promise?"

"To hell with the promises, I've got a better idea" his clothes flew in all directions and he was with her on the bed and her long shapely legs had wrapped themselves around his hips.

She was quickly aroused. "This is not what I call spanking" and her words of argument trailed away as she moved against him.

When he opened his eyes she was sitting up looking at the pictures in the folio. "Oh yes, she is very beautiful this black girl." She stretched back and pulled him down to her and put her lips up to his ear "But tell me, is she as good as I am?"

CHAPTER XVI

THE PLAN AND ITS CONSEQUENCES

ank Wilson, Jason's roommate and personal instructor, had reported the questions about Jason that had been raised by members of that rather mysterious group of well heeled Americans a few weeks earlier.

Red acquired a master key for the barracks where Jason's room was located. Hank was away with the main body of the regiment so the coast was clear in the nearly vacant barracks. Red found absolutely nothing incriminating in Jason's room until he managed to pick the lock on a small strong box and found the contents included correspondence and records of bank transfers mostly bearing names other than Creighton. The name Jason Parker came up several times but much more often Red encountered the name Jason Buchalter. If Red had needed any further evidence that Jason Creighton represented a security problem he now had it. He was also convinced that the beautiful blonde, Sandy, was also involved in this threat to NATO security. Red made detailed notes and took a few of the bank statements to support his notes and carefully re-locked the strong box. If Red had had any reservations about the implementation of the proposed plan he no longer had any doubts. Jason and the beautiful Sandy were just a pair of Goddam commies, he thought as he left Jason's room. Well they just weren't going to achieve their objectives, whatever they were, not on Red Mombirkett's watch.

On Thursday evening Red drove past the cottage Jason had rented and noted that Jason's little BMW was parked outside. Quite a fancy little car for a lowly Private First Class and Red's personal investigative effort now suggested that Jason was on someone else's payroll besides Uncle Sam's. In addition to Jason's little car Red noted that Sandy's bicycle was also leaning up against the side of the cottage. No rehearsal had been scheduled but Red could not doubt that

Jason and Sandy were actually making music together."The lucky son of a bitch, "Red muttered to himself as he drove away but thinking that it was almost time for Jason to share the wealth with his good friend Red.

On Saturday evening they were all at the gasthause for their regular weekly presentation. The program was a complete success and Red, Jason and Sandy agreed to meet at the cottage the following day and Gerda begged off on behalf of herself and Woody but promised to send a picnic basket. Red had not told Jason of the shift he would be required to do at the communications center from noon until 4 p.m. on Sunday. He would save that until Sunday morning when he would agree to meet Sandy at the cottage and Jason would join them at the end of his shift. This would give Red a few hours alone with Sandy.

When Red informed Jason of the extra shift on Sunday morning he promised that he would meet Sandy at the cottage and Jason could join them later. Jason agreed with the plan having no reason but to trust his best friend.

Sandy was already at the cottage when Red arrived on Sunday at about noon. He told her that Jason would be along at the end of his shift. Sandy was not unduly concerned. Over the weeks since Jason had joined the combo Sandy had become increasingly comfortable with Red particularly since the incident at the pub when Red and Woody had protected Jason from receiving a severe beating. This same situation was always a possibility at some of the rougher bars but the presence of Red and Woody always made Sandy feel just a little more secure.

Sandy had brought the big picnic basket that Gerda had promised but they decided not to open the basket until later. Nevertheless, Red popped the cork on the big bottle of champagne he had brought and poured a large glass for each of them. He had actually removed the same cork earlier in the morning and had added just a little Schnapps to the contents to add a bit of kick to the wine.

The fortified champagne had the desired effect and Sandy was showing the effects after less than a glass. Red pulled her to her feet and turned on the small record player. An area area of the floor had been cleared and could be used for dancing and Red now announced that he was going to teach Sandy some new dance steps. As the tempo of the music varied from piece to piece Red was pleased to note that she pressed herself closer to him during the slower numbers. They sat down on cushions on the floor and Red poured another glass of champagne for each. Sandy protested just a little claiming that the champagne on an empty stomach was making her just a little tipsy.

"We'll open the basket in a moment but first, how about giving old Red one of your special kisses. Sandy was hesitant but Red persisted. "Come on Sandy, what's a little kiss between friends ..... best friends. We should always do nice things for our friends and your kisses are very nice. Their lips touched but Sandy drew back almost immediately. Her speech was just a little bit slurred as she said "Red you must promise not to ------ me." The use of the word that had shocked Jason did not have quite the same effect on Red as he became just that much more excited. "Don't be silly Sandy, I just want to kiss you. I promise I won't do anything you don't want me to do."

It was a long warm kiss and Sandy responded although her mind told her to hold back. Her body would just not obey and the arms that should have been pressing against his chest and pushing him away were now firmly wrapped around his shoulders. Then she felt him on top of her and when she tried to tell him to stop his lips on hers sealed off any sound. And then it was happening. She didn't want it to happen but her body seemed to have a mind of its own as he moved against her. She managed to get out one long plaintive plea but it was too late; her treacherous body had betrayed her and she only heard his deep breathing as he said her name over and over. "Oh, Sandy oh Sandy, that was really wonderful, you are so special."

Sandy sat up and straightened her clothing. Now she was crying "Red, you did it and I didn't want you to do it. You promised you wouldn't but you did."

"No Sandy darling I promised that I wouldn't do anything you didn't want me to do. But, Sandy, you really wanted me to do it. Now you're telling me that you didn't want to do it. Don't worry, no one will know about it. It will be our little secret."

The tears were still welling up in her beautiful blue eyes as Red tried to comfort her. "Here, drink a bit of wine and I'll pour you a cup of coffee." Red opened the picnic basket a pulled out the thermos of coffee.

He poured her a cup of coffee and managed to add a small dollop of Schnapps from his pocket flask as she emptied her wine glass. She was still sobbing softly as he continued in his attempts to comfort her. "Don't worry," he repeated, "Jason won't know anything. Just forget it even happened. I don't think I can because you are very special to me. I've wanted to do that ever since the very first I saw you nearly a year ago." He stroked her hair and put another cushion under her head so she could finish her coffee. The soft sobbing subsided and her breathing became deep and regular.

Red checked his watch and noted that it was about a quarter after three. Jason would be arriving shortly after four and Red decided he had lots of time to set the scene the way he wanted. He quietly covered the sleeping Sandy with a thin spread from the sofa and she didn't even move. Perhaps the wine, sex and Schnapps had resulted in her passing out. He quickly checked the dresser drawers and struck gold. In the bottom drawer, hidden behind some spare blankets he found a package of condoms. He took out two of the small individual packages and slipped the remainder under the cushion on which her head was resting. He opened one of the individual packages and put it on the floor beside Sandy and he put the other small package in his shirt pocket.

At four o'clock Red kissed Sandy very gently on the forehead and noted that she was still completely out. He removed the spread and opened her blouse. Her bras was hooked in the centre and on unhooking the bras her breasts were completely exposed. He noted that her miniskirt was fastened by a hook at the top of the zipper. He deftly unhooked the fastener and drew down the zipper and the miniskirt fell limply on each side. Her tiny bikini panties had really offered little resistance the first time but Red decided that he could probably remove them without waking her up. He hooked his index finger under one of the straps and succeeded in moving it down to the middle of her thigh before he heard any sound from her and she was moaning "Oh Jason. I love you Jason." She was dreaming that she was with Jason. He quickly disengaged the bikini strap from the one leg and left it dangling limply across her other ankle. He decided that it was now or never and he covered her putting his lips on her and felt her arms and legs close around him. As he released her lips the sounds came again as she moved against him. "Oh Jason, oh Jason, I do love you, " The sounds increased in both volume and tempo as her head moved from side to side until the final sounds became little more than a long heavy sigh and Red collapsed against her.

It was at this precise moment that Jason arrived to see his beautiful Sandy lying there naked in the arms of his best friend. His first reaction was a soul wrenching scream followed by a stream of epithets aimed at both of them. Red jumped to his feet warning Jason "Watch your language boy!" And as the epithets continued Red knocked Jason down and knocked him down again when he scrambled to his feet. Sandy was just coming to her senses and quickly covered her naked body with the spread. As reality penetrated her awareness the tears started again punctuated by screams to Jason telling him how much she loved him.

After knocking Jason down the second time Red pulled on his clothes and dragged a groggy Jason out to Jason's car. "Now, drive! That's an order soldier!" As they drove off they could still hear the screams from Sandy.

When they got back to the barracks Red directed Jason into his own parking spot and took him up the outside stairs that led to Red's quarters on the second level. Just about everyone in the unit was out on the NATO exercise so there was no one to observe the Staff Sergeant practically dragging the PFC into his quarters.

Red sat Jason down on his bed and told him to just shut up and sit there. He took out a large bottle of bourbon and poured two large drinks telling Jason "Just shut up and get a couple of these into you and listen. I know what you saw but you've probably got it all wrong. I didn't want to do it. Correction, that's a lie. Any man in his right mind would want to have sex with her. But she's your girl friend and you're my best friend. I couldn't do that to a best friend but she asked for it, she even pleaded with me. She told me that no one would know that this would be just our secret. Sure she loves you but this had nothing to do with love this was just sex and best friends should always do nice things for best friends. I still didn't want to but I'm only human. Then she pleaded with me to wear one of these condoms. I don't use the damn things but she had some in one of the dresser drawers." He showed Jason the little packet he had put in his shirt pocket. Red refilled their glasses with bourbon before he continued.

"Jason, I don't know where you ever got the idea that that is an innocent young girl. She's a real tiger and very experienced. Take it from me that there is only one way to get that experience."

Jason had not said a word. He finished the second glass of bourbon before he even tried to speak. "But Jesus Red I really love her. Why would she do that to me?"

"Women, "Red replied, "They're all the same under the skin, just bitches. Just think back to other women you have known. Were they any different?" Jason thought back to the beautiful little starlet in New York; she had dumped him also after promising that he was the only one for her.

"Now Jason just take some advice from a friend and an old soldier.Put as much space as you can between yourself and that little bitch just as quickly as possible. You're much too good for her but she wants to go to the States so badly she'll do just about anything to get you into bed again. Then when she gets to the States she'll be screwing all your friends. You should really look at this as a lucky break because you saw her for what she is before it was too late. I remember you telling me that you had provisional acceptance at a college in the states. Well next week is the deadline for applications. You can be on your way in 48 hours if you just say the word and there will be absolutely no hassle. So long as you are making passing grades in school you will be exempt from the Viet Nam draft."

The bourbon was now taking effect on Jason and he had toppled back on the bed was very nearly asleep. Red sat back in his big lounge chair and watched as Jason fell into a deep but troubled sleep. As he watched him groaning and twitching Red couldn't help but look back with satisfaction on his implementation of the plan to this point. The completed application for voluntary transfer lacking only Jason's signature, was in his office only about fifty yards away and with that signature Jason could be Stateside within 48 hours.

Red called the motor pool and requested a vehicle to pick up his own car which was still at the cottage. When he arrived he found the cottage deserted. Sandy had obviously left in a hurry because the picnic basket was still in the same position as it had been when he opened it to pour Sandy the cup of coffee. Red closed the window and locked the door and drove back to the barracks.

At about 5 p.m. Sandy arrived back at the Mansion on her bicycle. She went through the kitchen without a word to Gerda, Woody or Mannheim who were seated there. She was so obviously upset that Gerda did not ask the whereabouts of the picnic basket. Mannheim was the most concerned because he always relied on the effervescent Sandy to cheer him up whenever he got a little down. He was still worried about what he had told those Americans earlier in the summer and he was still afraid that some of the things he had said would come back to hurt someone he loved and Sandy was certainly one of that small group.

Mannheim went up to Sandy's room and knocked softly on her door. He heard her coming out of her shower but the only words he heard told him to go away; that she didn't want to speak to anyone. Mannheim persisted pleading that it was very important that she speak to him and she finally opened the door. Now he could see that she was crying and this made Mannheim even sadder. She was such a special person and he just hated to see her unhappy. "Please, Sandy, what's the matter. Was it something I said to those Americans?"

"No, Mannheim, it's nothing you said but don't ever mention Americans to me again. I hate Americans!"

As Mannheim made his way down the hall to his own room he decided that if Americans made someone he loved as much as Sandy so unhappy and if they always tried to get him to say things he didn't mean, well, then, he hated Americans too.

Gerda was also concerned about Sandy. It was a very rare occasion when Sandy was ever anything but happy and those occasions were always very brief and Gerda had a little bag of tricks that never failed to bring the smile back to that beautiful face. Later in the evening she took a sandwich and a bowl of soup up to Sandy and she gained entrance to the room only after threatening to sick Plato on her. Sandy protested that she wasn't hungry and that was unusual. Sandy was always ready to eat. Gerda did not have much success in getting to the bottom of the current situation except to hear Sandy's repeated statement that she hated men, all men and especially Americans. On hearing this Gerda decided that this was just a typical lover's tiff and under such circumstances such a level of hatred would have a duration of something less than forty-eight hours. Gerda was just a little more concerned when several evenings went by and Jason did not appear at the Mansion.

Sandy was heartbroken and just a little confused. She spent at least twenty minutes in her shower trying to wash off everything that had happened that day but then, after Mannheim left, she sat on her bed trying to recall what had actually happened. Her first decision was that she would not drink any more champagne. She just couldn't understand why she had not resisted the first time but it had happened so quickly and she had trusted Red. But the second time her body completely betrayed her. Now she realized that she had thought it was Jason making love to her so her body responded. It was only when it was over that she fully realized what had happened and her cries to Jason went unanswered. If she could only have spoken to Jason she could have convinced him that this was all a mistake but he wouldn't even speak to her. Meta and Helga had both been right, all men were bastards.

Jason slept until after midnight and awoke with a splitting headache. Red was stretched out on the lounge chair watching TV. On noting Jason's return to life Red recommended some of the "hair of the dog". Jason offered very little resistance and after a cup of coffee, two asprins and another large jolt of bourbon Jason decided that he would really survive.

Red told him to stay where he was for the night and Red would bunk down in the next room which was unoccupied. He told Jason to give some thought to the voluntary transfer because the deadline for academic leave was fast approaching. Red promised him there would be no hassle and he would be Stateside so fast that there wouldn't even be time for jet lag.

Jason had a good night's sleep and on Monday morning he told Red that he wanted that voluntary transfer. Red took him up to his office and the completed forms appeared very quickly. Red took him to the office of the Second in Command who was holding down the fort while the regiment was on exercise. The 2IC double checked the personnel policy regulations referred to on the application form and witnessed Jason's signature. The 2IC promised that the completed form would go to Corps HQ that day by courier and he advised Jason to commence his clearance procedure immediately.

Jason was in the transit unit at Frankfurt Airport at noon on Tuesday and that evening was on a scheduled flight for JFK in New York.

At about 3 p.m. on the same day Red got his final anonymous telephone call and could barely conceal his exuberance as he reported the successful completion of the mission. The "Package" would arrive in New York at 0900 hrs on Wednesday, August 21st and gave the caller the flight number. He was informed that his successful completion of this mission would be duly noted by the Director of Personnel on his personal file that would be considered by the next promotion board. Nothing spoke with greater accuracy on just how good a soldier S/Sgt Billiebob Mombirkett really was than the degree of pride he derived from the successful completion of this mission without experiencing the slightest twinge of remorse.

Late in the evening of Tuesday, August 20th the Senator called his wife to tell her that Jason would be arriving at JFK at about noon on the following day and gave her the flight number. The final audition at Julliard was scheduled for 9 a.m. on Wednesday, September 11th. A corporate jet would arrive in Columbus at 9 a.m. on Wednesday to take her to New York. Jason would be on leave for as long as he was in fulltime attendance at Julliard just as long as he maintained the grades required to indicate satisfactory progress. The Senator suggested that she take Jason along with her on her scheduled visit to see her father in Dallas and to attend the board meeting on Friday.

When Jason arrived at JFK he was greeted by his mother and whisked by limousine to the special terminal for executive jets and they were in Dallas for dinner at her father's mansion. Jason tried a long distance call to Hank back in Germany but Hank was not available and he remembered that the regiment would be still on exercise. Hank did call back on Sunday, August 25th, and told him of the dramatic developments that included Red's sudden death and that they were looking for Woody because he had been involved in some way in Red's death. Everything was very quiet around the Mansion and Hank hadn't seen any signs of life there on his two visits back to the barracks. Jason asked him to return his car to the dealer he had arranged his lease with. The dealer would know where to send the final statement. Hank was very curious about Jason's sudden move but Jason just didn't want to talk about it.

CHAPTER XVII

RED RECEIVES A "DEAR JOHN"

On Friday, August 23rd S/Sgt Red Mombirkett received two letters. The first was from his wife Allison telling him that she had decided to sue for divorce on the grounds of mental cruelty in that he had continually refused over a period of seven years to make any effort to establish and maintain a normal environment for his family.

Red's initial reaction could be summed up in very few words. "Bitch!" "Mental Cruelty Horseshit!" He had given the ungrateful bitch the very best of two worlds.

The second letter drew a more protracted and emotional response. While he had been home on leave in April his suspicions had been aroused by a number of things. First the kids had been talking about someone they called Uncle Juan - not Uncle John they insisted - who they claimed was a great baseball player. There had been also a number of mysterious telephone calls in which the callers just hung up when Red answered. Finally, and most conclusive in Red's opinion, Allison just didn't seem to be as ready for "bedtime" as she had been during previous leaves. Her response in bed just lacked a lot of that enthusiastic participation he had come to expect and, Red would argue, fully deserved, considering the sacrifices he was making in giving Allison exclusive North American rights to the Great American Sex Machine. As a result of his suspicions Red had asked his dad, known as Big Red, to do a little checking on his daughter-in-law.

The second letter on this day was from Big Red. Red's suspicions had been right on target. Uncle Juan was Juan Marino a very fine second baseman from the Dominican Republic who had been recruited by a major university in North Carolina on a full scholarship to play baseball for the varsity team. He came from a very good family in the Dominican and had already compiled nearly two years of acceptable university credits. To assist Juan to maintain an acceptable academic average, and remain eligible to play baseball, the university athletic department had hired a teacher to help him overcome a small language difficulty and maintain his grade level in other subjects.. They had hired Allison Magioli - really Allison Mombirkett who insisted on using her maiden name in her teaching career - and this combination proved to he highly successful on both the academic and personal level.

Young Juan Marino was tall, very graceful, very handsome and approximately half way between black and white which in North Carolina, as well as all other southern and most northern states, counts as black. He proved to be a charming, intelligent young man and while it was not love at first sight, the frequent tutorials presented both the "opportunity and proximity" mentioned so often by lawyers in divorce suits and had the predictable result. The inevitable happened and when it did Allison discovered another dimension to sexual gratification in which passion and tenderness could be combined for mutual satisfaction. Juan would be graduating in 1969 but had already been drafted by the Boston Red Sox and his initial contract would include a substantial signing bonus. He was deeply in love with Allison and she felt the same way about him. As traditional southerners her parents were not really that fussy about Allison's choice but when they compared him to Billiebob Mombirkett, Juan was a clear winner. In addition, Allison's father was a rabid baseball fan.

Red reread his father's letter a second time before the situation really sank in. Then he exploded "A goddam nigger, she dumped me for a goddam nigger! Just wait, I'll show that bitch and her fancy nigger."

Just before noon a courier arrived with legal documents for S/Sgt Billiebob Mombirkett. Red took them to his room and while he was not prepared to wade through the pages of legalese, the covering letter contained some information that was quite sufficient to keep his blood pressure at a dangerous level. The lawyer advised Red that Allison would be claiming full title to the matrimonial home on the grounds that Red had never made any significant contribution to the initial cost and ultimate purchase of the home which was now debt free with a valuation of approximately $120,000. When this little gem finally sank in there was a further stream of epithets and Red was ready for a drink, several drinks.

Red checked his private liquor stock and found he was down to three 26 ouncers of Jim Beam and considered that that should get him through the night. Red was already in a highly agitated state as he continued to review his current situation. He quickly drank about eight ounces of bourbon and each swallow was punctuated by "bitch. unfaithful bitch, goddam nigger lover, etc. etc". After his third glass of bourbon he had worked himself into a pretty mean mood.

Red went out in the long hall and started shouting obscenities at everyone he saw. He was looking for trouble and he found Woody. Woody had just come off three long 12 hour night shifts in the kitchen and he was now looking forward to a long weekend until he came back on duty for the night shift on Monday . He came out of his room just down the hall from Red's to see who was causing the racket. He'd had a few hours sleep and was looking forward to joining Gerda at the Mansion. Red saw him coming out of his room and immediately directed a stream of racial slurs towards the big cook. Woody could see that Red was really tanked up and in a foul mood and decided to step back in his room and avoid trouble. But Red came after him and increased the invective as he pushed his way through Woody's door. "Don't you try to hide from me you black son of a bitch. I've got a good mind to just beat the shit out of you. " Red took a long swig out of the bottle he was carrying in one hand.

Woody decided to try and reason with Red. "Come on Red take it easy. Let's go back to your room and we'll have a little drink together. Come on Red we're all friends here." Woody started to lead Red back towards Red's room but Red stopped midway, took another long gulp from his bottle and screamed "Just keep your black hands off me you black son of a bitch. You're another nigger who chases white women. How's that big blonde bitch of yours in the sack? I might just have a piece of that German bitch myself. I had some of that cute little blonde Sandy the other day and she loved it and just maybe now that her wimpish boyfriend is gone I'll go back for some more but perhaps I'll try some of that big blonde nigger lover of yours first. What do you think of that you black bastard?"

Red's words really stung but Woody decided that it was just the booze talking and that he might be able to talk Red down. "Red, Red, just take it easy. How about a little fresh air?" They were now beside the open door that opened out to the landing at the top of the two flights of stairs that led down to the parking lot.

"Fuck the fresh air. I don't need any fresh air. Don't give me any orders you black bastard." Now Red started swinging and raining punches on Woody's head and shoulders. He tried to get his arms around Red to smother the punches and to get as close as possible to Red so that he would have no room for his powerful punches. As he tried to protect himself he fell against Red and they both lurched against the railing at the top of the stairs. There was the sound of shattering wood as the railing broke and the two men fell the nearly fifteen feet to the ground in a tangled mass of arms and legs. Woody landed on top and got to his feet immediately. Red never moved.

A soldier passing by heard the noise and came over to investigate. "Hey this guy is really out. Someone call for an ambulance!" He bent over Red then reached down and felt for Red's pulse on his throat and drew his hand back quickly. "Jesus Christ, this man is dead!"

Woody heard these words as a small crowd of curious spectators began to gather and he slowly withdrew to the outer fringe. Woody really felt no guilt about what had happened. It had been an accident but Woody was afraid. Long experience in the culture of the South had taught him that whenever a black and white fought or even struggled and the white man was hurt, the black man was in trouble. There had been no witnesses so it would have been his word against Red's but Red was dead. Woody started walking away slowly and could only think that he had to get to Gerda and explain what had happened. He made his way towards the Mansion by a roundabout route and heard the ambulance siren in the distance.

As Woody entered the rear entrance he received a friendly greeting from Plato. Greta and Mannheim were in the kitchen and Woody crossed the room to the rear stairs and signaled to Gerda that he wanted to speak to her. When she joined him in her room she could see that the big black man was very troubled. "Gerda" he blurted out, "I'm really in trouble. Red is dead and they're going to blame me. There go all of our plans. But, Gerda, it was an accident. I swear it was an accident. He was very drunk and saying terrible things but I was just trying to talk to him and then he was punching me. We fell and now he is dead and they'll blame me."

Gerda and Woody hadn't noticed but Mannheim had followed Gerda upstairs and was now standing in the half-open doorway. "Gerda, what are the Americans doing to Woody. He's a good man and our friend. Why are the Americans always trying to hurt good people?"

"Mannheim, please leave us alone and don't tell anyone that Woody is here." She then closed the door.

As Mannheim turned to go back downstairs he noticed that Sandy was standing in her doorway. She signaled for him to come over and asked what was the matter with Woody. Mannheim told her that Woody had killed someone called Red and now the police would be after him. Gerda had asked him not to tell anyone that Woody was there. "We must protect him from the Americans." With that Mannheim continued on his way downstairs.

Back in her room Sandy thought about what Mannheim had told her. Red was dead. Woody had killed him. Sandy desperately wanted to talk to someone. Where was Jason? The scene at the cottage flashed through her mind again and she remembered what Red had done to her and tried to remember just how it had happened. She had asked Gerda when Helga would be back but was told that Helga was still in Paris and that she had been in hospital there for a couple of days for food poisoning or something like that. Jacob had called and told Gerda that Helga was quite all right and would probably be back on Sunday. Sandy wanted to see Helga very badly because she was very worried. She would have spoke to Gerda about her problem but thought it would be better to speak to both of them. Sandy was certain that she was pregnant.

Back at the scene of the accident the ambulance arrived at about the same time as the Military Police. The latter quickly taped the area off with crime scene tape and ensured that nothing in the area was touched. Only one soldier answered the call for witnesses and he told the police he had witnessed part of the incident from his room in the barracks just across the road about seventy-five yards away. He had heard a noise and saw two men struggling at the top of the outside flight of stairs. One was a big black man and the other was a big red headed man and one of them was shouting foul anti-racist epithets at the top of his voice and then the railing gave away and they fell to the ground. The big black man apparently took off because he was no longer at the scene when this witness arrived.

The regimental duty officer arrived and the 2IC a few moments later. There was another call for witnesses but none came forward. The duty officer pointed out to the 2IC that there just might be an additional witness. He pointed to a box on a utility pole just outside the barracks and identified it as a security camera. He also informed the 2IC that most of these buildings had security cameras in the central hallways and those cameras were always activated when the unit was away from the barracks All of these cameras were controlled from the central security office and he recommended that the security officer be instructed to seal the film from all the cameras in the area and that this film be held for the inevitable board of inquiry.

The 2IC remained at the scene until the MPs had completed their investigation and ensured that the scene was photographed from every possible angle. He then directed that the duty officer go directly to the unit security office and instruct the staff there to seal the film from all the cameras in the area of the incident and that applied to both outside and inside cameras. Those seals would remain in effect until removed by order of the President of the Board of Inquiry. The 2IC then returned to his office and called in his Administration Officer. He briefed this officer telling him that there were obviously racial overtones to this incident because the one witness reported a struggle between a black man and the deceased. The 2IC had a distinct recollection of an administrative order relating to the demise of American soldiers and specific directions regarding interracial incidents involving violence.

It only took the Administration Officer a few minutes to come up with the relevant administrative orders. First, all boards of inquiry into suspicious deaths of American soldiers would be chaired by the unit Commanding Officer. Second, all Boards of Inquiry into interracial incidents must be convened within forty-eight hours of the actual time of the incident.

The 2IC immediately got on the phone to his Commanding Officer. Jules was in his field HQ in the regimental defensive position as the exercise was winding down. The 2IC gave Jules a preliminary report and volunteered to convene the Board of Inquiry as Acting Commanding Officer in Jules' absence but Jules told him that he would be back in time on Sunday to meet the forty-eight hour requirement. He directed that his 2IC detail the other members of the board and prepare the executive order that Jules would sign as soon as he returned. The first meeting of the Board would be at 0800hrs on Monday, August 26th. Jules directed that all witnesses including the MPs should be available to answer the call of the President of the Board at that time.

He then went on to ask if the identity of the black man involved in the fracas had been established. His 2IC informed him that preliminary investigations indicated that the only person who fitted the witness's description would be Sgt Woodrow Washington who was a food specialist who had been on the rear party. As of the time of this telephone call, 2000hrs, Friday, August 23rd, they had been unsuccessful in establishing contact with Sgt Washington. He had come off three successive twelve hour night shifts at 0800hrs Friday morning and was now on pass until he took over the night shift on Monday, August 26th so he was not AWOL. Jules was informed that the film from all security cameras had been sealed and the security officer had been instructed to give the development of films from these cameras top priority and had promised that all films would be available by noon on Tuesday.

215

CHAPTER XVIII

FIELD MARSHAL BARON ERICH von FREIDERHOFF
1885 - 1968 - A MATTER OF HONOR

Helga arrived back at the Mansion Sunday evening. She had been discharged from the very exclusive private hospital on Sunday morning and Jacob had arranged to have the corporate jet pick her up in Paris and take her back to Frankfurt. He had been deeply apologetic about leaving her alone in Paris but he had to attend a World Bank meeting in Rome. He left Paris only after being assured by the medical staff that Helga was in absolutely no danger and that they would keep her under observation until Sunday just to be sure that the food poisoning had cleared her system. Helga was deeply appreciative of the professionalism of the hospital staff because both she and the presiding specialist knew that what had been publicly diagnosed as "food poisoning" had actually been a miscarriage. Helga fully appreciated just how mature the French were about such things, probably more so that Jacob whose analytical mind would wonder how his vasectomy had failed him after all these years and try to estimate the probability of such an event happening. And then, of course Helga was quite certain that her condition, now corrected, could be attributed to Jules and their visit to the Hunting Lodge in June.

On her arrival back at the Mansion Gerda could see that she was very tired and decided to leave the detailed report until Monday morning after Helga had the benefit of a good night's sleep in her own bed.

Helga checked in with her Grandfather and found that he had missed his chess games with the American colonel but the latter had been in Brussels for a week and was now out on a major exercise with his regiment. The old man was looking forward to resuming the chess matches the following weekend. He also mentioned that Sandra had not been practicing the beautiful music she had been learning with the help of that American soldier. He had not heard any Chopin from the music room for over a week now.

Helga spoke to Gerda on her way to her room and asked about Sandra and the American soldier. Sandy was asleep and as for the American soldier most of them were away on a training exercise but would be back in a few days. Helga decided that right now her priority would be a good night's sleep and she made her way to her room.

Jules convened his Board of Inquiry into the untimely death of S/Sgt Billiebob Mombirkett at a few minutes after eight a.m. on Monday. They heard evidence from the lone eye witness, the MPs, the Duty Officer and the Medical Officer. The latter advised the board that the deceased had died of a broken neck the result of a fall and that blood tests indicated that he had been highly inebriated at the time of his death. Certainly a fall from a height of between twelve and fifteen feet could quite possibly cause such an injury and such a possibility would only be increased by the weight of another person landing on top of him.

The unit security officer advised the Board that the film from all the security cameras, both inside and outside cameras, was now being developed and would be available for showing no later that noon on the following day.

It now seemed quite certain that the identity of the big black man who had struggled with the deceased was indeed Sgt. Woodrow Wilson Washington but the MPs had not been successful in establishing contact as of the time the Board had convened. Jules was quite sure that he knew where to find the witness. He directed that the MP Detachment Commander provide him with a vehicle and an escort of two MPs at 2 p.m. that afternoon for a task related to the Board of Inquiry.

Back at the Mansion Helga was receiving her detailed briefing from Gerda and Sandy. First came the shocker from Sandy that she was quite sure she was pregnant. In consideration of her own experience just a few days earlier in Paris, Helga might have been just a little more understanding of Sandy's predicament. But this was different. Helga was a grown woman whereas Sandy was only a child. Then there was the guilt factor. Helga would have loved to have someone to blame but she realized that some of the blame was hers. She had actually encouraged Sandy to spend time with Jason and was there anything else she could expect? She lashed out at Gerda but relented when she saw that Gerda probably felt worse than she did.

"And where is this young man Jason? What has he to say for himself?" Helga asked Sandy.

"I don't know" Sandy replied. "I haven't seen him since Sunday."

Now Gerda dropped the bomb. "He's gone, he's back in the United States. His unit transferred him, Woody told me."

This bit of information drew a wail of anguish from Sandy who had still hoped that Jason would come to see her. But the information had an even greater impact on Helga. All of the emotions she had felt, the sympathy for Sandy, the emotional drain of the miscarriage in Paris were now replaced by an overwhelming wave of rage. Later she would realize that to direct all of this rage against Jules was just a bit unfair. He was not solely responsible for her own pregnancy. It had not been rape. But that experience plus the apparent protection and transfer of Jason just tended to focus her rage. Then, Gerda told her that they were looking for Woody because a man they referred to as Red had been

218

killed and Woody would be charged with murder. This was the proverbial straw. Woody a murderer; just how ridiculous could these Americans get. Woody wasn't a murderer. He was just a big, nice, good natured black man who wouldn't hurt anyone. Now her rage was really focussed on Jules and she just couldn't wait to get her hands or her tongue on him. She didn't have that long to wait.

Jules arrived at the Mansion at about 2.15 p.m. in a staff car accompanied by two MPs. He instructed the MPs to remain in the car and he would call them when he needed them. Helga opened the door to his ring and indicated for him to enter. He could see that Gerda and Sandy were at the door at the far end of the living room. Helga called to them in German. "Where is the General?" and Gerda answered that he was out in the car with Mannheim.

Jules just started to say, "Helga I must see Woody" but he was stopped before he could conclude his remark. The look on Helga's face was very different from what he recalled from their last evening at the hotel near Brussels. He sensed that he was facing a very angry woman and as soon as she opened her mouth his opinion was confirmed.

"So here we have that famous black hero." Her voice was just dripping with sarcasm. "Here is that great black commander who inveigles his way into the confidence of unsuspecting people and then takes advantage of them by either impregnating them or acting to protect those who do by whisking them back to the United States where they will not face the consequences of their actions."

Jules really didn't know what hit him and it was apparent that she was just warming up.

"You are a rotten, scheming, black son of a bitch with no more social conscience than our pet Plato. But always so superior, looking down your nose at my Jewish lover who

219

was always so kind and generous to this family Then there is really no reason to wonder about those higher human instincts because you black bastard you have only been out of the jungle for a few hundred years. My grandfather was absolutely right about your inferior......" She stopped in mid sentence as her attention was caught by a frantic Mannheim now standing in the doorway at the other end of the room and pointing emphatically towards the old General's study. Helga immediately understood; the old General had come in by the side entrance and was in his study. Her question as to how much of her wild tirade aimed at Jules he had heard was quickly answered as the door to his study burst open and the old man lurched out with the Heidleberg Sword of Honor brandished above his head and obviously zeroing in on the sound of Jules' voice as he had attempted to defend himself from Helga's fierce attack.

"You rotten black son of a bitch I will teach you how you should deal with a man of honor!" He was only a few feet from Jules when his face was caught in a grimace of pain and he clutched his chest as his knees crumbled under him and he collapsed to the floor.

Helga screamed "He's had a heart attack, please, someone help him!"

Jules was already on his knees beside the old man. He gently turned him over and placed a cushion under his head. Then he commenced mouth to mouth resuscitation. Helga tried to join him but he waved her away. Between breaths he instructed her to call an ambulance. The CPR continued until the ambulance arrived in about ten minutes. Woody had heard the commotion and came down to help. After about five minutes Woody took over on the mouth to mouth resuscitation from Jules who was getting just a little drained emotionally. Helga, Gerda, Sandy and Mannheim were frantic and Jules tried to quiet them down until the ambulance arrived. The two MPs had come in from the staff car and they helped the ambulance attendants to carry the stretcher to the waiting ambulance. Helga and Mannheim went along with the old man in the ambulance.

Jules now sat back and rested for a moment before appealing in a loud and clear voice..."Will someone please tell me just what the hell is going on in this house? But first, Sergeant Washington will be taken into custody. Before the MPs take you back to the barracks, Sergeant, I can only tell you that for now you will be held as a material witness because the first thing we need from you is your statement on what happened on Friday. As of now there is only one eyewitness and all he could tell us is that you were involved in some kind of an altercation with the deceased, S/Sgt Mombirkett. This witness states that he heard someone shouting a stream of racial epithets and I doubt if that would have been you. We are now waiting for the film from the security cameras to be developed. We'll have that evidence by this time tomorrow. Until then you will be a guest of the Military Police Section."

There was no protest from Woody but Gerda tried to intervene. "Please Colonel, Woody is a good man. He wouldn't hurt anyone. That man Red was mean and nasty when he was drinking and he raped Sandy." But Jules held up his hand.

"Please, Gerda, I have convened a Board of Inquiry to find out what happened. You are probably right but a man is dead and the circumstances must be investigated and for now Sgt Washington is at least a very important witness."

Jules accompanied the MPs and Woody back to the regimental guard room and instructed the Duty Officer who met him there that Woody was not to be charged at this time. He would be held as a material witness until further instructions were received from the Board of Inquiry.

221

The Duty Officer told Jules that the 2IC had been trying to get in touch with him and Jules told the Duty Officer to inform the 2IC that he would be in his office at 7 p.m. and he would see him then.

After all the documentation was completed Jules told the driver of the staff car to take him to the local civilian hospital. In the waiting room Jules saw that Sandy had arrived probably on her bicycle and she was involved in a tearful discussion with Helga. Jules decided that it would be best to give them any time together that they needed and he waited in the hall. When Sandy came out still very teary eyed he went in. As he took a seat Helga came and sat beside him. Her eyes were also filled with tears.

"Oh, Jules, he's gone. They couldn't save him and I'm so sorry for everything I said to you. Sandy told me everything and now I know you were not to blame in any way. Sandy is pregnant and Jason is gone. I had a miscarriage and I really can't blame you. Sandy was my responsibility and I should have known that she was just too innocent to be exposed to so much temptation. I should have tried to keep Sandy and Jason apart but I just encouraged them to spend so much time together. The only person I blame is this man they call Red. He raped Sandy but now he's dead and it's poor Woody who's in trouble." The tears were really flowing now as she put her head on his shoulder. "It's so sad to think that Grandfather was sitting there in his study and listening to all of those terrible things I said about you and they were all untrue. After all you were the one person who had been so good to him and treated him with the dignity he deserved despite some of those ideas he had. He really intended to kill you with his Sword of Honor."

"Well, if I had been in his position and heard what he heard . . . . . he really did the only thing he could do that would be consistent with his lifelong beliefs. Now come on I'll give you a lift home. Both Gerda and your Sandy are going to need some comforting. I wouldn't worry too much about Woody because I think the security cameras will prove that S/Sgt Mombirkett or Red, as you call him, was responsible for his own demise. There is just one other thing I would like to add. I'm very sorry about your Grandfather. During those hours we spent together I developed a great measure of respect for the man. No, I couldn't accept some of his ideas but there was absolutely no doubting the sincerity of his beliefs but time had just passed him by and right now I'm not sure whether that's really for the good of mankind or not. He was probably one of the most impressive people I have ever met."

Jules dropped Helga off back at the Mansion and noted that Sandy had returned because her bicycle was beside the garage.

At 7 p.m. that evening the 2IC came to his office. He told Jules that he felt that he was in an awkward position because he wasn't quite sure as to whether he should be speaking to Jules as his Commanding Officer or as the President of the Board of Inquiry. Jules advised him to let him decide on which hat he would be wearing.

"I have been doing a little investigating on my own," the 2IC announced, "I trust that you will not regard this as interfering with the proceedings of the Board of Inquiry but the incident did occur on my watch. The deceased, S/Sgt Mombirkett appears to have been a very mixed bag. He was always rated as a good NCO but he appears to have had a dark side. I'll just tell you what I have discovered and you just stop me if you feel that any of what I have to offer should be heard by the Board under oath.

"As I believe you know, Colonel, Mombirkett was a career soldier, fourth generation in his family to make the army a career. He was married but always took his career moves unaccompanied. On Friday morning Mombirkett received what is known as "a Dear John letter" from his wife followed by legal documents from her lawyer which arrived later the same morning by courier. On Friday he also received a letter from his father and I took the liberty of reading that letter as I was going through correspondence in his quarters. Obviously, Mombirkett was a little suspicious about just what his wife was doing back in North Carolina and he had asked his father to check up on her. His suspicions proved to be correct as his father discovered that the wife had established a meaningful relationship with a student from the Dominican Republic, a baseball player on an athletic scholarship at a major university. Mombirkett's wife was hired by the university's athletic department to tutor the young ballplayer and ensure that he maintained his grades at the required level so he would continue to be eligible to play baseball. The other factor which, unfortunately, had some bearing on Mombirkett's reaction to this news, was that the ballplayer is black. Now Mombirkett was from rural Alabama but there is absolutely nothing in his record of service to indicate acts or expressions of racial prejudice. However, I think that it would be a reasonable assumption that news about his wife's new love interest did very little to improve the day he was having on Friday."

The 2IC paused as if expecting questions from Jules. There being none, he continued. "It appears that S/Sgt Mombirkett was drinking heavily on Friday afternoon and, unfortunately, the first person he encountered was Sgt Washington who has been in charge of the kitchen and dining hall we operated for the rear party. He had just come off three 12 hour night shifts and it would appear that he came out of his room just to investigate noises he heard. We can assume that Washington then became the deceased's target and focus of all his woes. While we still haven't seen the film from the security cameras or heard the sound track I'd be willing to bet that the deceased's comments to Washington were far from complimentary but we'll wait for the film to tell us what happened in the barracks."

The 2IC paused again but Jules gave no indication of having any questions. The 2IC continued. "On checking the personal papers of the deceased we found some items of interest. As you may know Mombirkett was the leader of a small music combo that played at the local pubs. In fact, Sgt Washington and his wife-to- be performed vocal duets with the combo from time to time. The keyboard player with the combo was Pfc Jason Creighton a recent arrival who was involved in the "in job" training program for communications specialists. Mombirkett was actually in charge of that training program for this unit and, during your absence, Mombirkett brought in an application for transfer to the non-effective list Stateside on behalf of Creighton because he wanted to enroll in college. The Administrative Order was pretty clear on such transfers and the deadline was this week so I approved the application. But in the deceased's papers there were some notes that indicated Creighton may have been really someone by the name of Buchalter and it appears that Mombirkett was conducting some kind of a clandestine security investigation on his own and it's just possible that the "spooks" or CIA were involved. At least Mombirkett was in possession of some authenticating codes that looked very much like those used by the CIA. I was under the impression that the CIA had agreed to work through established chains of command but now it seems that they still have their own little projects. It's probably no coincidence that when we had that strange group of Americans asking questions locally about a month ago one of the men they were interested in was Creighton. That's all I have right now and I can only hope that I have not caused any problems for your Board."

"No Curt, I don't think anything you have told me will compromise the work of the Board, "said Jules talking to his 2IC. "The Board may call on you to testify or at least submit some of the articles you have mentioned as evidence. I think that the film and sound track from the security cameras may enable the Board to wind up its deliberations in short order.

The decision that the Board must make is just how much of what you have told us really has any bearing on the death of S/Sgt Mombirkett. For example, just what did the deceased's extracurricular activities investigating on behalf of an unknown party have to do with his death if any? If the CIA was involved I think the appropriate action for us would be to yank someone's chain and have our own security people dump on those "spooks" from the CIA from the highest possible height. They have been told to work through normal channels and, what's more, they have promised to abide by that order and now it seems that they may be reviving their own little empire."

The 2IC reported that the security officer had promised to have all films and sound tracks available by 1100hrs on Tuesday, August 27th. He also assured Jules that copies of all the correspondence he had reported on this evening would be available for individual members of the Board when the Board convened on Tuesday morning if Jules, in his capacity as President of the Board, decided that such evidence had any bearing upon their deliberations. His final remarks related to S/Sgt Mombirkett and his record of service. Personal questioning of a number of other non coms and junior officers left him with the distinct impression that the deceased's clean record of service might just reflect twelve years of undetected crime instead of completely meritorious service. It now appeared that Mombirkett maintained a high standard of discipline in his section but the methods he used to maintain this standard may not have always complied with the Uniform Code of Military Discipline.

Jules thanked his 2IC for the very valuable briefing and he could see things starting to fall into place. He was looking forward to his next meeting with his faculty advisor, General Reichold, and the answers the General might have on some coincidences that had cropped up recently.

Just before the Board of Inquiry re-convened on Tuesday morning Jules' 2IC called him and told him that the security officer had received the developed films from the security cameras and had compiled a composite from the two cameras that had been directly involved fully supported by sound track. He suggested that if Jules called a recess at 1100hrs he would have the conference room set up for the showing of the film by 1115hrs. Jules told him that they would swear in the security officer just prior to the showing of the film and that they would be taking Sgt Washington's statement and questioning him commencing at 1000hrs.

At 1000hrs Jules called the proceedings to order and had Woody sworn in as the first witness of the session. Woody, resplendent in his seldom worn dress uniform, took the witness chair. He told the members of the Board of the incidents that had occurred on the afternoon of Friday, August 23rd. He was just a little nervous to start as he told of coming off his third consecutive 12 hour night shift at about 0800hrs that morning, and spent a couple of hours taking care of administration and ordering supplies. He told of sleeping for a few hours and having been awakened in the afternoon by a loud commotion in the quarters. He recounted that he had stepped out of his room to investigate and encountered S/Sgt Mombirkett in the hallway being very loud and obviously very drunk. Woody told of how he had tried to step back into his room but Mombirkett pushed his way in behind him using some very abusive anti-racial language. He told of trying to talk the deceased down, to cool him out and lead him back to his room but the insults became even worse as Mombirkett said some terrible things about Woody's fiance' and a young friend of his. Then he had started punching Woody and Woody tried to get his arms around the deceased to protect himself from the heavy punches and, as they struggled, they found themselves outside the door leading into the quarters from the outside stairs. They lurched against the railing, the railing gave way and they fell to the ground and he had landed on top of the deceased.

The first question from a member of the Board was to ask Woody about the actual words the deceased was using in what Woody had described as abusive language.

Woody told the Board that he just didn't like to use those words and Jules came to his rescue advising that they would be seeing the film and hearing the sound track within the next hour and it might be just better to hear Mombirkett actually using the words than to have the witness repeat them.

The second question was asking Woody why he had left the scene. "Well, sir, someone said S/Sgt Mombirkett was dead and I was just scared. I come from the South and when a black man and a white man fight it's usually the black man that gets in trouble. I wasn't really going anywhere but I just wanted to see my friend and tell her what had happened."

Jules called a recess so the security officer could set up his projector and sound equipment. When the equipment had been set up and tested Jules called the proceedings to order and instructed the secretary of the board to swear in the security officer.

Everything in the two films supported Woody's evidence. They showed Mombirkett obviously very drunk and in a foul mood staggering along the hallway with a bottle in one hand. They also heard his foul abusive language as he forced his way into Woody's room. They watched as Woody tried to talk to Mombirkett, to reason with him and lead him back to his own room. Mombirkett then made some foul abusive remarks about Sgt Washington's fiancée' and a young friend of the couple. Finally Mombirkett became even more abusive and physical as he started swinging punches at Woody as the near empty bottle flew across the hall. It was exactly as Woody had testified; he was trying to hold the deceased's arms to control the punches. Then they were on the second floor landing leading into the quarters from the outside flight of stairs and the force of their combined weight was too much for the wooden railing. The railing shattered and they fell to the ground. Woody landed on top and got up immediately but the deceased never moved.

As the film completed its run the lights came back on and Jules spoke to the members of the Board. "I think we should congratulate the security officer for the excellent and highly informative presentation. After seeing that film, hearing the sound track and combining that with Sgt Washington's evidence it is my recommendation that we call Sgt Washington in and have him released from custody." Jules looked up and down the table and received the anticipated nods of agreement. "I also recommend that this Board consider returning a finding of accidental death through misadventure in the death of S/Sgt Mombirkett. Major Branson, our 2IC who was in command at the time of the incident, has been doing a little investigating on his own and has come up with a fairly convincing explanation for the actions of the deceased on that fateful afternoon but I don't believe his evidence would have any bearing on the task assigned to this Board. It is my direction, subject, of course to any disagreement on the part of any member of this Board, that the Secretary of the Board show the finding of this Board to be accidental death." Jules paused again but it was obvious that his direction had the unanimous support of the Board. "Thank you Gentlemen and now, just before we conclude the Board's deliberations please bring Sgt Washington back in."

Jules advised Woody that he was to be released from custody immediately and returned to duty status. Woody was told that the film evidence exonerated him completely and he should be commended for his efforts to defuse a potentially dangerous racial situation.

Before adjourning the Board of Inquiry Jules instructed the Secretary of the Board to produce the required documentation and transcripts of the evidence the Board had taken. The security officer had advised that copies of the relevant film and sound tracks were available and should be included in the final package. He then thanked the members of the Board for their service and adjourned the Board.

CHAPTER XIX

JULES AND GENERAL REICHOLD

THE FINAL MEETING

The funeral of Field Marshall Baron Erich von Freider-hoff was held on Saturday, August 31st and became a much bigger event than had been anticipated by local residents. The name struck a chord on the national scene and lengthy and laudatory obituaries appeared in all national publications speedily written by journalists who one week earlier had forgotten that the old man was even alive. There were tributes from many governments, veterans' organizations and other national political groups who paid tribute to the Field Marshall's efforts following World War I to restore Germany's rightful place among the nations of Europe.

At the request of representatives of the German Defence Forces Jules arranged for a gun carriage and a local riding stable provided a jet black stallion to be led by a representative of the German Defence Forces with riding boots reversed in the stirrups as was the time honored tradition for cavalry officers. On the gun carriage Jules suggested that the Heidleberg Sword of Honor be laid on top of the casket. The honorary pall bearers were very elderly German veterans who had served with the General during World War I and the actual pall bearers were volunteers from the German Defence Forces.

The funeral cortege proceeded from the Mansion for about two kilometers to the small church which had been near the centre of the original estate and where the cemetery contained the graves of many generations of the von Freider-hoff family. After the brief church ceremony and the final tributes at the graveside most of those attending the funeral returned to the Mansion for an official reception. Before leaving the churchyard Helga took both Jacob and Jules for a very brief tour of the cemetery. She pointed out the grave of the old General's wife, the grave of his youngest son and the memorial markers for his two other sons, his two daughters and for his three grandsons. Jacob and Jules left Helga for a few moments at her grandfather's grave and she was still teary eyed when they returned to the Mansion where Gerda was holding down the fort.

Jules did not know very many of those attending the funeral and reception. General Reichold was there representing the Commander of NATO and he introduced Jules to a number of senior officers who were representing various European Governments. It gave Jules the opportunity to confirm a final meeting with General Reichold to discuss the tapes which covered the final two afternoons that he had spent with the old General. Reichold told Jules that he had indeed reviewed the tapes and they should meet as originally scheduled on Tuesday, September 10th. As for the previous meetings General Reichold would be available from 3 p.m. on that date.

As the final guests departed Helga and Jacob thanked Jules for all the help he had provided in making the old man's funeral a special event and Jules told them that it was the least he could do as a measure of the respect he felt for the old man. Helga told him she would be back at the Mansion the following week and asked him to be sure and drop in to see her.

On Thursday, September 5th Jules noticed that Helga's car was parked beside the Mansion and that evening dropped in to pay his respects. They sat in the old General's study. Jules noted that the chess sets had been packed up and the tables had been removed for storage but everything else appeared to be the same including the Heidleberg Sword which had been restored to its former place of honor behind the old man's desk.

"I'm not sure just what to do with all of this," she waved her hand around the room indicating the many bookshelves full of books and several filing cabinets. "I just haven't had time to really think about what the future will be for the Mansion, members of the household and all my grandfather's belongings."

"Perhaps I could made a suggestion or several suggestions," said Jules. "I'm sure that many of the contents of this room have significant historical value and would be welcomed at a major university or at the Library of the German Defence College. The first step would be to catalogue all the material and that would fit very nicely with the final research I will require in support of my doctoral thesis. This project will take about a year and, with your permission, the cataloguing could start no later than January. Once you have a catalogue of everything here you would have several options. The option I would recommend is that the official catalogue be distributed to major libraries and they could make their bids for various items. The estimated value would have significant tax implications if donated to a tax-free institution. I believe you will be pleasantly surprised when you see the value placed on even the contents of this one room. But first I recommend the cataloguing."

"That's fine with me. Go ahead with your project. I'm sure the estate will meet an expense involved. Jacob has already advised me that there are several wine brokers very interested in all or part of the contents of the wine cellar. I was amazed at just how valuable some of the wine is."

"There would be no cost involved in the cataloguing. That would be part of my doctoral project and I think I know of someone who would undertake the cataloguing as an academic project." Jules then drew her attention to the magnificent chess set which was now stored in a handsome oak cabinet in one corner of the room. "Yes I'm sure your wine cellar will attract some very high bids but I think you will also be pleasantly surprised at the value of that chess set. Just to satisfy my own curiosity I described the set to both the Sotheby and Christie auction houses in London and both told me that this is only one of two sets made by a famous Italian craftsman for the then King of Prussia. The other set is privately held in the United States after being bought at auction for nearly one million pounds. If this is actually the other set both auction houses would recommend a reserve bid of one million pounds. And, Helga, there is absolutely no doubt in my mind that this is the missing set."

"Well, " Helga replied, "That would certainly solve the mortgage problem and it might just make it possible to implement another idea I have been toying with. I'd really like to keep this old place. It's been in the family for so long. I thought that it might make a nice small guest house and conference centre with a fine dining room and, needless to say, an excellent wine cellar. I think both Woody and Gerda would like that idea also Mannheim who has lost all interest in going to the United States.'

"That just might be a very good idea," replied Jules. Remember you also have the former family hunting lodge and the area NATO now uses for training. The lease on that property comes up in January and I'm sure that the German Defence Forces would be very interested in purchasing both properties for both their own use and for leasing to NATO. That would provide any capital required for renovations of your little hotel."

"Yes, that sounds like a wonderful idea." Helga sounded nearly enthusiastic about the idea. "I must speak to Jacob about this. He is so good on business plans and the Rhine Group holds the mortgage. But, regardless of the possible guest house plan, you can go ahead with your project and plan to start the cataloguing whenever you're ready."

"Now, how is everyone else making out?" Jules asked.

"I guess you mean Sandy. She's is still broken hearted and, of course, still pregnant. She'll have her baby and Gerda already sounds like a grandmother in waiting. Sandy states she has sworn off men for life and that should last until the baby is born. Woody hopes to complete his service here in Germany and I think both he and Gerda would be quite happy to stay here. Mannheim has given up completely on his plans to immigrate to the States. He doesn't think Americans are very nice people, present company excluded, of course. The guest house and dining room might work very well for those three, Mannheim would make a very good wine steward."

As Jules prepared to leave Helga told him there was one more matter to be settled and warned him that she was not prepared to accept any resistance on his part. She had decided that the only person who had emerged from this encounter with any semblance of the quality of honor so highly valued by her grandfather was Jules. She was absolutely devastated by the memory of how her grandfather had died thinking those terrible ideas about Jules that she had planted in his mind and ideas that had been proven groundless. Only Jules had been completely honorable in the entire matter and had not only always treated the old General with sincere respect but had tried valiantly to save him when he suffered his heart attack. As the sole survivor of the von Freiderhoff family Helga told Jules that she insisted that Jules accept the Heidleberg Sword of Honor because that is what her grandfather would have wanted had he known the truth at the time of his death. Jules attempted to protest but Helga was absolutely adamant. The Sword would remain in its present setting until she received instructions on its disposition from Jules.

CHAPTER XIX

JULES AND LT-GEN REICHOLD
THE FINAL MEETING

On Tuesday afternoon, September 10th, shortly before 3 p.m., Jules checked in at General Reichold's office in Frankfurt. The aide advised the General that Jules was there and the General came out to greet him.

"Come right in. The rest of my day is clear unless an emergency arises. Unfortunately this will probably be our final meeting between now and when you are requested to defend your thesis before the full board. It has been over a month since we last met and a very eventful month. The death of the old General was most unfortunate but the month since we last met has given me the opportunity to review the cassettes you delivered since our last meeting and I also had the time to review all of the tapes right back to your first visit. The result is that I am even more impressed with what you have accomplished and it would appear that you achieved most of the objectives that you set for the sessions with the old General. I was back in the States last week and spent one day at the university. The review board is very impressed with your plans for your thesis and recognizes just how imaginative an approach you have selected. The commentaries of the old General will provide another dimension in our understanding of just what happened in Germany during those crucial years between the wars."

"Yes Sir, I agree that it has been a very eventful month and I was fortunate to meet most of my objectives in my discussions with the old General but I cannot escape some feelings of guilt in making use of the recordings without his permission. However, I do have the full permission of his - granddaughter. She seems to appreciate that I had developed considerable respect for the old gentleman during all those hours we spent together. She has also given me permission to catalogue all the contents of his study and library and I fully expect to find much of interest there."

"Another sentiment aroused by my complete review of the cassettes was one of envy." The General paused and selected his words carefully. "I found myself just kicking myself for never having looked for such a valuable living source of information when I did my own thesis. I was here in Germany and the old General was probably available but I'm afraid my skill in chess would have never commanded the respect of your skill at the game and I think that was the key to your success. Perhaps there was an element of luck in how you met the General and had the support of his granddaughter right from the start but good management of the situation was a more important factor. The cataloguing of the General's study and library should prove very interesting but I doubt if you will have more than one more year in your current posting and it sounds like a major undertaking to be added to your command responsibilities."

"Oh, no, "Jules interceded. "I do not plan to do the cataloging my self. My fiancé', Malina, is also a history major and has had extensive experience in library science. We met at Oxford when I was completing my MA and she is now the Assistant Headmistress at the private girls' school where my mother is Headmistress. We plan to marry in December. My mother is becoming anxious for grandchildren."

"Well, "replied the General, "That should work out very well because it looks as though your next posting will be a faculty appointment back at the Point. That's still very unofficial but it certainly sounds like a logical move. However, I don't think I have to remind you that logic is not always the motivating force in personnel management."

"Well that is just about what I expected and it would certainly be ideal for me. My mother wants to retire in two years and my fiancée' will be in line for the job as Headmistress and we might just have a grandchild for my mother and father to spoil in their retirement."

"On the subject of the cassettes," offered the General, "I really don't think there is that much to discuss. The old General was certainly a gold mine of information and I just can't help wondering where we would be today if Hitler had been just a little more receptive to his advice. Just think of how things would be today and ten years or so into the future if Hitler had not been in such a hurry. What would have happened if he could have reached some accommodation with France and Great Britain that would have enabled him to concentrate on Eastern Europe and Russia? Russia certainly did not have many friends in Eastern Europe and it would appear that countries like Poland, Czechoslovakia and Hungary would have been quite receptive to a defensive alignment with Germany to protect them from the Russian threat on their Eastern borders. Belgium, Holland and the Baltic states would have been easy to neutralize and if German treaties could stabilize Europe the United States would have been only too happy to concentrate on the threatening noises being made by Japan. Yes, Colonel, I think the old General had it right but Hitler was just in too much of a hurry to listen to him."

"I won't really know until my fiancée' and I complete the cataloguing," said Jules, "but there just may be a book somewhere in this. I agree that the old General probably had it right but he was right because he arrived at his conclusions based upon principle rather that expedient. He sincerely believed in the qualities that he attributed to the Teutonic Ayrian race. I could never agree but there was no doubting his sincerity or the depth of his belief. For proof all we have to look at is the price he paid in support of his beliefs. Honor, discipline, patriotism, courage, responsibility and leadership were all qualities that he imbued in his sons and daughters

238

and, through them, in his grandsons. Just think of the price he paid all in the forlorn hope that Germany would rise again as the Germany embracing all those values that he held so dear. It is so easy to say that time had just passed him by but surely there are some lessons in there for all of us. Life would be so much simpler if we could just get back to some of those values."

"Such idealism is to be commended but we live in such a different world today," said the General and Jules had the distinct impression that he was being studied very carefully.

"You had it right when you said earlier that this had been a very eventful month. I was called back just before the end of our exercise when my 2IC advised me that there had been a violent death in my unit and it appeared that one of my sergeants had been involved and was missing. First impressions were that it had been an inter-racial incident. Perhaps it was pure coincidence but the victim was S/Sgt Mombirkett and I immediately recognized that name as one you asked about as possibly the son of a former Master Sergeant whom you had served with in Korea. The sergeant who was suspected of being involved was a cook and was the same one that I had interviewed when he had applied for permission to marry the old General's housekeeper. My 2IC did a little investigating on his own and found that Mombirkett had been involved in some security project that just may have involved the CIA even after their promises to work through normal channels. At least my 2IC found some authentication codes that looked very much like CIA codes."

Jules paused as the steward was admitted to the office and poured coffee for them. When the steward departed he continued. "My 2IC also found that there also appeared to be some connection between S/Sgt Mombirkett and a security flap we had about a month ago when there were several Americans poking around in our area asking questions and the questions appeared to be centered on members of the old

239

General's family and household staff and at least one member of my unit who we knew as Pfc Jason Creighton but S/Sgt Mombirkett found that this may not have been his true identity. While I was away on the exercise Mombirkett brought in an application from Creighton for transfer to the non-effective list to enroll in a college back in the States. My 2IC was in command during my absence and it seemed that the application conformed to current Personnel Administrative Orders and he approved the application and Creighton was gone within forty-eight hours. After Creighton departed an inspection of his quarters, and certain documents in Mombirkett's possession, suggested that his real name was Jason Buchalter and that name certainly rings a bell.

"To further complicate the situation, during the Board of Inquiry into S/Sgt Mombirkett's death, the security cameras both inside and outside the quarters revealed that he had become very drunk on that afternoon after receiving a "Dear John letter" from his wife that morning telling him that she was suing for divorce. There had also been a letter from his father whom Mombirkett had obviously asked to do a little checking on his wife. His father informed him that his suspicions about his wife had been correct and told him that she had established a relationship with a ballplayer from the Dominican Republic on a baseball scholarship at a major North Carolina University who she had been tutoring. Yes, the fellow from the Dominican was black and it seems that Mombirkett went right off the rails. He went after the very first black he saw and that just happened to be our cook, and prospective bridegroom, Sgt Woodrow Washington. The film and sound track from the security cameras revealed Mombirkett as we had never seen him before. Sgt Washington did his very best first to avoid him and then tried to talk him down, cool him out. However, all he really did was make matters worse as Mombirkett became even more abusive. He used every racial epithet I have ever heard and then started verbally abusing Washington's friends. He bragged that he had seduced Creighton's or Buchalter's - whatever his real name was - girl friend from the Mansion and it now appears that it was probably rape. He threatened the same for Washington's fiancée' the housekeeper from the Mansion."

Jules paused to drink his coffee. The General was very quiet but studying Jules very carefully. Jules continued. "Sgt Washington continued in his efforts to cool out Mombirkett but without success. Then the punches started and Washington is a big man but Mombirkett was quite an accomplished boxer and the punches were landing. To protect himself Washington wrapped his arms around Mombirkett and their struggles took them out onto the outside landing at the top of the two flights of stairs leading down to the parking lot. They crashed against the wooden railing and the railing gave way and both men fell a distance of between twelve and fifteen feet to the ground with Washington landing on top of Mombirkett. Washington got up immediately but Mombirkett never moved and was pronounced dead at the scene."

Jules paused again but the General remained very quiet. "Based upon the film and sound track from the security cameras my Board of Inquiry returned a unanimous verdict of accidental death in the death of S/Sgt Mombirkett and Sgt Washington was released without prejudice and was even commended for his efforts to control the situation. As President of the Board of Inquiry it was my decision that the evidence gathered by my 2IC which included the "Dear John letter", the letter from Mombirkett's father, the CIA authentication codes and the papers questioning Pfc Creighton's true identity not be presented to the Board. It was my opinion that such evidence had really no bearing on the terms of reference for the Board. However, I have asked my 2IC to put together an official complaint on the apparent renewal of CIA clandestine efforts in my regimental area."

The General was continuing his silence and his eyes were concentrating on Jules. "All of this is very interesting and it would appear that both you and your 2IC are to be commended on your efforts to gain a full understanding of the circumstances surrounding Mombirkett's unfortunate death. The coincidences that appear to arise must be noted and it would be quite reasonable for me to consider the entire sequence of events in the light of your earlier remarks that compared the type of leadership the old General advocated and the more manipulative techniques of man management we tend to use today."

The General's tone of voice appeared to change as he seemed to be taking a very deliberate approach to defending his position. Jules thought he detected just a touch of anger or exasperation in his voice. "Colonel, I have always been suspicious of coincidences. I have also always been very annoyed with subordinates who disguise their true meanings by using something similar to the way lawyers use hypothetical arguments in court. You should also excuse me for becoming just a little pissed off after being exposed to your very thinly disguised lecture on morality. The one factor that you have been smart enough not to mention, but we both realize you know, is the rumor on that usually reliable West Point "Old Boys' Net" that I'm under active consideration to head the CIA with strong support from my old friend and Point classmate Senator Buchalter. When we add this little bit of information the conclusion is inescapable - the General is being rewarded for services rendered."

Just for an instant Jules thought of interceding but was really at a loss as to know just what to say. The General's assessment was so accurate that Jules was even more certain that he was absolutely correct in his reading of the situation. It was also obvious that the General's anger was increasing as he continued. "Colonel, I have never had the slightest doubt as to your intelligence and I'm sure that that level of intelligence will also make you receptive to some very good advice. The one weakness I have always encountered in junior officers has been their inability to visualize the big picture, the old "forest for the trees" syndrome. Recognition

242

of the big picture will often demand measures that are very difficult to justify on a local basis. Also, before you get your back up about how, just possibly, there may have been what you might call meddling with your command prerogatives you should realize that one of a commander's most difficult tasks is selecting the right people for the right jobs. Sometimes questionable tactics are required but some people might just drag their feet if asked to employ such tactics. If not asked they should look on the bright side and attribute it to their commander's effective utilization of available resources as he recognizes that there are subordinates who might reject the use of certain tactics. However, such an assessment should not be considered as reflecting a weakness in subordinates regarded by the commander as - shall we say - temperamentally unsuitable for such tasks. Such judgements of the commander should be recognized as special consideration that will ease the consciences of those passed over in the allocation of such tasks. But the "big picture" often demands that such tasks be undertaken."

The General paused and now became increasingly deliberate. "Colonel before you embark upon your next morality lecture to a senior officer you should give careful consideration to your own actions. Sometimes we refer to this as "People in glass houses etc., etc." One example would be your little tryst in Brussels with the "great and good friend" of one of the most influential men in Europe. We can rest assured that the security people at Rhine Group have all the details although it would also be safe to assume they will be very discreet just how such information is disseminated. Their dossier on you would also contain a detailed account of the day that you and the same young lady spent at the Hunting Lodge. I recall that you did brief me on that visit but you quite obviously considered me too young to hear the more intimate details. I'm also sure, Colonel, that the Rhine Group dossier on you and the young lady would include the details of the miscarriage she suffered in Paris recently. Colonel, you obviously have a very bright future in this man's army but it will not be enhanced by morality lectures to superior officers. Righteous anger, Colonel, is a privilege of rank. The big picture, to put it very bluntly, is that to ensure a level playing field in the Washington game, we must have powerful friends and to keep such friends on our side we must be prepared to help them in their hours of need. Senator Buchalter is not only a personal friend of mine but he is a proven friend of the Armed Forces in an arena where we need every friend we can get. When someone like the Senator has a problem we must be prepared to offer whatever help we can."

The General's comments filled in all the blank spaces and Jules now had a full understanding of the "big picture" and while he questioned the tactics employed he could appreciate the General's motivation and he could understand just why the General was highly pissed off with him. Nor was he finished.

"When I first met you Colonel I was really of two minds about you. One impression was that you were a very capable young man with a very bright future. The other was that you were just another smart-ass nigger. Now, I suggest you get out of here before I change my mind!"

The End

EPILOGUE

Or

A READER'S SCRAP-BOOK

Many times after I have finished reading a book it has been with a vague feeling of dissatisfaction in that I was left wondering just what happened to the characters who were left on the scene at the close of the fictional account of portions of their lives. The more I enjoyed the book the greater the feeling of dissatisfaction.

I have often thought that it would be so wonderful if someone out there in the "never-never land of fiction" could exercise a little magic and put together a scrap-book telling us what happened to the characters who had combined to hold our interest for a few hours. It is probably highly presumptuous of me but in the rather vain hopes that some readers of my book have similar feelings I offer my account of some of the more interesting things that could have happened to some of my characters and I will call it……..

…………A READER'S SCRAP-BOOK

A clipping from a Washington, DC daily newspaper in November 1969.

CAREER ARMY OFFICER TO HEAD CIA

Washington, DC. The Senate approved a committee recommendation that Lt Gen Carl Reichold be confirmed as the next head of the CIA. The vote was 70 to 30 in support of the committee recommendation after some heated debate in committee. The new CIA Director's chief supporter was the powerful minority leader from the Senate Armed Forces Committee, Senator Buchalter. General Reichold is a much decorated veteran of WWII, Korea and Viet Nam where he is currently deputy commander of Ground Forces. His Ph D thesis is regarded as the definitive document on Germany's social development between World War I and World War II.

A clipping from a North Carolina daily newspaper in March 1970.

MOMBIRKETT CASE DISMISSED

FATHER ACCUSES ARMY OF COVERUP

Charlotte, N.C. An action initiated by the father of the late S/Sgt Billiebob Mombirkett was dismissed by Federal Justice Brian Wilson. Roger Mombirkett had asked for a decision of wrongful death in the case of the death of his son and challenged the disposal of his son's estate. Outside the court the father of the deceased claimed that there had been a cover-up in the death of his son in which his son's commanding officer, Lt Col Jules Pelladeau. an African American, asd President of the Board of Inquiry, had absolved Sgt Woodrow Wilson Washington, also an African American, of all blame in the death of his son by returning a finding of accidental death.

In a second action Roger Mombirkett sought the disqualification of the widow of S/Sgt Mombirkett's widow, Allison Mombirkett (now remarried to Juan Marino) as principal beneficiary of the deceased's estate because she had commenced divorce proceedings prior to the death of the deceased. The accidental death verdict of the Board of Inquiry had increased the value of the deceased's estate through indemnity clauses to $750,000 which the deceased's widow had committed to the establishment of a school for underprivileged Dominican children to be known as the Magioli - Marino School. She will be joined in this endeavor by her present husband, Juan Marino, star second baseman for the Boston Red Sox. They will both spend the baseball off season in the Dominican Republic assisting in the operation of their school.

In his decision the judge commended the widow and her new husband for undertaking such a worthy project in memory of her first husband. Justice Wilson was highly critical of the actions of the deceased's father describing it as an action motivated purely by greed. Justice Wilson announced that he had reviewed the entire Board of Inquiry proceedings and that he agreed completely with the findings of the Board of accidental death on which, as he noted, the Board's finding had been unanimous.

263

A clipping from a Dallas daily newspaper published June 22nd, 1968

ITALIAN AMBASSADOR THREATENS TO TAKE CASE OF IMPRISONED MUSICIAN TO UNITED NATIONS.

NOTED ITALIAN CONCERT PIANIST BEING HELD ON STATUTORY RAPE CHARGES

Dallas, Tx. The Italian Ambassador was in Texas yesterday to protest the treatment of famous Italian concert pianist Umberto Fillini now being held in Harris County on charges of statutory rape. The Ambassador claims that the musician was kidnapped from his hotel in Los Angeles and transported illegally over state lines to Texas. The Ambassador also claimed that the musician is travelling on a

(Clipping from Dallas daily newspaper June 25th. 1968)

THE CASE OF THE MISSING MAESTRO

ITALIAN AMBASSADOR CLAIMS MUSICIAN HAS BEEN KIDNAPPED AGAIN

Dallas, Tx. Umberto Fillini has disappeared again and the Italian Ambassador charges a prominent Texan family with his kidnapping following his release on $200,000 bail yesterday. Italian diplomats at the maestro's hotel claim he had been seized by a group of gangsters as they exited the hotel on a false alarm fire alarm. The Ambassador claimed that he had a private jet waiting at the airport to transport Fillini hack to Washington where he would reside until his case was scheduled in the Texas court.

An investigative reporter from this paper discovered that the flight plan filed by the Captain of the Italian private jet was not for Washington but for Rome via Gander, Nfld. When asked to comment on this report the Italian Ambassador refused to comment except that he would use all methods at his disposal to protect the rights of Italian citizens.

265

ITALIAN AMBASSADOR CLAIMS TEXAN COMPLICITY IN PAINFUL ASSAULT ON FAMED MUSICIAN

Dallas, Tx. The mystery of the disappearing maestro has been solved. An ambulance called to a rural motel in Harris County yesterday found that the famed Italian concert pianist, Umberto Fillini had been the victim of a very painful operation which when applied to animals is defined as "gelding". Texas Rangers called to investigate the incident could find no record of who had rented the room in which the musician had been found but indications were that the operation had been undertaken at another location and performed by a professional. The unsigned note found with Fillini offered nothing more than advice to the noted concert pianist that he would be able to concentrate on his music now that the source of other distractions had been removed.

The Italian Ambassador claimed outrage at the tendency of Harris County law enforcement agencies to regard this serious assault as an amusing incident. The Attorney-General of Harris County apologized to the Ambassador and stated that the charges against Fillini of statutory rape would be withdrawn in consideration of his painful injuries and added that the charges had been withdrawn at the request of the prominent family who had originally laid the charges. The Ambassador also objected to the remarks of the Judge who, in dismissing the statutory rape charges told Fillini that he should look at the bright side. After all he had been

charged with the same offence 30years earlier but now, if ever charged again, he would have the ultimate defence.

The Ambassador insisted that the case should be fully investigated and accused "Big Jim" Taylor, prominent Texan rancher and oilman, and his three sons of involvement in the assault. Also involved, according to the Ambassador, was Paul Taylor, cousin of "Big Jim"who isGodfather of the young lady involved and current head of the Department of Veterinary Medicine at a leading university in the state of Texas.

Clipping from London daily newspaper from March 1st, 1980

POPULAR GROUP PLANS WORLD TOUR

London: Jason Buchalter leader of the famed rock and roll group "The Chastity Belts" announced yesterday that the group will embark on a world tour commencing in July of this year.

This will be the very popular group's first major tour in five years during which the group's leader has been on the concert pianist circuit on which Buchalter received critical acclaim as probably the world's most versatile musician. This will also represent the first tour for the group's leader, Jason Buchalter, since his marriage to the beautiful German model Sandra von Friderhoff adopted granddaughter of the late Baron Erich von Freiderhoff at the ancient family home The Enclave von Freiderhoff in Freiderberg near Frankfurt. Buchalter will be joined on this tour by his new bride, also an accomplished nusician, and their eleven year old daughter who is being acclaimed as a musical prodigy after being discovered by the famous Italian concert pianist, Umberto Fillini, who only recently returned to his role of highly successful teacher after having recovered from the paidful injuries he had suffered in an accident in Texas while on his last US concert tour.

(Clipping from a Washington daily newspaper from June 1st, 1980)

THE END OF A GREAT CAREER IN SENATE

BUCHALTER CALLS IT QUITS

Washington,DC. Senator Richard "Buck" Senator will return to a fulltime role as CEO of Compass Inc where his wife, Patricia Buchalter and daughter of the late Howard Conrad, the founder of Compass Inc, is Chairman of the Board Buchalter, after serving four terms in the US Senate, has announced that he will not seek nomination in the 1980 election. Long regarded as a leading GOP presidential candidate the very popular war hero was one of the leading casualties of Watergate when then President Gerald Ford received the GOP nomination in 1976 after assuming the Presidency on the resignation of President Nixon.

FIRST AFRICAN AMERICAN TO COMMAND WEST POINT

GENERAL JULES PELLADEAU TO ASSUME COMMAND

Washington, DC. The Secretary of the Army has announced the first appointment of an African American to command West Point. General Jules Pelladeau will be promoted to General and will assume command of the corps June 1st.

General Pelladeau graduated from West Point in 1954 third in his class. He won All Americam honors as co-captain of a very successful football team and several honorable mentions as an All- American in both track and basketball. He completed his MA on a Rhodes Scholarship to Oxford where he was also a member of the famed Oxford boat crew.He completed his Ph D in Modern European History at Cornell and his thesis on Germany military resurgence between World War I and World War II has been published under the title *Hitler and the Field Marshall* has received wide critical acclaim and the Pulitzer Prize.

General Pelledeau is maried to Dr Malina Pelladeau Head mistress of the Upper Hudson School for Girls who was co-author of *Hitler and Field Marshall*. They have three children. He is the son of Major (USA Ret) Romeo Pelladeau former Food Services Director at West Point and the White House.

The following represents a clipping from the Jerusalem Post from June 30th, 1975.

TOP ISRAELI HONOR TO BANKER JACOB WISEMAN

Jerusalem, Israel.
The Israeli Cabinet have announced that their most prestigious award, The Star of Israel, will be awarded to Jacob Wiseman for his many outstanding efforts in support of the emerging State of Israel. Mr Wiseman holds Swiss, German and Israeli citizenship, the latter being conferred on him in 1970 also in recognition of his tireless support for the State of Israel. He is economic advisor to the State of Israel and to the Secretary-General of both NATO and the UN. He is a director of both the World Bank and International Monetary Fund.

As Chairman and CEO of the Rhine Group Mr Wiseman is recognized as one of the world's most influential bankers. The news of this latest honor was announced today in Jerusalem by the Secretary to the Israeli cabinet and in Frankfurt by his Executive Assistant and Vice President of Public Relations with the Rhine Group, Sandra von Freiderhoff. She also announced that Mr Wiseman would be honored by the German Jewish Citizen's League in recognition of Mr Wiseman's many years of support for Europe's Jewish Communities.

The following represents an extract from a release from the Tourist Bureau of the Federal Information Service on June 1st, 1980 and has been translated from the original German.

POPULAR FRANKFURT AREA CONFERENCE CENTRE MARKS 10th ANNIVERSARY

Freiderberg. This represents an extract from a recent interview with Helga von Freiderhoff the Managing Director of the Enclave von Freiderhoff which has become one of the most popular Small Business Conference Centers and Guest Houses in the Frankfurt area. Helga von Freiderhoff is the Grandaughter of the Ninth Baron Field Marshall Erich von Freiderhoff who passed away in 1968.

The success of her business venture is attributed by the Managing Director to a number of factors. First there is her partner, Jacob Wiseman, Chairman and CEO of the Rhine Group who was able to impress the Federal Government as to the importance of subsidizing such ventures in the private sector. A second factor was the wisdom of her Grandfather, the Ninth Baron, to collect one of the finest wine cellars in Europe when so many outstanding vintages were available at very attractive prices. The proceeds from the sale of of some of the more valuable wines together with the outright sale of the family's private hunting preserve and Hunting Lodge to the German Defence Forces who would share the lease with NATO Forces provided the funds required to rebuild the wing of the Mansion that had been leveled in World War II. Also of great value were certain items in the estate of her Grandfather which had included a rare chess set sold at auction for nearly $2,000,000 and the Field Marshall's collected books and papers which were donated to several federal institutions in return for significant tax writeoffs.

271

An additional factor was the presence of a nucleus of the staff to establish and operate a first class dining room offering both German and American cuisine The German cuisine is provided by her long time housekeeper, Gerda Washington, an outstanding cook and the American cuisine is provided by Gerda's husband, Woodrow Washington, formerly a food specialist with the American Armed Forces. Gerda Washington is responsible for the day to day management of the entire operation and her nephew, Mannheim Hillstrom, is the Chief Wine Steward with additional responsibilities to supervise maintenance of the entire establishment.

The success of the establishment has been enhanced by the addition of tennis courts and access to a nearby championship golf course. The premises are nearly fully booked for small business conferences and to accommodate a few carefully selected tour companies which specialize on visits to famous old family homes.

Later this year the Enclave von Freiderhoff will be closed for one week to accommodate a happy family event when Jacob Wiseman will wed Helga von Freiderhoff his longtime companion. A second wedding to be held on the same day will join world famous concert pianist Jason Buchalter and Sandra Von Freiderhoff the adopted daughter of Helga von Freiderhoff and adopted granddaughter of the late Field-Marshall Baron Erich von Freiderhoff Ninth Baron von Freiderberg and currently the executive assistant to Mr Wiseman and Vice-President of Public Relations for the Rhine Group.

The guest list for these happy events will include the parents of the bridegroom Senator and Mrs. Buchalter who is theChairman of the BoardEOof Compass Inc.and with the recent death of her father she will become the Chairman of the Board and will be succeeded as CEO by her husband who will be retiring from the Senate within the next year. Also in attendance will be General Jules Pelladeau Commanding officer of the US Military Academy at West Point and his wife who was the co-author of the best selling Pulitzer Prize winning book *Hitler and the Field Marshall* which told the story of the Ninth Baron von Freiderhoff and his valiant efforts to save Germany from the unfortunate alliances that led the country into World War II.

POST SCRIPT

Charles Frederick Allen

Fred Allen was born in Moose Jaw, Saskatchewan and raised in Fredericton, N.B. He was educated in several Fredericton public schools but, by his own admission, just didn't make it through Grade VII when he landed a job as a bellboy in the old Barker House. There was no salary, just tips with a small guaranteed nightly income from delivering the wares of a well known bootlegger who operated from the hotel's elaborate lower level gentlemen's washroom. He also had the distinction of caring for the famous Coleman Frog which can now be seen in the York Sunbury Museum. As a term of his employment at the Barker House he was sworn to secrecy on the origin - and authenticity - of the famous frog. After six months of dusting the giant frog several times a week, he swears that the secret will go to his grave with him.

Fred was saved from cleaning spittoons and dusting the Giant Frog, and possible incarceration for his dubious extracurricular liquor deliveries, when he was hired in the same capacity by the Queen Hotel, Fredericton's leading hostelry. There was still no salary but meals and a uniform were provided. Uniforms were "hot stuff" with the girls in the late 30s so there were certain fringe benefits.

Fred was then saved from a life of answering bells by the outbreak of war and the mobilization of the 104th Battery, the militia unit he had joined at age fifteen. He spent five and a half years overseas with service in the UK and Northwest Europe. On demobilization in 1946 he was accepted as a mature student by the University of New Brunswick. He found university much more to his liking than public school and was a gold medallist and triple prize winner in his junior year. On graduation he was awarded a Beaverbrook Overseas Scholarship but was obliged to withdraw because of a prior military commitment.

He served in the Royal Canadian Artillery and the Royal Canadian Horse Artillery until 1968 with service in Northwest Europe, exchange postings in the United States and service with the ICC peace keeping mission in Indo China. He also served with the 79th Field Regiment, 1st and 3rd Regiments, RCHA, and as an IG (Instructor in Gunnery) at the School of Artillery in Shilo, Manitoba. His final posting was as Resident Staff Officer serving four universities in Southwestern Ontario. At the UWO and WLU he had the designation of Associate Professor of Military Studies but the true indication of his status in the academic hierarchy was that he had a parking spot in the "Red" lots.

On retirement from the Armed Forces in 1968 Fred joined the staff of Sir James Dunn C&VS in Sault Ste. Marie as a teacher of mathematics. He became well known to teachers throughout Ontario for his efforts to improve teachers' pensions and served for seven years as the elected representative of Ontario's Secondary School Teachers OSSTF) on the Teachers' Superannuation Commission now the Ontario Teachers' Pension Plan Board. On his retirement he was awarded an honorary life membership by OSSTF for his service to education in Ontario. More important, the staff at his high school (Sir James Dunn C&VS) made him an honorary graduate of the high school leaving him only to find a cooperative public school principal to complete his academic record.

During the 1980s and early 90s Fred planned, conducted and participated in dozens of workshops and seminars on retirement planning for teachers throughout Ontario. For eight years he was publisher of <u>Teachers Money Matters</u> a monthly newspaper designed to inform teachers on all matters relating to financial security.

Fred has resided in Thornhill, Ontario, for eighteen years with his wife of fifty-four years, Nell. They have three sons and a daughter, six grand children and six great grandchildren.

This is his third novel and a fourth book is in the active planning stage. The fourth book to be published under the title ....*From Among My Souvenirs* will consist of reminiscences from his several careers and those wonderful years growing up in Fredericton.

****